HIS TO KEEP

QUINTESSENTIALLY THEIRS: ONE

SERENA AKEROYD

G. A. MAZURKE

DEDICATION

To Sascha, Andrei, Sean, Kurt, Devon, and Sawyer.

For being charmers.

For worming your way into my heart.

And for being rampant rabbits and having four children whose story I just had to tell…

FOREWORD

Hello darlings,

This is an MF romance book.

Simple.

This is Valentin and Alice's story. One hero, one heroine.

However, both Valentin and Alice have multiple fathers from some of my Reverse Harem books. You do **NOT** have to read those RH to enjoy this novel.

I've written these next gen books for original fans of those RH series, but also for my fans who love MF romances. I promise, you can fall for Valentin and Alice without ever touching those books.

Now, it wouldn't be a Serena Akeroyd novel without some trigger warnings, would it?

What? In a holiday romance?

Yes.

I'm a fucker.

I know this. LOL.

This is not your average holiday romance...

As always, there'll be a bonus scene once HIS TO KEEP hits 200 reviews in my Diva reader group: www.facebook.com/groups/Serena AkeroydsDivas

Much love, and happy holidays!

Serena

xoxo

PLAYLIST

If you'd like to hear a curated soundtrack, with songs that are featured in the book, as well as songs that inspired it, then here's the link:

https://open.spotify.com/playlist/oHdVNXLPoC7GUccIez7jLv?
si=f3cfe8293ea7465d

TIN & ALICE

PART 1

ONE

ETTA

Lawrence Fortsythe was a creep.

Grade A.

24ct.

He was also an ass-kisser. One who was quite content to spend hours at a time with his mouth shoved firmly between my father's buttcheeks.

Graphic?

Not as graphic as what I was hearing.

At the interview my father, Edward DeSauvier, the King of Veronia, was having with him.

About me.

And I wasn't freakin' invited.

To a conversation about my own goddamn life.

"You know how well Alice and I get along, Your Majesty," Lawrence blustered.

Alice.

Ha.

I had many names because that was one of several things

members of a royal family had in abundance. While my parents and siblings all called me Alice, the only man I loved called me Etta.

Lawrence Fortsythe was *not* the man I loved.

"I know you're friends," Father intoned calmly, but I could sense he was distracted.

Well, Father was rarely *not* distracted.

That was life as a king.

This time, however, we'd had an earthquake in the northern territories. I was as concerned as he was. That was why I'd come to his study—to help.

His ante-office, a space that was usually brimming with staff, was curiously vacant now as Father's assistants were working in other parts of Masonbrook Castle—the DeSauvier family's royal seat.

My hand poised to knock on the door, I'd heard Fortsythe's guffawing laughter that reminded me of Donkey from *Shrek*, and curiosity had me listening in.

Why?

Because I didn't understand how a man like Fortsythe was continually granted an audience with my father.

Until now, that is.

Now, I knew.

Father thought we were friends.

Ha.

"We're more than friends, Your Majesty," Lawrence protested.

My eyes flared wide with annoyance.

Liar.

"You are?" The volume of the TV increased. "Lawrence, now isn't the time for this conversation—"

"Sir, I want Alice to be my wife."

My eyes did more than just flare this time.

They almost bugged out of the sockets like I was in an episode of *Tom and Jerry*.

He wanted to marry me?

"I wondered when you'd build up the courage to ask for her

hand," Father muttered, still distracted, but somehow, that made his answer worse. "You'd make a good consort, Lawrence—"

Mouth dry, I froze.

Lawrence, a man as annoying as a house fly, was—

Father seriously thought we—

WHAT IN THE ACTUAL FUCK WAS GOING ON HERE?

"The privy council would certainly approve. Alice is... flighty."

Stung, I backed off.

I wasn't sure what hurt worse.

Knowing I was about to be married off against my will, or my father believing I was flighty.

Flighty.

A part of me wanted to storm inside the office, damning politeness and protocol to hell.

I wasn't flighty.

I *questioned.*

That was my sin.

The privy council were my father's advisors. They were appointed by the cabinet of the ruling government, and they had a direct effect on what we could and couldn't do as a family.

We were autonomous to a certain extent, but the council could make things difficult for us.

If I wanted to go study something, the subject as well as the university location would have to be approved by them.

If I was flighty, it was their damn fault for never agreeing to the courses I wanted.

Hands balling into fists, Lawrence's bluster turned into white noise as my ears switched off, my senses shutting down as a sense of fatality hit me.

I was Veronia's future queen and I was about to be married off at nineteen.

Had I always known this would be my fate?

This might be the new millennium, and my familial situation

might be unorthodox—having three fathers wasn't exactly traditional —but the DeSauvier family, for all that, was still stuck in the 1800s.

My cellphone buzzed.

The vibration sent tingles of sensation washing through me. Waking me up.

Gulping, I reached for it, and when I saw Tin's name on the notification, I closed my eyes a second.

Here was the man I loved.

Here was the boy who'd been my best friend before we'd become lovers.

My secret boyfriend.

The man I wanted to spend the rest of my life with.

Eyes opening once more, I licked my lips as I tapped the notification and found a photo he'd taken on his trip to the US.

His gap year was something I was jealous of because the privy council had denied me the request, citing security reasons, and that meant he was on his own.

Alone, when I wanted nothing more than to be with him.

His happiness warmed my heart, however.

Tin was beaming a grin at me, his hand hovering in the air like he was holding the 'Welcome to Las Vegas' sign in his palm, and that was when I saw fate unfolding before me.

Knew it like I knew my name was Crown Princess Alexandra Lisetta Diana Eugenie Alice DeSauvier.

Knew it like I knew I'd be the queen of this great nation at some point in the future.

Just like I knew that when that happened, Lawrence Fortsythe would *not* be my consort.

Valentin Dubois would be.

TWO

TIN

As the plane began its descent toward the private airstrip, I stared at it, dying to get my eyes on her.

My hands as well.

It had been too damn long since we'd been together.

This gap year was supposed to help me figure out what I was doing with my life, was supposed to help me make a massive decision about my career, and instead, it had rammed six thousand miles between me and the woman I loved.

"Dumb, Tin. Real dumb," I muttered to myself as I squinted through the gleam that not even tinted windows could counteract.

The DeSauvier crest was emblazoned on the private jet, the sleek bullet slaloming toward the runway, bringing my girl back to me.

I was on my way to meet her on the ground but, truth be told, I wanted to see her look for me.

I wanted to see her seek me out.

Not because I was a jerk.

Not because I was playing with her feelings.

But because some days, it was hard to believe that Etta DeSauvier, the future queen of Veronia, wanted *me*.

As the plane came to a final halt, and once the checks were complete, I gnawed on the inside of my cheek, waiting for the steps to lower.

Then, she was there.

Standing in the entryway, her royal guards behind her, her hand covering her eyes, shielding her gaze from the sun, as she peered out onto the tarmac.

A shaky breath soughed from my lungs, relief and need warring inside me as I rushed away from the gate and toward the doors that'd lead onto the runway. A move that was only possible because there were Guard Elect waiting in the wings to grant me access to their charge.

The second the doors opened, I burst outside into the raging heat and called out, "Etta!"

A beaming grin split her face almost in two, and she hurried down the stairs, looking less graceful than usual as she screeched and raced to reach me.

We collided in a hug, and though I wanted to slam my mouth onto hers, I knew that would change everything.

There could be paparazzi waiting in the wings.

The guards were watching—they could tell her father, the king.

I wasn't an appropriate suitor.

That was probably where some of my insecurities lay.

"My God, it's good to see you," I growled under my breath as I hugged her tight. Enough that when I twirled her around, her legs flew back and she laughed, the sound happy.

Happier than I'd heard her in a while.

"I want to kiss you," she murmured in my ear as I let her land.

"Later," I told her, but I knew there was heat in my eyes.

How couldn't there be?

I wanted her as much as she wanted me.

More, maybe.

I was in the land of sin, but no woman appealed to me like she did.

"I'm going to let you go now, but only because the Guard Elect might think it's weird that we're hugging for this long. Okay?"

She blinked at me but pulled back, muttering, "I hate this."

"Me too." I longed to cup her chin, but I couldn't. So I sighed. "How long do I have you for?"

"Meredith is arriving in two days' time—"

"I thought you didn't like her?"

Peeping a smile at me, Etta admitted, "I don't. She's more of a social climber than wisteria. *But* her bachelorette party is here in Vegas, so I asked to be invited."

"And she was more than happy to extend the invitation?"

"Of course. It's a coup for her set."

I shook my head. "A coup. To have you hang out with them." My lips quirked up at the corners. "I guess I should kiss your feet more."

"Not unless you've developed a fetish since you've been gone."

"You're in luck. My only fetish has been my hand. It's gotten better acquainted with my dick." I saw relief war with need in her expression, the emotions mirroring what I'd felt upon seeing her. I didn't allow her to comment, just said, "I'm surprised your parents let you come earlier than the others."

"I wasn't allowed to fly on the same plane with them anyway, and you're here, so Mom worked her wiles on the dads."

Etta was like me—had multiple fathers.

No, we weren't raised in cults. Just had very liberal parents. Well, *sexually* liberated, at any rate. I wasn't sure if a king could be liberal exactly.

My lips curved at her remark. "Wiles you inherited."

She sniffed. "Hardly." Her eyes gleamed. "What are we doing tonight?"

"Things that require a bed."

A shaky breath escaped her. "I was hoping you'd say that." She cleared her throat. "Andrea's sick."

My brow puckered as I glanced back at the plane. "Sick? Andrea's never sick."

Andrea was Etta's shadow.

Literally.

It was only now that she mentioned her name that I realized she wasn't here, looming over us, casting me disapproving glares when I stood too close to Etta.

Andrea, Etta's body double, had what my Scottish father called 'a face like a smacked arse.' Beautiful the woman might be, but she acted as if a smile were worse than genocide.

"She started puking when we hit the Atlantic." Etta bit her lip. "It's..."

"It's...?" I questioned when her voice tapered off.

"I'm a horrible person," she wailed.

I grinned. "Because Andrea being sick means that she won't be watching every move we make for the next two days?"

She sucked in her cheeks and nodded. "Horrible, right?"

"It's not like you made her get sick."

"Oh, my God, Tin! Of course I didn't. Jeez." Etta shoved my chest, making me laugh.

"Methinks the lady doth protest too much," I teased, knowing full well that of the two of us, the only one capable of poisoning someone was me.

And that wasn't a character trait I was particularly proud of, either.

It was, however, one that MI6 wanted to exploit.

"How do you make someone puke? Leave their chicken out too long so they catch salmonella?"

I snickered. "You'd make a great serial killer. Death by vomit. I think it'd be kinder to be slashed to shreds."

Etta rolled her eyes at me. "Yeah, okay, Mr. Bundy."

Still chuckling, I slung my arm around her shoulders and murmured, "Reach into my back pocket."

"Not your front pocket?" she demanded with a pout.

Grinning down at her as she pulled out the photograph, I watched her eyes soften. "Where did you get this?"

I shrugged. "Mom was going through old photos before we left."

"And you brought this with you? I need to send you better pictures."

Tapping her on the nose, I shook my head. "This is us. Where we started." It was a picture of her with soapsuds on her head and me with a soapsud beard.

"Where will we end?"

Something in her eyes made me squirm, and that was unexpected so I fell back on, "In a bed."

She shoved me in the side. "Jerk."

"Hardly," I argued. "Would a jerk bring you this?"

"True." She smiled down at the photo. "No wonder the folks think we're more fraternal than anything else."

"Joke's on them." I felt anything but fraternal about my Etta. "You ready to party?"

"So long as it's in a suite in a hotel somewhere and you're naked, sure."

My lips twitched. "That's my kind of party."

THREE

ETTA

The second he pressed his mouth to mine, I sighed.

Coming home.

That was how this felt.

And it was still so new. *So* new. We'd only stolen time for ourselves twice since we'd taken the next step, but sinking into his embrace made me realize how badly I'd been pining for him.

How deeply I'd missed him.

Neither had a damn thing to do with Lawrence Fortsythe.

I breathed into his kiss as I settled myself against him, my soft curves pressing into the hard lines of his body.

"Are we really alone?" he muttered against my lips.

"As alone as I'll ever be," I rasped. "Mika and Yann are in the hotel room next door and Andrea's puking. That's the guards accounted for."

To celebrate, I dragged off my cardigan and slingshot it across the room before I went to work on the buttons on his shirt.

"You did that with hate," he teased as I shoved the two halves of his shirt aside, planted my hands on his pecs, then straddled him.

"Hate?" I scoffed while his fingers molded to my hips. "You know I *loathe* cardigans."

His lips curved as he watched me grab the hem of my cami and start to strip it over my head.

"Shame for you that it's a part of the princess uniform."

I'd have made a gagging noise, but that wasn't sexy.

I wanted him focused on my breasts, not on my boring pearls and the smart clothes I had to wear that were the opposite of sexy.

That in mind, I unfastened my bra and threw that aside too.

Arching my back as I exposed them, the dazed look in his eyes made me melt as he cupped my breasts.

When he slipped his fingers over the upper curve of them, I shivered, all the tiny hairs standing on edge in reaction.

The reverence in his touch made my head fall back, especially when he reached up and traced them over the line of my throat.

He stunned me then by gripping me by the nape and drawing me down against him, not stopping until there was barely an inch separating us.

When bare flesh met bare flesh, we both shuddered. He drifted his fingers along the sides where my tits bulged. I didn't realize how sensitive I was there, and I shivered again.

"You've no idea how many times I've jacked off thinking about these."

Peeping a smile at him, I told him, "You should have video called me."

"I should have, but the time zones." He grimaced. "I wish you'd been able to come with me."

"I do too."

I might have been a few months older than Tin, and had celebrated my nineteenth birthday three months ago, but Veronia wasn't like the more modern countries.

The heirs to the thrones in the Netherlands and the UK were allowed to head off on charitable ventures before college. I wasn't allowed to do that.

His hands smoothed over my waist. "We'd have had a lot more fun together."

"In bed. You wouldn't have visited the Rockies or gotten to see Niagara Falls—"

Nose wrinkling at the bridge, he argued, "How do you know? We could have done that through the day and then gone to bed really early. I'd never have been so well rested."

"You have a point," I said with a laugh. "Plus, if this is your idea of backpacking around the States, then I missed out big time."

Behind me, there was a six-star hotel suite that had impressed even me, but nothing compared to the sight of him below me.

I was fortunate enough to experience luxury on a daily basis. Heritage and history were bread and butter to me because I lived in a centuries' old castle. I didn't take it for granted, but I sure as hell preferred what I was looking at right this second.

Something he agreed with... "Would have stayed outside if it meant I could be with you."

My throat choked. "I'm so sorry, Tin."

"Hey! Don't be sorry. It's not your fault."

I wanted him so badly, my need was there, deep in my core, but regret made tears well in my eyes and lodge at the back of my throat.

Regret and desperation went to war inside me, but he seemed to sense that too because his mouth reached for mine, and he didn't plunder, he savored.

Gently, he brought me back to him.

"Whenever I get you, I'm grateful," he rasped before he thrust his tongue against mine.

Why couldn't I be normal?

I didn't say that. Instead, the desperation riding me from before, I cupped his hips and started to bite back with the kissing version of fighting talk.

When I rubbed my breasts against his chest, we both moaned and our kisses stilled as I ground into him.

In the pause, I said the only thing I could think to say, "I missed you."

"Missed you too, Etta," he whispered back.

That was the story of our relationship.

Something that conversation I'd overheard was hopefully going to change.

I let my lips whisper over his jaw, down to his throat, where I sucked on the flesh there. I could smell the couple shots of vodka he'd had, but beneath it was Tin.

Always Tin.

His groans vibrated against my lips as I sucked down hard, wanting to mark him. Needing to leave a little bruise behind.

Tin was free like I would never be, and that was the only way I could stake a claim.

Moving down, I pressed my lips to his pecs, nipping the tip of his nipple, before I felt his hands settle on my ribcage. I jolted in surprise when he clutched at me then twisted us around, but found myself staring up at him this time.

There was a smile on his lips, but deep in his eyes was the hunger I needed to see. A hunger I always felt but rarely had the chance to savor.

A lifetime in this bed wouldn't be enough.

It'd never be enough.

With me underneath him now, he grabbed a hold of my skirt, the boring schoolmarm, knee-length excuse for clothing, and began dragging it down my hips.

As I helped him by shimmying out of it, he grabbed my panties at the same time, exposing every inch of me to him.

Did he know how much trust it took to do this?

How much faith I had in him?

My sister, Christel, last year, had gone with a guy who'd taken photos of her and had tried to sell them online.

We'd been lectured about the importance of security *and* chastity in the aftermath.

All while the king shared his wife with two other men.

Hypocrisy.

But I shoved that aside as I focused on him, focused on his desire and the need there.

He looked at me like he was a kid in a candy store and I was a massive bag of gummi bears.

It was then I knew he'd been faithful to me.

How he touched me, his fingers skimming over the length of my thighs, how he gently pressed a kiss to the tip of my nipple, how he reveled in my nudity by running his hands down my arms, it all left me feeling one thing and one thing only—*loved*.

I shuddered against the sheets, feeling even more exposed and needing that. Needing to feel his reverence. Not because I needed to be worshipped, but because I needed to know that how I felt for him was returned.

My mouth quivered as I shared a truth with him. "I was scared when you came to the US."

His hands didn't stop their exploration as he told me, "The crime statistics aren't *that* bad—"

"No. There are women who—" I bit back a gasp as he caressed my nipples, squeezing and pinching them softly until he did it hard enough to sting.

"Women who, what?" he asked, but I heard a sternness in his voice.

A sternness I hadn't heard before.

It didn't stop me from speaking, but it made me shy.

"You could sleep with."

He blinked at me. "Why would I sleep with them when all I want is you?"

Those damn tears made me choke up again.

"You're a guy, Tin. You're hot and rich and eighteen. You're in Vegas and you're partying—"

He dipped his head and tested the resilience of my nipple with his teeth this time.

I groaned, my hands raking through his hair to keep him in place as he taught me pleasure could be painful.

"I repeat," he murmured before his tongue soared over the curve of my breast.

Down my belly.

Around my navel.

Along my pubis.

To the slit that was already wet for him.

"Why would I want another woman when I have you?"

I cried out when he fluttered his tongue there. Around my clit. Through my folds.

He hummed as he tasted me, and I stared wide-eyed at the ceiling. Only realizing at that moment it was mirrored.

My eyes bugged as I watched him savor me.

And this time, I really did feel like a goddess being worshipped.

His back arched, the muscles delineated and strong, his hands digging into my thighs, the tips burning a brand that I felt in my core.

I watched the show he gave me, truly feeling his words.

He wanted me.

Me.

Not Princess Alexandra.

Not Alice.

His Etta.

I cried out when he sucked on my clit.

I didn't understand how he could be so good at this, but I didn't think it was because he'd practised on another woman. I just imagined that God had been kind when he'd given me Tin as a soul mate.

My legs tightened around his head as he thrust his tongue into me, and then, as he did, it was like he exploded.

It was crazy.

Insane.

Wonderful.

He flung himself back and off me, his hands snapping to his fly as he exposed his dick. He gripped it harder than I ever would, and he fell on me.

Thrusting the tip through my folds, lubricating the shaft with my juices, his mouth moved to mine as he pressed it to my slit.

I was tight.

He was big.

As the crown pierced me, I moaned into his lips, my hands and nails digging into his back, but he was slow.

Patient.

Loving.

Always loving.

Tears leaked from my eyes as he slowly filled me, letting me acclimate to him.

We stayed there, kissing for what felt like an endless amount of time, and he thrust his tongue against mine again, savoring me once more before he started rocking his hips.

Slowly, at first.

Gently.

Not too fast. Not too hard.

Then, he swiveled his hips, doing something that had him grinding into my clit.

A cry escaped me and I clutched at him, needing to feel more of that, needing to feel the roar of pleasure as it started to consume me.

Digging my heels into his ass, I began encouraging him to move, and he listened.

He always listened.

I felt sure he was the only person in my life who ever did.

He ground into me, riding me incrementally faster until my head was arched back against the pillows and I was thrusting into him as he rocked into me.

When the wave of pleasure came, it hit me out of the blue.

I screamed.

I couldn't stop myself.

The other two times, we'd had to be secretive.

But not today.

I screamed and I enjoyed it.

I loved the freedom of declaring my pleasure to the four walls of our room, adored that I could be myself here and that he'd celebrate that, never chide me for it.

He groaned, his body powering into mine as he found his own release.

I watched us from above, taking in the show, all while we began to drown in an ecstasy I knew we'd only ever find together.

FOUR

ETTA
FOUR HOURS LATER

Tin was of the persuasion that because his biological father was Russian, vodka belonged in his veins and not the bottle.

And on this occasion, I wasn't going to argue with him about it.

Normally, I'd fret about his liver and tell him that he'd get erectile dysfunction before he was thirty.

Tonight, I encouraged it.

God, I was such a shitty girlfriend.

I'd be an even shittier wife.

Get him drunk, that had been the plan. Somehow get him into a cab. Drive to the nearest chapel. Have Marilyn Monroe or Elvis officiate the ceremony. Sneak back into the hotel. Somehow have sex.

Was that rape?

It seemed kind of rapey to me.

But it wasn't, was it?

I was forcing him to marry me. Not to have sex with me.

Tin *wanted* to have sex with me.

We'd already done it twice since I'd arrived, and that was four hours ago.

As I pondered the minutiae of consent, and how this was breaking *every* single rule in the handbook, I also thought about Lawrence.

About the kind of man he was.

Agitated, I watched Tin sink back another shot of vodka, grateful that the 'getting him into a cab' part of the evening was done with.

I was well aware of the ticking clock, even more aware that if Andrea hadn't been laid up with food poisoning, she would already have caught us by now. It was by sheer luck rather than management that my other guards, Yann and Mika, believed I was a good girl.

I wasn't.

Guiltily, *nervously*, I asked, "Tin? Do you want to be with me?"

He let loose a chuckle that made my lips twitch as he curved his arm around my shoulder and dragged me into him.

"Luv yoo, Etta. Soooooo much. Wish was normal. Wish me and you could be us. Not normal." He heaved a sigh. "Not a prinssss."

Translating that took some effort, but I felt a little less guilty.

Well, not enough to stop this whole thing.

Tin would understand in the morning, wouldn't he?

He'd get it then, right?

Agitated, I rasped, "If I were just a girl you knew, would you want to marry me?"

He sighed again. "Not just a girl. You're Etta. She of ten names."

"Not ten. Five," I corrected as a streak of pain hit me like a bolt of lightning. "What if I *were* just a girl?"

"S'pose so. You and me, I, you and *I*, we is, no." He grunted. "Why's the world moving?"

"I'm never letting you get this drunk again," I told him grimly.

He smacked his lips. "Not drunk. Happy. I'm with my girl."

Hope hit me. "Is that what I am?"

"You're nobody else's," he snapped, sounding possessive enough that I'd admit it made my heart race.

"You want me to be yours?"

"You are mine. Forever and ever, amen."

His words weren't consent.

I knew that.

But they made me feel less shitty about the path I was taking.

"Lawrence scares me, Tin," I told him, well aware that he wouldn't remember what I was saying.

"Who's Lawrence?" he grumbled. "I'm Tin. Valentin."

"I know you are."

"You're scared of me?"

I blew out a breath. "No. Of course not."

"Who you scared of?"

"Lawrence."

"Who's he?"

I sidled closer to him. "Never mind."

In his current state, he wouldn't understand what I was trying to tell him. Christ, he might not even remember *who* Lawrence was.

I'd never told him that Lawrence gave me the total creeps.

That he hovered around me like bees around honey.

I'd spoken about him to Tin because Lawrence was a nuisance, but that was pretty much it.

And my current situation was so Victorian in nature that Tin might not believe me.

Drastic times, I feared, called for drastic measures.

"I wish you'd proposed," I whispered under my breath.

But I knew he wouldn't.

Tin wouldn't do anything without my father's approval—he'd been raised that way—and Father, the *king*, would never have agreed to our union because of who and what Tin was.

The child of a notorious family.

Five fathers.

One mother.

All six parents infamous for their feats and achievements.

Nothing about Tin's family was discreet.

"I propose a toast," Tin crowed, raising his vodka bottle to his lips and taking another swig.

I snagged the bottle away and smashed my lips against his as a distraction.

Tonight was already going to be a clusterfuck.

I didn't need to end it with a visit to the ER for my soon-to-be husband to have his stomach pumped...

PART 2

FIVE

Some people were born to be regular.

Crown Princess Alexandra Lisetta Diana Eugenie Alice DeSauvier wasn't one of them.

It just wasn't something she was capable of. She tried, I knew, but it wasn't doable.

Everything about her was royal. From her haircut—a cascade of waves that were trimmed to hang just below her shoulders—to her clothes...

Even now, though she was heading into class, a class where other attending students wore slouchy jeans and tees, Etta wore a pencil skirt with a blouse tucked in at the waist.

There was no denying that the navy pinstripe did things for her olive skin tone, and the crisp white shirt showcased her figure to perfection beneath a swinging peacoat that gave her a jaunty flair, but she looked like she was about to open a hospital.

No joke.

Especially when I took in the high heels that no woman would wear for class—not unless she was trying to flirt with her professor.

While that might have been a possibility, I knew her schedule.

Her next class, Art History, was taught by a woman, and Etta did *not* bat for the other team.

Not unless things had changed in the last four years anyway...

And I highly doubted that was the case.

Not because I had a big head which, admittedly, I did—literally—but because of the kind of connection we had.

It didn't go away.

It couldn't.

And I'd tried to push it aside.

Many times.

To no avail.

There was no getting rid of the ties that bound us together; this I'd come to accept.

So, no matter how much I'd angered her, upset her, or irritated the living shit out of her, I didn't think I'd made her question her sexuality.

As I studied her ass, which swayed thanks to her heels and tight skirt, I whistled under my breath, taking a moment to fully appreciate the sight before me.

Slouching back in my seat, I watched her for as long as I could before I reached for my cell.

Me: *How are the folks?*

Rosie: *In general?*

Me: *Well, yes. There are a lot of them, so in general.*

Rosie: *I don't do generalizations. You should talk to Jack for those.*

I rolled my eyes.

Me: *Why didn't I realize you'd be even more pedantic now that you're in university?*

Rosie: *I'm not pedantic. I'm detail-oriented. If you were a cow, wouldn't you want me to be that way if I had my hand inside you?*

Me: *Appreciate the mental image, sis. Do I want to know?*

Rosie: *We're learning about cows and birthing. It's fascinating.*

Me: *Sounds like it. Thought you wanted to specialize in horses?*

Rosie: *I do. Duh. But you can't just become a horse vet. You have to become a regular vet first. I thought you were supposed to be smart?*

My lips twitched.

Me: *I am.*

Rosie: *Sounds like it. Pfft. Anyway, GENERALIZATIONS coming up. Mom's pissed.*

Me: *Why?*

Rosie: *One of the heads of her charities is under investigation.*

Me: *For?*

Rosie: *Umm, Papa said something about fraud.*

Me: *Papa as in Andrei?*

Rosie: *Yep. He's investigating it.*

Whichever charity head was being investigated would wish they hadn't been born if my mom was unhappy and *Papa* was on the case. He made a bloodhound look like a teddy bear.

With ties to the Bratva, he was the one man you didn't want to piss off.

Me: *Can't imagine Dad's happy either.*

Yes. There was a difference. My siblings and I had five fathers. *Dad* was Devon.

Rosie: *Nope. Dad is VERY unhappy. I think he called in MI5 and MI6, but they told him they don't deal with stuff like that.*

I grinned.

Me: *No. Bit like sending in Iron Man to clear up the aftermath of a rave.*

Rosie: *A bit. Lol.*

Me: *What about Father?*

Father was Sean. A formal name for a formal man. But, not with us. And definitely not with his daughters.

Rosie and Bethan were the apples of his frickin' eye and could do no wrong.

Rosie: *Well, he called in Scotland Yard too. But they were more interested in trying to get him to help with this serial killer who's going around killing Johns.*

Me: *Johns? Like men called John?*

Rosie: *Nope. Guys who use prostitutes.*

Father was a British criminologist. He'd solved so many cases he should have had his own police procedural show.

Me: *Well, that's a first. Normally those nutcases go for the sex workers.*

Rosie: *See? That was what I said.*

Me: *Let me guess, you told Father the serial killer was a feminist?*

Rosie: *Haha. I did! Know-it-all.*

I chuckled.

Me: *Just where you're concerned, Nosy Rosie.*

Rosie: *Grr. Remind me why I'm not listening to my lecturer so I can talk to you?*

Me: *Because you love me?*

Rosie: *Sometimes. Why not just ask the folks?*

Me: *Gotta talk to them about something.*

My gaze drifted to Casterby where the outer doors to one of Madela's most prestigious colleges were swinging to a close behind the last tardy student.

To where Etta was about to be bored alive by her lecturer in this semester's final class.

Etta wasn't like Rosie or me. She didn't have a natural inclination toward academia, so I could only imagine she was dreaming about winter break and all the studying she didn't have to be doing.

Rosie: *What do you have to talk to them about?*

Me: *Something that might upset them.*

Rosie: *Like what?*

Me: *Work related. Doesn't matter. Just checking on things.*

Rosie: *Hmm. Well, if it's about you quitting, I think Daddy knows. He mentioned something over the phone this morning, and he was all cryptic. More cryptic than usual, I should say.*

My brows rose.

How the hell did Dad know I'd quit?

Sure, MI6 had been my old employer, and they used him to crack code from time to time, but...

Shit.

What was the point in wondering?

Dad knew everything.

That was a fact of life my siblings and I had to come to terms with when we were younger.

Me: *Well, that changes things. How are Vati and Daw?*

Vati was Kurt—our German father. *Daw* was Sawyer, our Scottish one.

Rosie: *They're okay. You mean health-wise, yeah?*

Me: *I do.*

Rosie: *Mom's got Daw on some high-fiber thing that he says is her way of trying to fatten him up.*

Me: *With fiber?*

Rosie: *I don't even want to know.*

Me: *Lol. Vati?*

Rosie: *Fine. His last check up was on Wednesday. He got the seal of approval from his doctors.*

Me: *Phew.*

Rosie: *What you have to tell them... you think it might give them a heart attack or something?*

Me: *Just checking that wasn't on the horizon.*

Rosie: *Hmm. Well, you should be okay. Dad's not been sleeping, but no change there.*

I winced.

Dad—Devon—had worse insomnia than me.

When she said he hadn't been sleeping, that meant it was approaching a week without him getting any rest.

He and Sawyer were mathematicians, and while, idly, I wondered what had Dad so obsessed, I typed:

Me: *Shit.*

Rosie: *Yep. Papa is all obsessed because that cryptocurrency exploded this week...*

Andrei was a Russian, quantitative economist. He got hard-ons over shit like that.

Rosie: *Vati got approached about another screenplay.*

Kurt was a German, Pulitzer-prize winning author with several Academy Awards under his belt as some of his books had been adapted to the silver screen.

Rosie: *Father's busy trying to sort out the roof at home.*

Our family home was an ancient pile of bricks in Surrey. There was always something in need of repair. It was normal with a house that size and age.

Sean had taken the entire estate under his wing with a zeal that made me wonder if he wished he'd gone into architecture rather than criminology.

Rosie: *Both Dad and Daw are fascinated by something that has a lot of Xs and Ys in the title.*

Knew it.

Me: *That's why Dad's not sleeping?*

Rosie: *Yep. Mom's fine. You know how she is.*

Me: *An Energizer bunny?*

Rosie: *Lol. You said it. Not me.*

Me: *Okay. Thanks for the heads-up, Rosie.*

Rosie: *You're welcome.*

Me: *What about you, Jack, and Bethan?*

Rosie: *It's almost Christmas. You need to come home for a catch up.*

Me: *I will. But I have stuff to do right now.*

Rosie: *:P You always say that. Bethan's fine. She's loving St. Andrews.*

Bethan wanted to be a human rights' lawyer.

Rosie: *Jack's driving Dad crazy because he keeps crashing his cars and he won't listen to his lectures about probability.*

Me: *Sounds like everything is very normal.*

Rosie: *Yep.*

I noticed she didn't talk about herself.

Me: *You and Bash still not talking?*
Rosie: *GTG.*

I smirked to myself, totally unsurprised that she hadn't answered that question.

Bash was... well, he was a part of our family but on the outskirts. That was totally a choice of his own.

He and Rosie had a love-hate relationship.

I figured she hated him, he loved her.

I had no idea why she was so all or nothing with him. Still, that was a conundrum for another day.

Knowing the family was okay, that I wouldn't trigger any heart attacks, I bit the bullet.

I connected the video call to Mom's phone.

Sean answered, "Are you there?"

My father's face appeared on the screen.

Ever serious, his brow was puckered as he stared at me.

Dogs barked in the background, like usual, and they made me smile.

Mom had a thing for Yorkies and, ever since I was a kid, we'd had a small pack wandering the grounds like they ruled the roost—which they totally did.

"No greeting for the prodigal son?" I taunted, unsurprised that Father had answered Mom's phone. There weren't many, if any, secrets among them I didn't think.

"You have to return home to be the prodigal son." Mom's wry voice echoed in the background. "As far as I'm aware, you're not here. If you were, then I'm pretty sure the laundry would be overflowing and the fridge would be empty."

Within seconds, she was there, her warm eyes twinkling as she smiled at me.

Father moved his hand to cover hers which she rested on his shoulder, and the sight, as always, settled something inside me.

Five dads, one mom.

Some kids might say two parents were too many to handle, never mind six, but for me, it was perfect.

The love between them all was just a life goal in the making.

It had proven to me that love was not selfish, but giving.

That was part of the reason I'd been so fucked up over what Etta had done.

"What can I say? I'm a growing boy."

A snort sounded in the background, as *Papa* chided, "Shouldn't you have stopped growing by now?"

Dad, a Brit, complained in low tones, "What does laundry have to do with the fridge?"

Daw, ignoring both Dad and *Papa*, muttered, "What mischief are you up to, lad?"

The gruff Scot's voice had my lips twitching even as I snarked, "It's rude not to be on the screen when you talk to someone."

A sniffing sound was all I heard before Father grunted, peered over his glasses, and started tapping the screen.

I wasn't surprised when the call disconnected; I just waited for him to call me back.

After two minutes of staring at the craggy walls of Casterby College, wondering if Etta had fallen asleep in Art History like I had when I'd taken the class, I accepted the call when my phone rang.

As the screen flicked on after buffering for a few seconds, I found myself staring at the breakfast table as a whole.

That, of course, meant I'd been put on the big screen, with all of my fathers and my mother in attendance.

Not that it came as a shock.

Breakfast was a big deal in my house. And ever since Mom had made my fathers slow down after *Vati's* second heart attack scare last year, breakfast could last upward of three hours.

They all stayed around the dining table, reading papers, grazing on the superfoods Mom shoved down their gullets, drinking tea and coffee.

In fact, it was getting to be a family ritual, one even I appreciated when I was back home and taking part in the process with them.

"How's everyone?" I asked.

"Your mother's driving us mad," Sean chimed in.

"Why?"

He grunted. "Christmas this and Christmas that."

"Two weeks to go!" she cried. "There's a lot to do and not much time left to do it!"

"Fourteen days is plenty of time," he argued, but I saw the amused gleam in his eyes and knew he was purposely goading her. "I got the roof fixed in a week."

She harrumphed. "The roof was easier to repair."

His brow rose. "Next time there's a problem with it, I'll let you handle it, hmm?"

Mom cast him a look that represented so many things I didn't want to understand... Especially when she turned bright pink.

God help me.

I loved that my parents were in love, but seeing it was really believing it.

Clearing my throat, I asked, "You fixed the roof, Father?"

His eyes lingered on Mom for a couple more seconds, but he finally deigned to grace me with his attention. "Yes. No more leaks in the west wing. The damn thing is going to drive me insane."

"You shouldn't live in a money pit."

Father snorted. "Your mother loves it here."

"I do, just not when it's Christmas," Mom countered. "It's crazy all the things we have to do in the village.

"Plus, Devon's no help. Your dad isn't sleeping as usual," she said glumly. "You're just as bad as him. How many hours of sleep are you getting? You've got shadows under your eyes the size of the moon."

"Gee, thanks, Mom," I retorted. "I'm getting plenty of rest."

Not exactly a lie. Not this week, anyway.

"You don't look like you are," she argued. "I swear, what with you and ET over there, you'll worry me to death."

My lips twitched.

ET was her nickname for Dad.

I could genuinely see why she compared the two. He was innocent in a way that invited protection, all while being one of the smartest men I'd ever known.

"For God's sake, Sascha, don't mother the lad."

Daw's bark made me realize I'd zoned out.

I did that a lot.

Especially when I dealt with my parents en masse.

Not because they were boring, but because having a conversation between seven people took work.

When my brother and twin sisters were involved, sweet Jesus, getting a word in edgewise was like going for gold at the Olympics.

"She can mother me," I slotted into the conversation, just to watch Daw's scowl darken.

I smirked at him as he narrowed his eyes even more.

The shock of red hair atop his head hadn't faded, and I was sure Daw wore it long to piss off Father, who was still in possession of a lot of it, but no one had a mane like Daw's.

Cancer might have kneed him in the balls twice, and he'd lost his hair twice, but it still grew back like his feet were in fertilizer.

"What are you smirking at?" he groused.

"I'm the one who gets care packages if she mothers me." I shrugged. "I'm not about to turn those down, am I?"

"Care packages?" Daw grumbled some more. "The lad's on the continent, for God's sake. He's not in the Middle East."

"I was two weeks ago."

Mom's eyes widened. "You'd better be joking, Valentin."

The full name. Ouch.

"I can't say. It's classified."

Dad's head tilted to the side while his eyes remained on the tablet in front of him—the only indication he was interested. "What clearance level?"

A laugh escaped me. "You can know."

Dad hummed. "I'll tell you later, love."

I rolled my eyes, but I wasn't too mad.

You couldn't really get mad at Devon—Dad.

Sure, you could get exasperated, but he'd just look at you like you were from another country and he didn't understand your language, then he'd proceed to ignore you and return to whatever he was doing which, of course, was far more interesting.

Still, even though I wasn't mad, I had to chide him for it.

"What's the point of clearance levels if you're going to tell people who'd be better off kept in the dark?"

"You know how your mother worries, son."

"Don't make out like I'm a nag," came her waspish retort. "My child goes off to only God knows where at the drop of a hat and on the government's tab... you can't expect me not to worry."

Though her concern made me wince, I muttered truthfully, "Mom, that's all over with now."

That caught everyone's attention.

Even Dad gave me his focus, going so far as to switch off his tablet to peer at me.

"How is it all over with?" she inquired carefully, and I got the impression she was trying not to get her hopes up, which I understood.

The second I'd told her who'd headhunted me from Cambridge, I knew she'd been terrified.

It wasn't like I'd gone on any 'missions,' and it sure as hell wasn't like I was James fucking Bond or something, but I'd definitely traveled on His Majesty's budget.

And what a budget.

If I'd traveled like Bond, I'd have been happy. It had been Ryanair all the way.

Skinflints.

"I mean I have one more mission." I licked my lips. "Here, in Madela."

"Veronia?" she questioned, her surprise clear.

Dad, picking up on what I was saying without words, frowned. "Why one more?"

"Because I'm where I should be."

"But you're in Madela," Mom queried. "Why would the Foreign Office send you there?"

Another lie. I hadn't worked for the Foreign Office, but MI6.

Father sniffed. "I told you he had feelings for Alice."

She shoved him in the side. "Don't start Mr. 'I Know Everything.'"

My lips twitched. "Father's right."

Papa cleared his throat. "When Edward pops his clogs, son, she'll be queen."

"The boy's a genius. I think he worked that out for himself," *Vati* said dryly.

He wasn't wrong.

I *was* a genius.

Went through college at fourteen and, at eighteen, after I scored my Master's in Criminology, I'd been hand selected by MI6 where I liaised with the Foreign Office on the regular—see, the best lies were couched in the truth too.

"Etta's mine," I told them simply. Because it *was* simple. As simple as their relationship. No matter the complications life threw underfoot. "Enough to overlook the fact I'd be a consort to the Crown."

Mom pulled a face. "Don't make me the grandmother of the heir to the Veronian throne, Tin. Please."

"But you'd pull it off so well," I remarked, and though I was definitely teasing, I meant it.

Mom had an elegance about her that was undeniable, but more than that, she had the best heart.

If anyone could deal with the scrutiny that was about to fall on our family, it was Sascha Dubois-Bennett.

"You mean it, don't you?" she whispered, her eyes widening.

"I've loved her since we were twelve."

The admission came freely now. Freely when I'd been fighting it for so fucking long.

I couldn't even say what I'd been fighting. The future? The past?

Overlooking her position had been impossible, and for a kid like me, who'd been raised the way I had? Living in the fishbowl of the Madelan royal court had felt insurmountable.

But after a few years of doing random shit for the government, of working on jobs that had opened my eyes, I'd woken up and smelled the coffee.

Enough that I knew what I wanted.

More so, I knew to take what I wanted with both hands before it was taken from me.

Grateful that the wounds on my torso, the bulky bandages, were covered by a thick flannel shirt and down coat—it was cold as hell in Veronia's capital today—I focused on Mom's pursed lips.

Did she disapprove?

Really?

I'd be surprised if she did.

Years ago, we'd lived in Veronia. Dad, *Papa*, and Daw—Devon, Andrei, and Sawyer—had worked hard to kickstart the Veronian economy in the wake of a rebellion that had destabilized the country itself.

As a result, our families were close.

In no small part because Etta's parents were like mine—she had three fathers and an American mother.

Our family was part of a group of very few people who knew that, and our friendship had not only been forged on that secret, but over twenty years of trips and shared vacations as well.

We had a holiday home in Madela, for God's sake, built on the Duchy of Ansian and Lorrena—the duke was Etta's Papa.

We had known each other since we were toddlers, and while, for a time, our relationship had been almost fraternal, my feelings for her now were anything but brotherly.

I tuned into Mom's conversation when she snapped, "Tin, are you listening to me?"

Daw frowned. "Are you taking your meds?"

"Of course I am."

For once, I wasn't lying.

My ADHD was under control for the most part, and though I had been known to skip my meds, after the 'incident,' I'd been religious in taking them.

Why?

Because I was more introspective of late, and focusing, which was never easy for me, was more difficult than usual.

"I said," Mom grated out, "have you realized what the repercussions are?"

"Kurt hit the nail on the head, lass. The lad's a genius. Of course he knows." Daw's defense of me made my lips curve.

It was usually how it worked with them.

They all ganged up on her on my behalf.

"Did you know what the repercussions would be when you took on five men?"

Her cheeks flushed, but Daw snorted even as the others shot her wry smiles.

"He has a point, Sascha," *Papa* told her, his tone droll.

"I know he does, but for God's sake, he's talking about Alice here. You know what she's like."

Dad pulled a face. "What's wrong with her?"

Mom sighed. "She's difficult."

And that was why I fucking adored the shit out of her.

Etta was like no other woman I'd ever come across, and she'd been mine for a long time.

"Anyway, I called for a reason," I stated, interjecting into an argument between Father and *Papa* over, what sounded like, this morning's edition of *The Times* and an article they'd just published on the DeSauviers.

"Not just to announce that you're intending on dating the future Queen of Veronia?" *Vati* tacked on wryly.

I wasn't surprised at his chilled tone. Very little actually riled *Vati*. It was why I found it so easy to talk to him.

He stared at me intently and, so minutely that I knew no one else would notice, he dipped his chin in soft encouragement.

Because Vati *knew*.

He'd known for the past four years, and not once had he urged me to share the truth with my other parents.

He'd let me live my life. Had let me make bad decision after bad decision and all without judgment.

Knowing I always had him at my back, I whispered, "Do you remember my gap year?"

Father blinked. "The year you spent in the US? After you graduated Cambridge? What about it?"

Time to bite the bullet.

"Etta visited the States when one of her friends was getting married. It was a bachelorette party."

Mom frowned, her stare taking in my intent as well as the seriousness of my tone. "So?"

"Well, we hung out for a while."

The urge to pull at my collar was immense. But I wasn't wearing a suit, and my T-shirt was not restricting me at all.

The reason I felt like I was choking was because I knew she was going to kill me.

It was why I'd waited until I was across the English Channel, firmly in Europe, and a few thousand miles away before I shared the truth.

Why I'd needed to know from Rosie if everything was okay back home.

"I repeat, Tin, so?" She huffed. "Although why you'd think it necessary to keep something from me—"

"Well, we met up, *hung out*," I interrupted meaningfully, then, when she stared at me some more, evidently refusing to get where I was coming from, I cleared my throat. "It was during that time when I was in Vegas."

"What are you trying to tell us, Tin?"

"We got really drunk one night and..."

"And what?" She laughed, but it sounded a little forced. "You got married in front of Elvis?" She laughed again, but her eyes were kind of wild, like she was just waiting on me to tell her she was talking crap.

But she wasn't.

I gulped. "Well... yeah."

SIX

ETTA

The second class was out, I released a deep breath.

This course had been the privy council's idea. An attempt to help me settle down but, in my opinion, I was way too young to settle.

I didn't see why I should have to, period, but shit was different when you were the future queen of a country.

Shit was, in fact, *shit*.

There were more rules, more responsibilities.

It never ended.

Ever.

Like a reminder I didn't need, my cellphone buzzed.

Daddy: *Come to my office when you get home.*

Shit, what the hell had I done now?

While being at the university was making the dads, as I called them, cut me some slack, I wished they'd cut me some more.

Because college was here in Madela, I was on their leash, and I hated it.

I hated Art History even more.

Everything about the course, from the reading list to the professor, irritated the hell out of me.

Unfortunately with my crappy grades, it was the only course the prestigious college had been willing to accept me in.

I was, in more ways than one, a complete failure in my parents' eyes, but they were stuck with me and I with them because I never did anything *bad* enough to be cut off.

Getting Cs and Ds in school, while bad for the family's rep, wasn't exactly execution worthy.

Neither was liking to go to one or two parties every once in a while.

I was rarely in the press, fulfilled every shitty engagement the privy council and my dads insisted upon, and pretty much did as I was told.

Except for my one rebellion.

A rebellion nobody even knew of.

A secret I held to my chest because it was so delicious.

So naughty.

So perfect.

Me: *What have I done now?*

Daddy: *Nothing. I wanted to show you the timetable for this year's Yule events.*

Relieved I wasn't in trouble, I still groaned inwardly.

Yule's timetable.

Fun.

With a sigh, I packed my cell phone into my purse and grabbed the rest of my crap together.

With winter break ahead of me, and Christmas with the folks in the near distance, I'd need to hold onto my secret with both arms.

Not because I wanted to share the truth with my family, but because it would keep me sane.

Only knowing that in this, I couldn't be controlled, kept me going.

When I thought about how often my father spoke of marital alliances, I relished the knowledge that I couldn't marry who they thought was best for me.

Nobody was best for me unless I picked them, but unfortunately because my choice had national, as well as international, implications, they thought they had a say.

And when I said 'they,' I was including the government in the collective.

Yes, my love life was part of a wider political play.

Wasn't it awesome being a princess?

Tucking my purse over my shoulder, I couldn't help but notice how everyone was so earnest as they packed away their laptops.

In class, everyone was always taking notes, staring at the professor with an intent that was so engaged, as though she were Jesus on the mount.

Me?

I took a few notes on my cellphone and that was it. I didn't want to be here. I was here under duress, and while I kind of tried, I also kind of didn't.

Spoiled? Yeah.

But it wasn't my choice to be here.

I'd have far preferred to help Papa out in his greenhouse, except that wasn't allowed and this torment was.

As I began to climb the steps out of the lecture hall, I froze when Professor Granger declared, "Alice DeSauvier, can you stay back, please? I need to speak with you."

Of course, because my name was Alice fucking DeSauvier, the entire student body had stilled.

Each goddamn student sucked in a breath that culminated in a silence so shrill, they'd hear it in America.

When everyone turned to peer at me over their shoulders, I forced myself not to blush.

Compelling my face to behave was par for the course when you were queen-in-waiting.

Sometimes, on occasions like today, I had to dig my nails into my palms, but that came with its own irritation—it stopped me from wanting to rake my nails down the bitch's face.

She couldn't have just said, 'Alice?'

Could she?

Oh, no.

She had to use my full name.

Just *had* to draw attention to the fact that she wanted to talk to me, undoubtedly, about my shitty paper on a shitty topic I didn't give a shit about.

Well, she could wait.

If she was going to attempt to publicly humiliate me, two could play that game.

So I plunked my butt down on the nearest seat and waited for the room to clear. As my row emptied, I didn't make a move until the professor and I were practically alone.

Not just because the nosy bastards would try to listen in, either.

Something would always end up in the papers even though everyone in my classes had been made to sign an NDA by the Guard Elect, our version of the Secret Service.

Nah, the reason I stayed seated was because I *could*.

Dick move, sure, but Granger was one big dick.

She was only my professor. I was her princess.

If she wanted me to be Alice DeSauvier, then I'd be her all the way to the bank.

As I trudged down the few stairs to the podium, hearing a couple lingering voices in the back, I moved toward the desk where Granger was waiting on me. All the while, I rued the day my daddy, George, had dated the bitch when they were in university together.

According to him, she was bitter because he'd never called her again after their last date. While, in the eyes of the world, I was only his niece, Granger kept making me pay for my 'uncle's' mistake.

As far as I could see, he'd been pretty damn smart to coyote ugly the bitch.

"Ms. DeSauvier, did you even read the course directive?" She waggled a printout that was titled, 'Rembrandt—The Lost Years,' at me.

"Yes, I did," I told her calmly.

"Well, I'd never have guessed. I didn't ask for you to psychoanalyze Rembrandt, and poorly at that... I asked for you to—"

Before she could continue dissecting my work in a loud voice that had to carry to the final few people still slowly exiting the hall so they could listen in on this conversation—seriously, sloths moved faster than some of the students—I raised a hand to stem the tide of her words and demanded, "Is there a point to this?"

Her eyes flashed and her chin dropped in agitation.

She hadn't expected me to bite back because I never had before. But today, I *had* to.

Today, Yule loomed in the distance.

And today, I had nothing between me and January when term restarted, other than family events where I'd be in the goldfish bowl of life at court.

Saying I was in a bad mood was like saying the Mariana Trench was *deep*.

"This, as it stands," she hissed, "is worth zero points because you didn't read the directive properly."

I shrugged. "Fine."

Though I didn't show it, I'd admit I wasn't altogether happy with that. I'd put a lot of work into the assignment.

As usual, I missed the mark.

She pursed her lips, looking ever more like the prune she was. "Your disinterest in this course shines through everything you do."

"Picked up on that, did you?" I asked dryly.

She ground her teeth—that wasn't the first, nor would it be the last time that I inspired that particular reaction in someone, so I didn't take offense.

"What's the point in your being here then? You're taking the place of someone who'd actually like to attend this class."

That someone might find her tedious lectures interesting, which were recounted in a dull as dishwater voice, seemed highly unlikely to me.

But I decided it was prudent not to insult the woman further. She couldn't help being boring.

"Do you have a boss, Professor?" I inquired politely.

She scowled. "What does that—"

"Do you have a boss?" I repeated, interrupting her to enunciate the question clearly.

Her eyes glittered with irritation. "Yes. Of course I have a boss."

"Then consider yourself fortunate. Because you only answer to the dean and perhaps a board of governors. Me?" I pointed to myself with a finger that was tipped with a pristinely manicured nail. "I answer to my father, who happens to be the king. I also answer to a government and a council of royal advisors.

"They insisted I take this course. I didn't want to, but when your boss tells you to do something, you do it, don't you?" At her tight nod, I shot her a tired smile. "Therefore, we have no choice but to make the best of things.

"Whether or not someone more worthy than myself merits my position in this class, it isn't by royal decree, whereas my being here is."

She shook her head. "That's ludicrous!"

"You're preaching to the choir, sister." I reached for the paper she'd been wafting around. "Now, would you like me to rework this or have you given up on me entirely?"

A few moments later, with the paper in my hand and a weary rebuke to actually read the questions rather than go off on a tangent of my own making in my ears, I headed up the stairs to the exit which was empty except for Andrea, my guard—the only one I permitted to follow me.

Of course, there was a SWAT team in my vicinity—a veritable battalion of bodyguards that my fathers insisted upon, and while I didn't blame them, neither was I about to have them in my face. Hovering around me every time I needed to use the restroom.

The second the doors to the lecture hall were closed behind me, I released a relieved breath.

The outer corridor, lined with artwork from the undergraduates' finals last year—anything from Buddhas fabricated out of paper mâché to classics that would give John Turner, Picasso, and Marcus Gregory a run for their money—was thankfully empty.

While my classmates had undoubtedly enjoyed watching a princess having her ass reamed, most of them didn't want to watch it enough to stick around when school was out.

Thank God.

Something would, undoubtedly, appear on Twitter later on, but my secretary was used to that.

As I pondered whether it was wise to key Lucy into the situation, I headed for the door the second Andrea peered outside, opened it up, then surveilled the area.

After she uttered something into her discreet earpiece, she nodded at me.

Andrea never smiled, and considering she looked like a stacked Angelina Jolie, I thought that was a damn shame.

Her dark eyes were rich as chestnuts, but they were always cool. Always untouched.

They'd picked her as my body double, but I didn't see the resemblance.

Andrea was gorgeous; I was just me.

Even though she'd guarded me for the past six years, we weren't close. She never allowed it and, frankly, I'd stopped caring a long time ago if we couldn't be friends.

As it stood, I'd learned as much about her as I could because the prospect of being guarded by a stranger was abhorrent to me.

I knew, for example, that Yann, my other guard, was having issues with his thirteen-year-old daughter because she wanted to start dating, and I knew Mika's dad was ill enough to require a permanent move into a nursing home.

Whatever I could learn, I remembered.

My guards were more to me than just a badge.

At Andrea's direction, I stepped toward the glass doors. As I glanced outside, I frowned when I saw the man, his face half shielded by his upturned coat collar, standing on the top step just beyond the entryway to Casterby.

I knew he wasn't a threat because Andrea wouldn't have allowed me to leave the building if he were, but his presence had red flags shooting up around me as I took him in.

There was something about him I recognized—that solid jaw that was turned into his coat collar to evade the bitter cold outside, that silky skin that reminded me of fresh cream, and that shock of white blond hair which, in the bleak sun, couldn't decide whether to refract as silver or gold.

As I stepped through the doors, I called out, "Tin?"

If I sounded wary, that was because I was.

Tin had been my best friend up until I'd shepherded him into doing something I shouldn't have done.

He hadn't forgiven me, not that I blamed him. He was my husband, but I'd forced him.

While our marriage had given me a freedom he'd never be able to understand, it had lost me the one friend I had who loved me for me. Who loved me despite the fact I was the Veronian royal family version of Calamity Jane.

His eyes sparkled a bright blue as he turned to face me, and the smile in them surprised me considering the last time we'd spoken, *truly* spoken, there'd been harsh words between us.

The smile made my heart skip a beat and my bones started to melt. He'd always been the epitome of masculine beauty to me, the man I measured every other against.

It had been four months since I'd last seen him at our family's regular get-together in August.

We'd all traveled to the summer palace in Laurela and spent twelve days doing whatever we wanted.

Outside of Yule, it was the only time we were permitted a break, and Father never scheduled any engagements during that period.

Tin had shown up during the vacation and had stayed for a

weekend before pleading a work emergency and getting the hell out of Dodge.

He'd barely looked at me in that short time and didn't speak to me once. And God, that had fucking hurt. Just having him close enough to talk to, but so distant he might as well have been in Russia, had been a torment in itself.

For him to leave so soon? Every masochistic bone in my body had mourned his loss.

So, while seeing him here was an unexpected delight, for him to be evidently waiting on me came as a surprise.

"Hey, Etta."

My heart went thunk in my chest at the name only he called me.

My royal name was Princess Alexandra, but my family called me Alice.

When I registered for classes, I always registered under Alice in the vain hope for anonymity, which lasted only long enough for them to catch a glimpse of me.

But to Tin? I was my second name—Lisetta.

Which he shortened to Etta because he said I had a voice that could rival Etta James.

The yearning to go to him was strong. Every part of me wanted to be nearer to him, needed to be close.

Even though another part of me pondered over playing it cool, it had been so damn long since he'd called me that, since he'd come looking for me, that I just walked toward him.

When his arms opened?

I started to cry.

I was so focused on him that I didn't hear it at first.

The soft popping sound.

My ears were rushing with blood as the urge to be close to the man I'd loved since I knew there was more than familial and friendly love had overwhelmed me. But his face?

It morphed from sheepish and welcoming and, wonders would never cease, *warm* to horrified and...

No. It couldn't be.

Scared?

Why?

"Etta!" he screamed, like I wasn't a few feet away. "Duck!"

He ran toward me, his body tense as he hustled closer, and I twisted around to see if what was freaking him out was affecting Andrea too.

She was always calm under pressure, so I took her as my measure of whether to freak out or not.

Only, when I turned around, I didn't see my shadow.

That was unusual in itself.

After a second of scanning, I found her—*on the ground.*

A bullet between her eyes.

And I screamed until my lungs burned and I had no choice but to allow Tin to tackle me and drag me wherever he saw fit.

SEVEN

I'd known there might be an active threat against her, but knowing of a potential issue and seeing it were two different entities entirely.

I heard the pop, knew what it was, and saw that she hadn't recognized it at all.

Even as my heart soared at the happiness on her face, a happiness that was founded in my presence, everything inside me froze as I saw Andrea, the guard who'd been at Etta's side for years, murdered before our very eyes.

After screaming, "Duck!" I surged forward to shield her.

The threat came from behind me, so I tucked her into my embrace even as I anticipated the next shot—one I thought would pierce my chest from behind.

I accepted my death, welcomed it if it would save her, but fuck, I didn't want to die.

Not when she was in my arms.

Not when the love of my fucking life had just looked at me like she would forgive me for all the years I'd left us out in the cold.

Determined that today wasn't going to be our first *and* last day together in years, I pushed her toward the hall she'd just left.

I felt her freeze as we came to the same level as Andrea's body, but I forced her to move, snarling, "Move, Etta, dammit. We need to get inside."

This wasn't her first brush with violence or death, and I knew that was why she'd frozen up on me, but if we weren't going to be sitting ducks then I needed to secure us in the building.

In the end, I hauled her inside because moving a brick wall would have been easier.

The second I shoved us into Casterby, a few rapid-fire shots blasted and screams soared in waves around the campus as people recognized the sound of gunfire and reacted to the active threats that were a part of life in this country.

With the chorus of terror and violence, I managed to get us a few feet away from the glass doors, and the second I did, I felt the damp stickiness against my stomach...

Fuck.

Adrenaline could mask pain so, for a moment, I wondered if I'd been shot, but after a quick check, I realized some of my stitches had burst from my original knife wounds.

Because that didn't matter right now, I pulled Etta away from me and, cupping her cheeks, snapped, "Etta, focus. Did you get hit?"

Her bright green eyes were hazy, the pupils tiny pinpricks as she stared into mine without really seeing anything.

I shook her, needing her to get back online. "Etta! Dammit, concentrate."

After a second, she whispered, "Andrea's dead."

"Yes, baby, she is." I ran my hands across her cheeks and smoothed over her jaw until I was cupping the back of her head. "But can you tell me if you were hurt?"

I didn't think she was, but until I knew whether she was injured or not, I wouldn't be able to focus on anything else.

"N-No," she stuttered before she pushed forward, not stopping until she was resting against me.

This was a side of Etta she didn't really let anyone see.

The vulnerable side that gave a shit about her people, her staff, who knew their names and as much of their family as they'd share. No one knew Princess Alexandra cared so much.

Hell, not even Mom knew how deeply Etta felt.

Me?

I knew.

I knew because the love she had for me was endless.

Eternal.

How could someone with that capacity for love be cold and unfeeling?

As she butted her forehead into my chest, she whispered, "Someone else died for me today."

"It isn't your fault *now*, and it wasn't your fault in Marrakech."

She swallowed, the memories of the embassy there being infiltrated clearly raw in her mind.

I got it.

Fourteen of the DeSauvier's security detail had died to spare the lives of the royal family...

Etta had been twelve at the time and, that summer, I'd heard our mothers talking about the nightmares she'd suffered in the aftermath.

That was when I'd known I loved her.

That was the first time she'd had to kill to protect herself.

No small child should have to do that. No small child should have to act on the self-defense she'd been learning from a young age.

Being a princess wasn't as easy or as charming as everyone thought.

Because I needed to get her moving, I rasped, "Did you know I loved you then?"

She tensed. "What?" Her eyes were wild with grief and fear but they were focused on me.

That was what I needed.

Her focused on me, shoving the rest of the world aside.

"Why do you think I stuck to you like glue that summer? I didn't leave you to your own devices at all. I wasn't about to let your sorrow overwhelm you.

"That was true then, and it's true now." I hugged her to me and whispered, "You didn't ask to be shot at, Etta. You didn't ask to be a target. This isn't your fault. The blame lies with whoever wanted to harm you."

She swallowed, and a shudder washed through her as she huddled in my embrace.

It felt so damn good to hold her, to have her here in my arms, but this morning, when I'd landed in Madela, I'd never expected this would be how my afternoon would end.

This was just me being cautious.

Chatter was chatter.

As prevalent as opinions and assholes.

I'd never imagined...

She flinched when, outside, there was a rapid flurry of shots followed by screams that sounded far too close to home.

"They'll have the situation under control soon. You know Andrea wasn't working on her own."

Her brow puckered. "I smell something." Her hands, flat against my chest, began to move.

For a second, I thought she was feeling me up, then I winced when she brushed the bandages that were sticky with my blood. "Christ, Etta," I bit off when she touched a tender spot.

"My God, you were hit!" she shrieked, pulling back to look over me.

Her eyes were filled with a terror so thick that I wanted to cry for her, but instead I grabbed her hands, and, holding them firmly in my own, told her, "The wounds are a few days old."

She frowned, but I saw the fear disappearing, fading away as she demanded, "What happened?"

My nose wrinkled. "You know you're married when your wife starts to nag you."

She tensed again and her fear was replaced with wariness. "That's the first time you've called me that."

I shrugged as I reached up and placed my hands on her shoulders. "It's the first time I've wanted to call you that," I admitted.

No man liked to be manipulated, and I knew Etta had led me to the altar. Maybe not kicking and screaming, but she'd planned it.

"I have so many questions," she whispered. "So, s-so many, but I need to know if you're okay first."

Because we both worked the same way, I understood.

But now wasn't the time.

With her more responsive, I needed to get her somewhere safe.

"Little incident in Cizre."

Her eyes widened, and though Etta was shit at most things school-related, she'd had a thing about geography since we were small.

"Turkey? What were you doing there?"

Now definitely wasn't the time for this conversation so, ignoring her question, I gruffly informed her, "I'm okay. Just a few cuts," before I started hustling her along. "We need to move, Etta."

She nodded even as she whispered, "Been a long time since you called me that."

It had been a long time since I'd *wanted* to call her that, since she'd been that to me.

I didn't say that as I pulled her toward the nearest door though.

I had no doubt her security detail was handling the shooter, and that the gunfire we'd just heard had been from her guards and not the active threat, but that didn't mean we were safe.

The classroom ahead of me was distressingly free of shelter.

There was a desk on a dais and the seats were in a hive shape.

That was it.

Fuck.

"Seems like an obvious place," I rasped, "but, the desk. We need to get under it," I told her, even as I winced at the prospect of having to bend down—just getting out of the damn car had been a nightmare, never mind crawling around on the ground.

The blood on my stomach was starting to darken my shirt—a quick glance told me that—but we didn't have time for me to bleed out.

"Won't they just head straight for it?"

"Yeah, but I'm packing."

Her teary eyes caught mine, and her consternation hit me. "You are? Since when?"

"Now's not the time for that conversation," I said grimly.

At my prompt and a gentle push, she started to descend the staircase. I followed at a slower pace, grunting with each jarring step.

By the time I made it to the dais, I was panting hard. Loud enough for her to demand, "Are you okay?"

My smile was tight. "I've been better, and I'll be better when your guards have things under control."

I dropped to my knees with a thud, unable to use core control to kneel. It made the joints ache with the force, but that was just one of many aches I was dealing with right now.

My brow puckered with pain as I slipped underneath, joining her in the relatively unsafe cocoon.

There were no legs to the desk, only solid walls beneath the tabletop, which was more of a curse than a blessing since I couldn't peer between it and the floor.

It galled me to hide instead of heading outside to help her detail contain the threat, but the wound was fully open now—I could feel it. Anything I did would only compromise her safety.

It would also have been the height of hubris and ego to think I could help in a situation I wasn't trained for.

My place was best served with Etta, keeping her contained, protecting her by staying close.

"What are you doing here, Tin?" she queried after watching me grunt as I tried to get myself situated.

Even crouched beneath a desk, fear etched on her face, she looked regal.

Like grace personified.

Whereas I was bleeding out onto the navy polyester carpet.

I wasn't the right man for her, I knew that, but I was the only man she'd ever have.

"The truth is complicated," I hedged.

She pulled a face even as she drew her knees up to her chest.

I was surprised when the seams of her pencil skirt didn't split with the move, but seeing her look so vulnerable didn't sit well with me.

It was only by chance that I saw it—a tiny glimmer of gold that twinkled in the faint light.

"You still wear it," I stated, touching the ankle bracelet I'd given her for her eighteenth birthday.

"Of course," she said, surprised at the direction I'd taken.

"I wasn't sure it would survive."

The chain was delicate, but it had a small cluster of charms that bobbed at the midpoint.

A shaky sigh escaped me. "I was so nervous you'd hate it when I bought it for you."

"Nervous? I always love your gifts."

I smiled through the pain. "A crown for a princess, a treble clef for the singer she should have been, and the Yorkie terrier for Hank... your only other friend besides me."

She swallowed hard.

"Why have you never gotten another dog?"

"Why haven't I gotten another best friend?"

Her words triggered a deeper agony than what I was already dealing with.

Etta, for all her flaws, was loyal.

So fucking loyal.

"It breaks, but I get it repaired," she said after a few moments where I remained silent. She swallowed then reached for my hand. "Tin, please, explain."

Her gaze drifted to my stomach, and the pain that flashed across her face looked worse than what I was actually feeling.

That was how love worked though, wasn't it?

I'd seen it time and time again with my parents and Etta's.

I gnawed on my bottom lip for a second then, after a few more, muttered, "You won't like it."

"I don't expect to," she rasped.

"There was a mission breach last week," I admitted. "I'm only a desk jockey. I'm not supposed to get hurt, but somehow, the group we were targeting found our base and this happened." I waved a hand at my stomach then regretted it.

She eyed it again like I had a snake sitting on my torso, then flashed her gaze up to me, and started slipping out of her coat.

When she'd made a tight bundle of it, she moved forward and pressed down against the wound with the coat, stemming the flow of blood.

The pressure was excruciating and holding back the cry of agony took more guts than were already spilling out of me.

A choked cry escaped me against my will, however, and I shoved my fist into my mouth to stanch it.

"A few cuts, my ass," she muttered under her breath.

"Husbands lie to their wives," I choked out, wondering when the black spots would stop dancing around the edges of my vision. "Makes them feel better."

"Best way to be unmarried is to think you can lie to your wife," she groused, the bridge of her nose pinching as she complained.

A sharp slice of pain speared me at the exact same moment as a wave of darkness seemed to engulf me.

I didn't have long before I passed out.

Fuck.

The idea of leaving her to defend herself was horrendous, but even worse was knowing that I might not wake up again.

Why had I wasted so much goddamn time?

The bitterness washed away and I told her, "I've lived without the woman I love for years, Etta—"

A soft cry escaped her. "Tin, stop talking. Conserve your strength."

"No!" I ground out. "I need you to know this. I shouldn't have cut ties with you. I denied us both—"

She pressed her hand to my lips. "Shut up."

Weakly, I reached up and snagged her wrist. "Listen to me. I know you love me, and you know I love you. I made us do without that but our friendship too.

"You hurt me, Etta. I felt like you used me, and getting over that wasn't easy, but I should never have done what I did. I should never have cut myself off from you because you're my happiness—"

Her shriek made me realize that my words had waned. They also made me realize that I'd closed my eyes, and when I opened them, those black dots were doing more than just sparkling at the edges of my vision, they'd taken over.

"Sorry." My smile was as weak as my voice.

A gasp escaped her, and I realized she was silently sobbing.

If that didn't break my heart, I didn't know what could.

"It will be okay," I reassured her, but when her face crumpled, I figured it didn't work.

I couldn't blame her.

I could feel the passage of time like my body was a clock.

The slow ooze of blood seeping from the wounds were the second, minute, and hour hands, and they told me that if her guards didn't secure the situation soon, I'd run out of all three.

"Tin?" she whispered.

Blinking dazedly, I muttered, "Yeah?"

"You know I *do* love you, don't you?"

"Sometimes," I whispered weakly, "that's all that got me through the days—"

The sound of the door opening had me tensing.

Adrenaline flared through me, giving me a second wind, and I sat up, jerking myself into a straighter position so I could reach for my weapon.

But the agony that triggered made my stomach rebel.

The wave of pain overtook everything else, drowning my senses to the point where I couldn't rely on them to help us.

Frozen, I cast Etta a beseeching look, saw she'd clapped a hand over her mouth to stem any noise she might make, but the terror in her eyes would stay with me until the day I died.

I just really fucking hoped that today wasn't that day.

I sagged back, my body acting of its own volition, and ordered, "Get my guns. They're holstered. Shoulder," I slurred, "and my left ankle."

I tried to stay conscious. I tried so hard to focus on the pain to the point where it would make me aware, but it was like a blanket.

It encompassed everything.

Suffocating my world in nothingness.

Banking the adrenaline like it had never existed.

I needed to protect her.

Only, my body wasn't going to let me.

Not sure of what would happen next, and feeling like my tongue was as thick as a slug, I managed to whisper, "Love you, Etta... forgive you," before everything went dark.

EIGHT

ETTA

The second Tin passed out, the tension in his body disappearing like it had never existed, I felt certain he'd died.

I stared at him with unseeing eyes because his stillness was terrifying, and then I heard the faint whisper of someone's footsteps and I knew, just like Tin had, that if it had been one of my detail, they'd have announced themselves.

Which meant, God help us, that the person approaching us was an enemy.

Someone who'd killed Andrea.

Who was here either to kill me or to take me captive.

With my lungs burning, and wondering where the fuck my security was because we trained for this way too often and it was all going wrong, I dug my hand into my mouth to stem the sobs that longed to break free.

Even as I cried, my brain kicked into high gear, and I knew I needed to get to the guns Tin was armed with and use the damn things.

Slipping my top lip between my teeth, I bit down, not stopping until the pain was so acute my brain focused on that rather than Tin, his limp form, and the words of forgiveness and love he'd granted me.

He loved me.

He forgave me.

And he was dying.

The sobs started up again, but knowing I had to protect him when I heard those footsteps move ever closer, I forced myself to touch his silent stillness.

Blood seeped through my coat, drenching it even as I found his holster.

The need to press down on his wound was unabating, but I had to keep us safe.

When I found his other gun, I reacquainted myself with the Glock and the Beretta, weapons I was unfortunately familiar with from training.

Blowing out a breath, I unclipped the safety on both and situated myself in front of Tin.

His prone body, hidden by my coat, made it difficult to see if he was breathing, and only the faint whistle between his lips every now and then gave me the reassurance I so desperately needed.

Armed, I braced for the recoil, and I forced myself to remain alert.

My entire being was focused on Tin, but he needed me to keep us both safe now. That was what he needed from me.

Not panic.

Not for me to break down and be useless.

He needed me to protect him.

Nobody had ever needed that from me before, and I refused to let him down.

Not when he was here for me.

Not when he'd forgiven me and we had a chance.

When a floorboard creaked about a foot away from me, I tensed and forced my eyes wide open so I wouldn't miss a thing.

Refusing to blink, I waited until a pair of feet approached from the side.

I recognized them as the jack-boots some of my uniformed guards wore.

A sob tried to escape me as relief filled me, but when the guard lowered down, slowly, and his face came into my line of sight, I didn't recognize him.

Our eyes caught and held, his wide and filled with something I didn't understand, but it made me scan him further, the need for reassurance as to his affiliation making me cautious.

That happened in less than a second. It might have felt like a lifetime, but it wasn't.

I saw his gun next, saw it wasn't pointed down at the dais now that he knew it was me, and I didn't think twice.

I'd been trained for this, and I used that training to defend and protect myself and my husband.

Within fifteen seconds, I'd fired both weapons.

I eliminated the threat against Tin and me.

One to the trunk.

And one to the forehead.

He dropped to the ground, eyes blank in death.

Kill or be killed—I hated that this was my life.

When the sound of sirens pierced the air, I wanted to shout hosannas to the sky, but we weren't out of danger yet.

Still armed, I placed one gun on the floor and, preparing to fire again, I peeped out from our position.

After scanning the area for other attackers, I sighed in relief when I saw we were alone.

Reaching for my cell, I sent out a text to the line my family used in an emergency.

Me: *In Art History classroom. Need EMTs. Valentin Dubois is bleeding out.*

And just in case that didn't light a fire under their asses...

Me: *I've been injured too. Hurry.*

The next few minutes were the worst of my life.

All I could do was put pressure on Tin's wound again, hoping that would do something, but I knew if the EMTs didn't arrive soon I'd be a widow before I could become a wife.

The doors slammed open and a voice called out, "Princess Alexandra, where are you?"

The sobs I'd been choking down escaped and, scrambling out from under the desk, I screamed, "Hurry! He's dying."

NINE

ETTA

"Hurry! He's dying."

That was a truth I was suffocating on.

I knew he was.

I could feel his strength fading from him, leaving me alone.

Always alone.

Seeing Yann and Mika made me feel safe, but the only thing that stopped me from breaking down entirely was the team of four EMTs.

"Fix him," I commanded in a tone of voice I'd never heard myself use before—one I recognized as being my father's.

The king.

When Mika tried to drag me away, I slapped at his hands and hissed, "Don't touch me. I'm not injured. I lied to make you hurry!"

After he let me go when I wouldn't stop slapping him, I focused on the care the EMTs gave my husband, not giving a damn about explanations or justifications.

Just needing to know he was stable.

A nod was the only reassurance I was given as the team spread out and worked on getting Tin onto the gurney.

His beautiful features were drawn, his skin pale and pasty, and if

I looked at his stomach, where the blood was no longer red but close to black, I knew I'd break down.

Mika pressed a hand to my arm. "Your Highness, they need to take him to the hospital."

I knew that, dammit. Where else were they going to take him? A veterinarian's office?

I started to shrug off his hold when he stated firmly, "*Without* you. We'll follow, but give them room to work on him. They don't need you in the way."

I resented that he was correct, but I stopped pushing against his hold on me and, instead, sagged.

I saw him nod and the EMTs, in barely the blink of an eye, were dragging Tin's gurney down the disabled access ramp.

For a second, I wanted nothing more than to crumble, to break down and disintegrate into a thousand pieces, but I couldn't do that.

My focus was on him, my body yearned to stay by his side, my whole being was with Tin, but I was more than just a wife desperate to know that her husband was safe.

I was Princess Alexandra.

I had a role to live up to.

So, I sucked in a breath and demanded, "UnReals?"

"Yes." Mika's stern retort had me nodding shakily. "The threat is contained for the moment."

And those were the key words.

'*For the moment.*'

Another breath flowed into my lungs as, in my head, white noise took over everything else.

"When isn't it 'for the moment?'" I snapped bitterly.

He dipped his chin in acknowledgement. "The UnReal threat has been a pest on your family for centuries, Your Highness. They're a scourge, but we're working on eradicating them."

My jaw clenched. "Pest control didn't work today, did it?"

Mika shook his head. "No, Your Highness. It didn't."

I'd lost my grandmother to their cause, and too many good men and women had fallen thanks to their evilness.

Now there was even more blood spilled because of whatever plot of theirs had just been foiled.

Yann stormed over, switching places with Mika who went to deal with another guard who beckoned him.

In the lull, I saw from how Yann was gritting his teeth as if he were trying to stop himself from crying that he was in pain, so I asked something I'd never asked before.

Something I'd speculated about for as long as I'd known them both because Andrea rarely, *if ever*, smiled.

Except at Yann.

"Did you love her?"

Yann blinked. "I don't know what you're talking about."

"Andrea's dead," I rasped. "Don't deny her—"

"I'm a married man."

"I won't tell anyone." I shrugged. "Did you love her?"

He hesitated a second, but then he dipped his chin again.

A silent acknowledgment.

Reaching for him, I grabbed his hand and whispered, "I'm sorry, Yann."

"She died honorably," was his wooden response, but he squeezed back.

"I promise," I said softly, "that I'll make them pay, Yann. I'll figure out a way to keep us safe from them."

He licked his lips. "Your father—"

He hadn't achieved that in his reign, and he was the most beloved DeSauvier King we'd ever had.

I expected Yann to point that out, to ram it home that I wasn't and never would be my father, but he didn't.

He squeezed my fingers once more. "If anyone could do it, Your Highness, it's you."

His faith in me came as a surprise.

But the level of warmth that filled me as a result was incomparable to anything I'd ever experienced.

I led my life at the Veronian government's pleasure.

At this moment, however, I knew what dedicating my life to public service truly meant.

I *would* do what no other DeSauvier had.

Why?

Because I'd have Valentin Dubois at my side.

He *would* not die, he would *not* leave me to do this on my own.

Mika returned, asking, "Your Highness? Did Valentin shoot the UnReal?"

Without looking at him, I shook my head.

"Andrea always said you had more mettle than any of us realized," Yann replied, his tone reflective.

"S-She did?" I sputtered, stunned because Andrea and I hadn't been close.

For all that I'd gathered she was having an affair with Yann, and that she'd been with me for years, I knew precious little about her that wasn't on her security file.

"She did."

Tears pricked my eyes.

Faith.

Andrea had had faith in me.

Yann moved aside, making me realize a cop had called for him.

I registered that Mika had returned because he placed one of those foil blankets around my shoulders and questioned, "Do you want to follow the ambulance?"

I did.

God, how I did, but I was a princess.

Not just any member of the royal family either.

I was the crown princess, the heir to the throne, and while the only duty that really mattered to me was Tin, I knew there was nothing I could do for him.

Nothing other than fretting in a hospital waiting room as I awaited news from a frazzled surgeon on his status.

Here, I could do something. Not much. But *something*. And I would.

First things first, I grated out, "Mika, make it known that Valentin Dubois is my husband, and, as such, is due the respect and treatment granted to the station of a member of the royal household."

My statement had him tensing, and his eyes widened even as his skin paled. Not much scared Mika, but I figured I'd just scared the ever-loving shit out of him.

"Your Highness, you can't be serious. How is he your—"

I raised a hand. "Now is not the time to argue. Make it known, Mika."

Andrea had known about Tin and me.

She'd disapproved too.

Even ill, she'd been a better guard than Mika or Yann. Maybe because she knew not to underestimate another woman where they did.

She, not they, had realized I hadn't been in my room.

She'd been the one to find Tin and me hobbling out of the wedding chapel, me propping him upright as he sang made-up lyrics to the wedding march.

She'd kept my secret, and now it was time to live up to the faith she had in me.

Mika's tension was evident, as was his desire to avoid making such a declaration over the radio.

He knew, as well as I did, that news of the shooting and subsequent updates would trickle down to my parents.

"I'll make the announcement about Tin if you want me to," I said stubbornly.

"When did you—"

"Does it matter?"

He shook his head. "I guess not. Andrea—"

"She knew," I confirmed, saddened by yet more proof of how Andrea had been utterly loyal to the bitter end.

God, what was I going to do without her?

"Mika, I want it known that Tin's my husband because it means something in this world, and I want him to have the best care imaginable. Do you understand?"

He bowed his head.

It was elitist of me, but I'd pull every string in the known universe to make sure that Tin made it out okay.

I couldn't even think of the word A-L-I-V-E.

He had to survive.

He just had to.

I could live in a world where he wasn't talking to me.

But one where he wasn't in it?

No.

Just, no.

"Do it," I commanded grimly, mouth firming when he still made no move to pick up his radio.

There was a staring contest, one I won because I refused to concede on this matter.

Tin was a DeSauvier now.

Whether he liked it or not.

And that came with duties and protocols and perks.

There was no way you couldn't take one without the other, and in this instance, I wanted him awash with the perks because the doctors would stop at nothing to save him once they knew who was under their scalpels in surgery.

An explosive breath burst from Mika before his hand snapped out and he reached for the radio, then he did as bid.

Finally.

Taking a step away from my guard, I moved toward the staircase I'd ascended such a short while ago.

A part of me listened to what he was saying, but my mind was awash with thoughts.

The last time I'd climbed these stairs, my only concern had been the upcoming dinners I'd be having with my parents and family over the festive season, but now, in the space of an hour, God, maybe even less than that, my world had totally changed.

I didn't wait for Mika to approach me. Instead, I returned to where I'd first met Tin on the top step, just outside the doors to Casterby College.

When Yann didn't appear from out of nowhere to stop me, I figured the threat was as clear as it could be, and I gave a silent 'fuck you' to the UnReals because there was no way in hell I wasn't going to Andrea.

She lay where she'd fallen, a pool of blood spilling around her upper body, seeping into the folds of the blanket that had been used to cover her.

The sight of her, so still when she'd always been the exact opposite, set me on edge. I half expected her to leap up and chivvy me inside where I'd be safe.

For years, every day, without fail because, in my memory, she'd taken criminally few vacation days for herself, she'd protected me.

And today?

She'd shielded me with her life.

It wasn't enough that she'd be honored with medals. Wasn't enough that our family would attend her funeral and that hers would receive compensation for her loss.

There were no words for this kind of sacrifice, but I knew how I could honor her further.

All around me, security personnel worked to contain the area.

The screams of before, the gun shots, and sounds of violence had been replaced with brisk military commands being barked out as the troops worked with the police to put things back under control.

In the distance, I could hear traffic, as well as the chopper that was either going to take me away from here or contained one of my parents who wanted to fly in to make sure, with their own eyes, that I was alive and well.

The tree-lined square beyond the gates to Casterby would forever feel the taint of this moment, and I cast a weary glance around, depressed and hurting, when I saw the blazing lights of several ambulances nearby which meant civilians had been caught in a crossfire that was intended for me alone.

As crazy as it was out here, my focus was on Andrea as I dropped to my knees beside her and whispered, "I'm going to miss you, Andrea."

"Your Highness?" Yann rasped behind me.

Realizing he'd made an appearance, I turned to look up at him and saw that, even behind his stoic mask, there were tears in his eyes.

Swallowing, I reached for the baptism ring every DeSauvier child was granted and worked it off my index finger.

It was warm from my body, where Andrea was already growing cold from the bitter wind out here.

Reaching for her hand, I cupped it a second in mine, wishing this weren't happening, wishing I could do something to keep her warm, before I worked the ring over her knuckle.

I heard Yann and Mika's gasps of surprise at the act of deep respect, but I ignored them and bowed my head before I got to my feet once more.

Staring around the chaos, I didn't let him steer me toward a waiting car. I headed into the fray where my people were bleeding.

Because of me.

Because I was the threat here.

"Can I do anything to help?" I demanded of a frazzled EMT.

"No, Your Highness," he blurted out in surprise when he saw me.

Mika sidled up to me. "We're willing hands," he declared.

The EMT blinked then asked, "Do you know first aid?"

"I do," Mika and Yann said almost simultaneously.

"Me too," I agreed.

Hell, I'd been trained in more survival techniques than a doomsdayer.

"Help is on its way but there was a pileup over in Saren—"

"Related to this?" I interrupted anxiously.

"No. Some logs fell off a three-wheeler. There are simpler injuries you could help with. A few people were hurt when others pushed them over." He shoved a case at Mika. "Don't do anything invasive. Just patch them up."

Mika nodded, and I didn't mind that they were talking around me because I knew Mika wouldn't stop me from helping.

A few steps away from the ambulance, I came across one of the girls from my class who'd hung back to watch the professor ream me a new one.

She was dazed, sitting with her back against a bench, clutching at her arm.

"Rhia?" I asked, crouching down to peer into her eyes. "Were you shot?"

Rhia's chin wobbled, and she slowly, sightlessly, moved her hand away.

In the distance, I heard the roar of incoming helicopters growing noisier as Mika dropped down beside me while Yann helped someone who was clutching his ankle.

Together, Mika and I worked on finding out if Rhia was in need of an ambulance next.

Which was where Papa found me.

The minute he saw me, parts of me drenched in Tin's blood and dotted with Rhia's, I knew he'd forgotten last week's recurring argument.

I saw his irritation with me, an irritation that was forged in my inability to do anything right, disappear.

With his arrival, there was a sudden surge in noise as sirens made my ears ring.

Though I longed to run to my papa, to hide in his embrace, Rhia needed me, and I stayed by her side until the EMTs approached and took her away.

That was when I was left alone with him, a man the press didn't even consider an uncle because he was the king's cousin, and who instantly hauled me into his arms and held me close.

The second I was there, leaning into him, I sagged, my control bursting like an overfull dam.

He was my papa, after all. How couldn't I find solace in his arms? Public eye be damned.

"Your mother is worried sick," he rasped in my ear, even as he squeezed me, telling me he was just as worried.

"Sorry," I whispered. "I wasn't injured. I just needed the EMTs to get to Tin."

"Don't ever scare us like that again," Papa snapped, but his arms tightened around me to the point of pain again—his relief clearly belying his anger.

"Is everyone safe?"

"Yes. You were the only one targeted," he growled bitterly.

That was when I understood the tight clasp of his embrace, and I didn't complain even though it was starting to hurt.

If anything, the pain was surprisingly grounding, and it helped keep me connected to the moment.

The last thing anyone needed was for me to go off the rails.

I needed to maintain my composure because royalty never had any alternative but to be in command of the situation. Whatever that situation might be.

Even now, there were millions of eyes on us.

I couldn't see them, but that didn't mean that wasn't our reality.

"I told you college was a bad idea," I whispered, needing to find some semblance of dark humor in this scenario before I burst into tears.

Peering up at him, I watched as his short laugh softened the unease in his face. As of this moment, the only thing about him that wasn't pale and white was the shock of red hair on his head.

"No change. You've always got to be right, don't you, sweetheart?" he countered, even as he hugged me tighter.

Dammit to hell. The tears were going to come anyway.

"I try," I whispered miserably.

"Are you okay?" he murmured a moment later.

"Been better." I pulled back to look at him, and I braced myself. "How mad is everyone?"

A twinkle appeared in his eye, and it surprised me considering the situation.

Papa could be surprisingly stern when he chose to be, and this clusterfuck definitely warranted *stern*.

"As mad as you can imagine. But we'll talk about that later. We need to get you home.

"Your mother won't believe you're okay until she sets her eyes on you."

And because the army was out, and the police were here in full force, I knew our Guard Elect would have put her under what was essentially house arrest.

That meant she couldn't come to me.

"No," I retorted, "I need to be at the hospital with Tin."

Xavier's mouth tightened but he nodded. "Of course."

I peered up at him. "I love him, Papa." I whispered that last word, and his gaze softened on me.

"You always did."

He was right.

I had always loved Tin and I always would.

The only reason I was on this earth was to stand by his side. Not to sit on the Veronian throne, but to be with *him*.

Nothing, not even this shooting, not the UnReal threat, would change that.

TEN

TIN

If I'd imagined waking up like this, I might have passed out sooner.

Okay, that might have been a lie… especially when Etta had been in so much danger. But to wake up with her at my side, tucked into me how she was, was a gift worthy of the upcoming Christmas festivities.

I knew it was royal privilege that enabled her to splay out the way she was.

Anyone else would have been made to wait out in the waiting room, but she wasn't your average visitor, was she?

I loved that her hair cascaded out in a wave, the bronze-striated, chestnut-hued locks liberated and drifting over the white sheets that covered me.

At some point, she'd changed into loose, comfortable clothing which wasn't dotted with blood and wasn't, most definitely, a part of her 'princess wardrobe.'

As I stared at her, glad to see she was resting and at my side, something inside me settled.

I was in pain, though I didn't doubt I'd been doped up. My body was stiff, my back fucking caned, but she was here, and while things weren't right with my world, not when she was still under threat, I felt a damn sight better than I had the last time I'd woken up in a clinic alone—which had been barely a week ago.

Fuck, this had not been the best seven days of my life.

A throat cleared, snatching my attention from my wife, and when I saw Edward, the King of Veronia himself, slouched in an armchair in the corner of my room, my brows lifted.

"Uncle Edward?"

His lips pursed at the title, but I didn't understand why. "Hardly 'uncle,' Valentin."

My family, the people who knew me, never called me Valentin. Except when they were mad at me.

As far as I knew, Edward had no reason to be pissed. After all, I'd gone a long way to making Etta safe this afternoon...yesterday afternoon...whenever the goddamn shooting had taken place.

So his failure to use my nickname, and how he corrected me, had me wondering what the fuck I'd done.

It wasn't like you could cause offense when you were lying unconscious in a hospital bed.

Warily, I queried, "What do you mean?"

Edward's eyes narrowed. "Look around you. Tell me what you see."

Brow puckering further, I glanced around the hospital room.

It looked like a standard clinic, and I'd been in enough over the years to know what a standard clinic was in pretty much most of the major countries in the world.

Those odd plugs and adapters that connected to equipment. IV lines and clusters of beeping monitors which, I knew, once the cadence made it into your head, were impossible to ignore.

The bed appeared to be standard... except—

Squinting, I saw a tiny impression on the sheet. It was faint, but it made me realize where I was.

This was no standard clinic, and the DeSauvier crest on the sheets revealed that truth to me.

When King Incumbent Philippe, Etta's grandfather, had been diagnosed with cancer a year before he succumbed to the illness, the family had added an extension to the palace.

Before, there'd been a medical unit, but this was pretty much a hospital in and of itself, and thus, they'd created a freestanding medical center that catered only to the royal family.

Which I wasn't... not officially anyway.

"Alice insisted we transfer you here after your blood transfusion," Edward continued tightly. "Maybe you'd care to explain why?" When my mouth worked for a few seconds as I tried to figure out what in the hell I could say to that, he swept on, "Why Alice would insist on installing you into a clinic that exclusively serves our family? Why she almost had a fit when I refused and didn't back down until you were moved here?"

Gulping, because I'd never seen him so pissed off, I muttered, "Did she tell you?"

"No. She didn't. She told her guard to inform the hospital staff that they were treating a DeSauvier."

Well, there wasn't much I could say to that except, "Fuck."

His face, as a whole, puckered like he'd started sucking lemons.

Though my mind raced, I had to wonder if Etta knew how much she resembled him when she was pissed off. He was clearly her biological father because, hold up a mirror to them both, she was the feminine version of him.

"Exactly," was his bitter reply and, nostrils flaring, he continued, "With the fallout from the shooting, this is the first time I've been able to visit you and, because she's been by your side for the past three days, without fail, it's the first time I've been able to see my daughter. And *you*."

I shot him a weak smile. "I'm relieved you weren't targeted."

"Yes, I'm safe. She—" His voice broke, revealing a chink in his armor that was rarely bruised. "Alice was the only one targeted."

He leaned forward, and it was then I realized he was wearing the crumpled remnants of an expensive suit.

His shirt was creased, his sleeves were up by his elbows, and his pants no longer had the central crease down them.

For Edward, with his dark hair tousled and unshaved jaw, this was about as messy as it came.

"How did her guards fail to secure the scene?"

His mouth tightened. "That is not the topic on the table. I'm tired of waiting for an answer, Valentin. Explain."

"The shooting happened three days ago?" was all I could think to say.

"Yes," came the taut response. "We almost lost you three times. Your mother is frantic, your fathers are close to a meltdown... so it's about time you woke up."

I cringed. "I mean, I'd have woken up sooner if I could've."

"Good to know. Now, why are you my son-in-law and how did I only find out about it three days ago?" He grunted. "For God's sake, you two have barely spoken to each other for the past few years..." Edward blinked at me as his words faded. Then, grimly, as if speaking the words aloud had made him realize something untoward had happened, he snapped, "What did she do?"

It might have been logical for him to blame Etta, but I'd always thought her folks never cut her any slack.

Well, except for Auntie Perry. She was chill. That was probably down to her being American and a commoner though.

"Nothing," I denied, irritated on Etta's behalf.

He squinted at me. "You're a rational child, Tin. Always have been.

"Your influence on her has been appreciated as a result. Like your fathers, you're steadfast and loyal. Like your mother, you're loving and kind...

"Nowhere in that character assessment does it make sense for you to essentially abandon a friend you've loved since childhood.

"On top of that, I've followed the rise of your star for King William's government. It has not gone unnoticed by my staff either.

"For some time, the Guard Elect has been monitoring you with a view to bringing you into the ranks because of your success in recent campaigns..."

While all his remarks percolated in my head, making me aware that he *knew* about my job, Edward's mouth flatlined in grim disapproval before he grated out, "So, Tin, I repeat, what did Alice do?"

I cast a look at Etta, who tipped her head to the side in her sleep. She was tired, and I sensed an unhappiness about her that I knew stemmed from our discord.

Her face was turned from her father, but it soothed me to study the woman I'd loved since my heart knew what it was to love in this way.

Seeing her filled me with peace. A peace I'd been missing since I'd left her behind.

"Nothing, Uncle Edward," I rasped eventually. "We just had a falling out."

Her eyes flashed open at that, making me wonder how long she'd been aware of our conversation.

But the question faded once I saw the gratitude in her gaze. A gratitude that was founded in my hiding the truth from her father.

Its presence rankled me on her behalf.

Etta's family was close knit, but it couldn't be denied that her fathers were harder on her than they were her sisters. But they weren't the future queen...

Edward sighed even as he reached up and pinched the bridge of his nose. "Always loyal to the last."

I cut him a look then spoke the words to her. "I love her, sir."

"That much is clear." He frowned, and before he could start with the inquisition again, I turned it around.

"Sir, how the hell did they get to her? Why wasn't her team on her faster?"

His eyes flashed. "Don't think you can change the subject on me, young man," Edward grated out, making me feel like I was five. "Her team has been dealt with. Heads are rolling with the Guard Elect.

"Mistakes were made, mistakes that people will pay for with

their careers..." He sucked in a sharp breath like he was trying not to get agitated—probably because the last time I'd been with them Auntie Perry had been worrying about his blood pressure—and ground out, "To get things back on track... You should have asked for her hand."

Well, that diversion hadn't worked as well as I'd have liked.

Grimly, I told him, "You had to have known she was mine, Uncle Edward. As much as I'm hers—"

"I'm not refuting that. Just saying there is a way of doing things, and the way you chose for yourselves is not the right one. Where did you even get married?"

"It wasn't in ideal circumstances," was all I'd admit to.

"We might as well tell him, Tin." Etta's voice was hazed with sleep.

Edward pinned her in place with a focus that could only be considered laser hewn as he demanded, "Tell me what, Alice?"

It amused me when she yawned, stretching her arms to ease the kinks that had to have formed while sleeping against the bed how she had.

It touched me to think of her staying so close at hand.

After all, we were in the palace—her family home. She could have gone to her bedroom, could have had the staff inform her when I woke up... but no.

Not Etta.

She always did dance to a different beat than everyone else.

Edward's mouth firmed.

Again.

Spotting it, and as aware as I was that it was his signal he'd reached the end of his temper, she muttered, "We married in Vegas. Elvis officiated."

Though her face was expressionless, I happened to see the slightest glint in her eye...

She was amused.

The minx.

To be fair, all these years later, and with Edward watching us like we were escaped convicts, it *was* amusing.

Something that was only exacerbated when Edward intoned, "Elvis?"

When he repeated the question, more to himself than us, it was clear that every inch of him rejected what she said as he stared at her, evidently unable to compute the truth.

Etta ignored him and told me, "I need to get your mom, Tin. We've been taking turns to sit with you."

"Uncle Edward said you didn't leave my side. Once."

I made sure to enunciate each syllable of the word, 'once,' and had to shoot her a tired grin when she pulled a face.

"Father!" she whined. "What did you tell him that for?"

But *Father* was still aghast at his daughter, the Crown Princess of Veronia, heir to his throne, getting married with Elvis as the officiant.

She, quite wisely, didn't wait for an answer, just huffed and informed me, "I didn't want you to wake up alone."

Her admission had me sighing.

Unable to bear any space between us, not after what had gone down in Casterby, I reached for her hand, wincing as the move necessitated me leaning forward slightly.

My words were fervent, "God, I missed you."

Her lips curved in the faintest of smiles. "I missed you too."

Her heart was in her eyes, and I knew if her father wasn't there, she'd have said something else.

I wasn't sure what.

Maybe she'd have told me what I needed to hear—that she loved me, even if I'd been a jackass.

Maybe it would just have been her clambering into the bed to give me an awkward hug—I wasn't averse to cajoling that out of her.

But Edward *was* here, and he was already astounded.

Considering Edward was the most unflappable man I'd ever met, that was a list I could include my fathers in, and that he was still gaping said it all.

No one could stun him like Etta.

Hell, I was almost proud about that.

When, heart still in her eyes, she made to get up, I tugged her back down. "Don't leave."

She smiled at me but shook her head. "They're staying in Masonbrook, in the apartments near me. I won't be gone long."

"Don't go," I repeated, even as my mind whirled with the news.

Patting her side, she reached for her phone. "Call her then. It'll make her feel better to hear from you. Everyone's been worried sick."

There was, as there had been with Uncle Edward, the faint note of accusation to her tone.

Exasperated, I muttered, "I didn't do it on purpose."

"Uncle Devon told us you've been working for British security."

I arched a brow—he had, had he? *Damn turncoat.* "You make it sound like a bad thing."

She blanched. "Isn't it? You could have been in danger."

"I wasn't. For the most part." Wafting a hand at my stomach, I stated, "This was a one-off."

Edward's raised brows told me two things.

One, he knew more about my record than I might have liked, and two, that my BS was enough to drag him from the stupor our marriage with a king who wasn't him had sunk him into.

Still, he was a wise man, and he knew better than to give Etta ammunition, so his brows were the only indication he gave me that he knew I wasn't telling the whole truth.

With the bit between her teeth, Etta could be a real pain in the ass. That side of her didn't come out often, but with things she cared about, it sure did.

Eying her cell, I placed the call to 'Auntie Sascha' and waited for Mom to pick up.

"Alice?" She sounded tired and drawn, but there was a note of hope in her voice that made my heart twinge. "Is he awake?"

"Mom, it's me," I said a shade awkwardly. "I'm sorry if I made you worry."

"Worry? Understatement, son." She sucked in a sharp breath, and I heard a tiny hitch as if she were trying not to cry, then I heard a rustling sound. Her voice was wobbly as she whispered, "Andrei, Kurt, Tin's awake."

In the near distance, which told me Dad was somewhere in her bedroom too, I heard him rumble, "Is he okay?"

"We'll find out," she told him. To me, she stated, "We'll be there in five minutes. Don't you dare go back to sleep until I set my eyes on you."

"There's no need to wake everyone up," I chided because I'd seen from Etta's screen it was four in the morning.

The lack of windows in here was really messing with my perception.

Security.

It was everywhere.

People didn't realize how invasive a gilded cage could be.

"There's every need," *Vati* muttered, keying me in on the fact she'd put us on speaker.

"You almost died, Tin," *Papa* rumbled in Russian. "She's, *we've*, been frantic."

"You know I hate it when you speak Russian," Mom grumbled, making my lips twitch. "Coming, baby," she added, and I had the feeling she was going to run here from wherever Auntie Perry and Etta had put them up in the palace.

"They don't normally stay here," I said softly when the line cut.

Etta shrugged. "I wasn't about to have them stay in their place on Papa's estate."

"It's only a short car ride away," I pointed out.

"I don't care," was her stubborn retort. "Your mom's been frantic ever since she landed. I can't say that I damn well blame her either."

My brow puckered. "I don't understand, Etta. This is a big deal—"

"You're my husband. You *are* a big deal." Her obstinacy rang through those words, as well as every arrogant royal streak in her body.

If I'd been capable of it, and if blood wasn't needed more urgently in other areas, that tone would have given me an erection.

"The public knows?"

"Yes." She raised her chin, just daring me to argue.

I whistled under my breath. "You triggered a shit storm, Etta."

Seeming to awaken from his stupor, Edward ground out, "Tell me about it." Then, his frown entered his eyes. If this was the sixteenth century, he'd probably have called for some guards to lop off my head. "*They* were aware of your marriage."

Edward's irritation was clear. And, to be fair, I didn't exactly blame him.

"Father, Tin just woke up. He isn't ready to be interrogated by you," Etta sniped.

I'd have smiled, but I didn't feel like being thrown in front of a firing range.

Instead, I tugged on her hand. "It's only natural he has questions. The country must be reeling from the news."

"It is," Edward inserted grimly.

"I told them the day of the shooting. They asked where I was, and when I told them I was in Madela, they didn't understand why."

"Hardly surprising considering your stays here have been far and few between." His nostrils flared, making him look the epitome of regal asshole. "I assume there's a reason for that if you're man and wife?"

It was a legitimate question. A solid one. The man might be in power because of the divine right of kings, but he was no moron.

Not willing to incriminate Etta, I told him, "Things don't always work out according to plan."

"You don't say," he retorted gruffly, his sarcasm clear.

I blew out a breath then winced when the move had my body protesting.

Spotting it, Etta whispered, "I'll get the doctor."

"No, it's okay—"

"We should have called for him the second you woke up." She glared at Edward. "Father, you should—"

"I wanted a word with my new son-in-law," was his unrepentant answer.

She licked her lips. "Hardly new. And it's not like you don't know him, is it?"

Edward tensed more at that, and I muttered, "Probably not the best comeback, Etta."

She surged to her feet. "Just because you wanted to marry me off to some asshole that would shore up the country's defenses doesn't mean you can give me the third degree.

"Lots of royals marry for love now. Hell, you did it yourself! So, in my mind, this is totally unnecessary and a bit like the pot calling the kettle black."

"I care for my daughter's wellbeing," Edward snarled, clearly taken aback by her attack. "I never had any intention of marrying you off. Jesus, Alice, is that what you thought?"

"You paraded enough eligible bachelors in front of me to start up our own reality TV show," she growled, making my brows rise in the process.

She'd always been a gutsy wee thing, but it seemed like she'd grown more spine in the years we'd been distant.

"I want to see you settled," was all Edward had to say to her claim.

"Settled? Like you were in your early twenties, you mean?" she snapped, further surprising me.

"It's different for you—"

Her hands fisted at her sides. "Is it? Really? Why is it? Because I'm a woman?

"You were allowed to lead a regular life until you got married the first time."

"Alice, that marriage was all duty. Nothing more, nothing less."

"Yeah, and look how that turned out," she argued. "The best

thing you did was the opposite of duty. Mama wasn't the best choice for queen, but look how perfect she is now!

"Just because something's odd on paper doesn't mean it isn't right.

"I know exactly what your problem is. It's his family. Your friends. Which makes you a hypocrite."

"That's bullshit."

Despite myself, I had to smile, especially as he rarely, if ever, cursed. "Is it though?"

I wasn't particularly offended.

How could I be?

He gritted his teeth. "You more than anyone understand the precariousness of my situation, Valentin."

"I do, and I'm not judging you."

How could I?

I was used to being one of two things.

A pariah.

Or, alternatively, an oddity that merited goggle eyes and creepy questions.

After a lifetime of handling the fallout from my parents' relationship, I couldn't be mad at Edward. Not when this was a cementing of ties between our two families that could bring us all under suspicion.

Yeah, suspicion.

Like we were doing something wrong.

"You might not be, but I am. The Dubois-Bennetts are our friends." She flashed me a glance. "I had to get Mom to negotiate with you for them to stay in the palace, for God's sake. Their son was injured."

"And he's being treated by the best doctors in the land," he snarled.

"Yes, because I had to trigger that protocol. It wasn't ideal, I didn't ask for this, and I sure as hell didn't ask to be shot at, for my guard to be murdered in front of me, or to have to kill—"

A gasp escaped her as she slapped her hand to her mouth.

Her words had Edward rubbing his brow, but deep in his eyes, I saw his regret.

"I'm sorry, sweetheart," Edward whispered softly. "If I could have spared you from that, I would."

I tugged on Etta's hand. "What happened?"

She blinked at me, her expression collected even as her eyes were troubled. Their green depths were usually as cool as the water on Madela's Lake Encharne, but were now as riotous as the Atlantic Ocean in midwinter.

"I used the guns you gave me."

"I wish I could—" Sighing, I squeezed her fingers. "I'll make sure you never have to go through anything like that again, Etta."

"That's the one promise you can't make, Tin. You and I both know that," she whispered sadly.

Bitterness had me shooting Edward a look, and rather than hold my tongue as was probably wise, I rasped, "No one will take her from me, Edward. No one.

"Not a king, not a prime minister, and not some UnReal bastard who bears a grudge against your ancestors. It's *my* duty to keep her safe because apparently you and your protocols can't."

Rage simmered in his eyes. "That sounds like a vow."

"That's because it is."

ELEVEN

ETTA

"I can't believe you didn't tell me."

Inside, I cringed. "How could I?"

"Vegas, Alice. Vegas?" Mom frowned at me. "God, what will Parliament say?"

I hated disappointing her because she wasn't the stickler in my family. She was, in fact, the only parent who gave me some freedom.

But what was done, was done.

I couldn't change that.

Didn't even want to.

"Why do you think I gave them a *fait accompli?*" I whispered, guilt making my shoulders hitch so high they were pretty much earmuffs. "They *can't* say anything, can they?"

Mom's brows lowered. "Dear God, your father's going to get nothing but hell for this from the privy council."

I knew she was right.

So I didn't say a word.

"I vouched for you, Alice," she continued, "I'm the only reason you could go."

"I know." My tone was miserable. Bleak. "I'm so sorry, Mom."

"It's a little late for apologies."

"Tin, our wedding, it's... I'm not sorry for that." I straightened my shoulders. "You might want me to be, but I'm not." Her outraged gasp had me swallowing. "I love him. He's my future. I can't regret something that will cement us together, that will never allow us to be torn apart." I turned to look at him. "Mom, he almost died. How... you couldn't live without my fathers. Why would you ask me to live without Tin?"

"None of us could understand why the pair of you had fallen out, and it makes even less sense now."

She got to her feet and started striding in front of his bed, back and forth, as if that would help her make sense of things.

I could almost guarantee that it wouldn't.

"We had an argument." I swallowed down the lie. "That's what married people do, don't they?"

"There's a difference between making your father sleep on the sofa and barely talking to each other for so long."

"I don't understand why this comes as a shock," I sniped, deciding it was wise to change tactics. "We've always been close. Why are you surprised that we love each other?"

Sascha, Tin's mom, flicked her hair over her shoulder. "Doesn't the fact you both love each other make it even more shocking that you two have barely talked for years?"

I sensed her disapproval and was hurt by it.

From the disparaging glances Sascha and Mom were giving me, and after what Father had said too, I figured they believed I was behind the wedding.

Tin might have defended me, might have even lied for me, but that didn't stop them from believing I was to blame.

I mean, I *was* in this instance, but I was usually the bad guy no matter what I did. That was why I'd gone through with this whole plan. Better to say sorry after the fact than to ask permission and be denied.

"We argued," was all I said.

"About what?"

I turned to Sascha, saw more disapproval, and rasped, "That's between Tin and me." Her eyes narrowed upon me, and maybe it wasn't a wise move to make, but I couldn't stop myself from asking, "You've never liked me, have you, Sascha?"

Her eyes widened at that. "Don't be silly, Alice. Of course I like you."

"Then why do you always give me such a hard time? Don't you think I get enough of that from four parents? All of them telling me I'm not good enough." Swallowing, I turned to Mom, "You and my fathers might not approve of me, but Veronia does. Veronia likes me. Veronia will celebrate our marriage. You'll see."

Mom's brow furrowed. "Sascha treats you no differently than she does Christel or Victoria."

"That's what you choose to focus on? Why? Because you know I'm right." My mouth tightened. "How you talk about me it's like I've been the rebel princess—"

"And it's not like you're living up to that title, is it?"

"Tin was my one rebellion. I've toed the line everywhere you've asked of me, but where my future husband's concerned, that *was* my choice to make.

"You had your decision; Father did too. Tin is mine." I sucked in a breath. "And I'm his."

Sascha's gaze was measured as she stared at my resolute expression then drifted down to how my hand was entwined with Tin's. Our fingers were bridged, and while he was resting, he clasped me as much as I clasped him.

"I can't believe we weren't there for it."

"How could you be?" I countered with a shrug. "Father would never have allowed us to wed. That was why it had to be done this way."

She pulled a face then shared a look with my mom. That look said it all—things they couldn't, *wouldn't* say out loud.

I half-believed that Mom was the reason Sascha didn't particularly like me.

Maybe it was inadvertent, but they were best friends. A lifetime of sharing stories about their problem children was probably enough to turn Sascha against me.

Not that I'd done anything *that* bad. Small fry in the grand scheme of things, but that didn't seem to matter.

"I think it makes sense."

I cut Devon a look.

As usual, he wasn't far from Sascha's side, her shadow even, but he was tucked away in the corner of the hospital room with a notepad on his lap and two tablets on the floor, with chamomile tea and water in tumblers around him.

Despite our conversation, I had to ask, "Didn't catch any sleep, Uncle Devon?"

His chin tipped down just a fraction. "No, Alice. Very little."

Sascha cast him a perturbed glance.

I was certain she worried about Devon more than she did her children, and not because she was a bad mom but because she'd raised very reasonable kids. All of them behaved far better than Devon did.

Well, not Jack.

Jack was... Jack.

Rather than comment on his lack of sleep, Sascha muttered, "Your sense and the rest of the world's sense don't often go hand in hand, love."

Devon sniffed. "That's hardly a fair surmise."

"I don't have to be fair. I just have to know you."

He rolled his eyes which had her sticking out her tongue.

Their playful side made me hope Tin and I could have that together again.

"What are ye two arguing about now?"

"Not arguing," Devon countered, not even glancing at Sawyer as he swaggered in.

The second Sawyer was behind Sascha's chair, he bent over and pressed a kiss to her head.

"Ye two are always arguing." Sawyer huffed then winked at me, making me shoot him a shy grin.

"Hi, Uncle Sawyer."

"Hi, lassie." His eyes twinkled. "Guess yer a part of the clan now, aren't ye?"

"I am." My cheeks pinkened and, pointedly, I said, "Thank you for being so nice."

He snorted. "Dinnae see what the problem is."

"Ha!" Devon exclaimed. "Sawyer agrees with me."

Another snort escaped Sascha.

"Aye, I do. God help us all. But you'll find most of this side of yer family get it, even if yer side don't."

At that, Mom winced. "Sawyer, don't say that."

"Why not? It's the truth, and I understand. The government here, the people, they've all got sticks up their arses.

"Lovely folk, warm-hearted, but old-fashioned." He whistled between his teeth. "Christ, they make me feel like I'm back in the nineties."

Mom winced again. "I know."

Her hand shot out and somehow, in that one statement, Sawyer did the impossible.

Mom had barely touched me since she had come to visit Tin this morning. Now, she leaned forward to grab my fingers and to squeeze them. "It'll be okay."

I knew it would be. We didn't have a choice to do anything other than work on damage control.

Thank God.

But still, I was grateful that she'd read between the lines and had taken the royal scepter out of her butt.

There was a grating noise as Sawyer dragged out another armchair from the side wall.

Overnight, since Tin had awoken yesterday, more chairs had

made an appearance. Enough for an entire conference of the now extended family.

Which meant, I knew, what was going to go down—a congress.

Great.

"Where are Jack, Bash, Rosie, and Bethan?" I queried, asking after Tin's siblings.

"Bethan's still stuck in Boston, Rosie can't leave because one of her horses is going into breech birth and might die without her," Sascha groaned. "Jack is en route. Bash said he'd be the responsible adult and travel down with him. Jack insisted on driving here when he learned Tin was stable. Little shit."

Sawyer grunted. "The boy likes his cars. Let him be. It's good practice anyway. He's got that race coming up in January, and boyo here ain't going naewhere. I won't let him."

His defense had Sascha scowling. "He should be here with his family." Her bottom lip wobbled. "And I wish it worked that way."

Sawyer snagged her hand in his. "He's got the best doctors in the world looking after him, Sascha, sweetheart. There's nae need to worry."

"If I had to fly down and we couldn't take the train, I don't see why Jack couldn't have flown too," Devon muttered, earning himself a scowl from Sawyer and a triumphant grin from Sascha—both, of course, went unnoticed as he was concentrating on his work.

"We're nae talking about that anymore. The lad will be here soon enough," Sawyer intoned. "Rosie and Bethan'll need to get their arses here for Christmas, Sascha."

"Damn, I hope Bethan will be able to catch a flight out of Boston. I never thought about that."

"How's she getting on at school?" Mom asked.

"Bethan?" Sascha blinked. "Fine, as usual. It's only Jack who's the problem child." She called him that, but she said it fondly.

It was like how Mom had a tender tone whenever she talked about Christel, but it was Christel who'd gotten drunk last year and had been filmed diving into a hot tub naked...

Mom laughed softly. "He's only sixteen."

"Almost seventeen," Devon corrected. "In fact, he's more seventeen than sixteen. And, if you really think about how time passes—"

"Dinnae be borin' us with yer claptrap about how we're all technically a year older than what we are," Sawyer grumbled. "I feel every year like it was a century; I dinnae need ye adding more onto my plate."

Sascha patted his hand but she was smiling as she did so. "Jack's doing well. He's on track for competing in Formula One."

Mom pulled a face. "Aren't you frightened?"

"Terrified. Every day," was Sascha's cheerful retort, "but I can't complain. I'm the one he inherited his love of cars from."

"How's Rosie finding Edinburgh?" She was studying to become a vet.

Sawyer preened. "She's half-Scot, ain't she? She's lovin' it."

My lips twitched. "Does she wear tartan to school?"

"Bet yer arse she does. Prefer her to be there than in bluidy Boston like Bethan, but it's only for some special meeting with Amnesty International. Beth's nae there fer long." Bethan was on track to become a lawyer. I knew she wanted to specialize in human rights. "She'll be back in St. Andrews fer the start of next term."

"Hey, I liked Boston," Mom chided.

"Ye would. Yer American. Just like Sascha." He shook his head, but he was preening as he said, "Nae history. My girls love their history and love the land of their ancestors."

"There's plenty of history," Sascha argued. "And since when did you give a damn about that anyway?"

That twinkle made a reappearance in his eyes. "Since I became an old bastard."

"Whenever you age yourself, you age me," Sascha complained.

"You have adult children," Devon pointed out. "Ergo, you're middle-aged."

"Ergo you should keep your trap shut," was Sascha's retort.

Evidently sensing a brewing argument, Mom butted in, "We're

going to have to arrange the wedding, Sascha. There'll have to be a vow renewal. You know that, don't you?"

My heart plummeted, even though I'd anticipated this back when I'd had my first wedding.

Sascha's nose crinkled. "Jeez. Really?"

"Yeah. I think Edward is going to sell it as a 'whirlwind romance' kind of thing." That statement went with air quotes. "Forged on a friendship that's been blossoming since they were children, and love is impulsive."

"Well, it's not a lie," Sascha remarked.

Just like Tin often said, Sawyer, sounding annoyed, retorted, "The best lies have a snippet of truth tae them."

His irritation had me staring at him, and his smile made me realize I had an ally.

He liked me.

He always had.

Most of Tin's fathers did, actually.

It was Sascha who had a problem with me.

Well, sometimes.

Mostly, I thought she didn't believe I was good enough for Tin.

Considering I was a future queen, I wasn't sure who *would* be good enough for him, but I got it.

She was protective of her family, and though her disapproval stung, I loved her for that.

"A vow renewal or a wedding ceremony?" I asked Mom, who was as much of a tigress defending her cubs as Sascha.

Sascha was more of a 'if I don't like something, I'll bust balls to change it' kind of woman.

Mom? She was a maneuverer. She used common sense and logic as well as my fathers' love for her to get her own way.

It worked too.

"Well, the nation might recognize American wedding licenses, but officially, your father has to agree to the match. Plus, Tin will need a coronation... so it's going to be a wedding ceremony."

"Is it wise when the UnReals are taking potshots at us to organize something as large as that?" I asked carefully.

"Security measures will be tightened, and it will be good for the country's morale. Especially in the aftermath of..." Mom sighed as she looked at Tin.

My poor husband.

He seemed destined to always be unconscious when his weddings were under discussion.

The first time thanks to vodka. A lot of it.

The second time, thanks to morphine.

Granted, he'd be more *compos mentis* than Vegas, but guilt speared me nonetheless.

Especially when I thought about the shitty chapel he didn't remember, the gin-sozzled Elvis with a gut as large as Nevada in a white jumpsuit with more rhinestones on it than a showgirl's, and how he'd slurred his vows as I practically held him upright all the while praying that Andrea, who'd been sick from the flight, wouldn't realize I'd sneaked out until after the license was issued.

What was done was done.

I could say that I regretted it, but it would be a lie.

I guessed I could say I regretted how it had come to pass, but not that I was Mrs. Valentin Dubois.

"Lass?"

I blinked, suddenly realizing I'd zoned out and, evidently, Sawyer had asked me a question.

"Sorry, Uncle Sawyer. What is it?"

"Your ma was just talking about the funeral."

My brow crumpled. "Yeah. The funeral." I blew out a breath. "When is it? I want to be there."

Mom's hand reached out and grabbed mine. Her fingers entwined with my own and she murmured, "I knew you would."

"Of course! She died protecting me," I muttered, annoyed that there'd been a question hovering over my attendance.

Anyone would think that I was an atrocious crown princess, but I wasn't.

Just because I marched to the beat of my own drum didn't mean that I was lax in my duties.

"The service is next week."

My brows surged. "So soon?"

"It's at her parents' request. Your father honored their right to decide." She rubbed her thumb over my pointer finger which was signet ring-free. "That was kind of you," she pointed out, obviously aware I'd given the ring to Andrea.

"Not kind enough." God, it was only a token of respect. My tone was fervent as I rasped, "I'd give Andrea her life back if I could."

Her smile was sad. "Your father wanted to keep you here, but I knew you'd want to be at the ceremony."

"Why? I thought he'd be all for me doing my duty."

If there was resentment to the words, then so be it. I loved my father, I truly did, and most of the time I even liked him. It was the king I had a problem with.

I actually thought it worked the same for him.

He loved and liked me as a daughter, just not as his heir.

"Your safety, darling. The threat is still active."

I shrugged. "When isn't it? Which DeSauvier hasn't had to deal with the UnReals? Plus, if you're going to throw Tin and me under the bus of a public royal wedding, what's the difference?"

Though she flinched, I felt no guilt for speaking truthful words.

A noisy sigh gusted from the door. "Unfortunately, she's right."

Mom's eyes lit up and her hand shot out to beckon Daddy forward. Energy seemed to sizzle inside her as she cried, "George!"

The most jovial of all my fathers swaggered in, a grin on his handsome face in response to the joy Mom had imbued in his name.

As I looked at them, I whispered, "It's so sad that the country can't see how happy you make each other."

Daddy paused on the path to Mom's side. "How unexpectedly romantic of you."

I huffed. "I can be romantic."

He bopped my nose with his finger then retorted, "I don't think so. Having Tin here must have resurrected that side of your nature."

I frowned at him, but he just smiled as he pressed a kiss to my crown before moving over to Mom and kissing her on the mouth.

"I'm not a romantic. I'm a pragmatist. I understand why you *can't* announce what you are to each other, but that doesn't mean I don't think it's a shame."

"Are you trying to win points with me?" Daddy remarked dryly.

"No. I don't have to. What's done is done." If I sounded smug, well, that couldn't be helped.

There was a wicked gleam in his eye as he said, "I find it ironic that Edward's losing his head over all this considering our relationship is the unorthodox one."

I cleared my throat. "Well, I didn't want to say anything..."

"No. I didn't raise a fool," he intoned, but he was smiling. The smile, however, died as he warned, "Xavier isn't happy about you wanting to attend the funeral either. It frightened him seeing you out in the yard beyond Casterby College."

"That was very noble of you, Alice," Sascha agreed.

Though the words were kind, they stirred something in me that wasn't pleasant.

"My people were injured because I was at that damn school, sitting in a class I didn't even want to take." I sucked in a breath. "The least I could do was tend to them when I wasn't even injured in the fray."

Sascha blinked at me, but Sawyer was the one who replied, "Ye always were a good girl, Alice. And I dinnae think Sascha meant to criticize. There's nae harm in being noble. It's a good thing tae be."

"It wasn't noble though. It was common decency."

"You can't have common decency," Devon pointed out, "you're royal."

Sawyer snorted. "Royal decency, then."

"Exactly," he muttered, his attention returning to his books.

"I saw the footage, and I have to admit, I understand why Xavier's terrified by the prospect of you attending the funeral," Daddy conceded. "You were totally exposed—"

"The threat had been neutralized," I discounted, uncomfortable with how everyone, including Devon this time, was staring at me. "And I *am* going to the funeral."

"I agree," Daddy said.

"Whether you did or not, I'd go."

His lips twisted. "I was about to tell you to keep your tongue skills sharp, but I see there's no need."

"I'm not that acerbic."

"Aren't you?" he argued. "I saw you cut down Prime Minister DeWitt the other day."

I narrowed my eyes at him. "The idiot deserved it. His foreign policies make Hitler look forward-thinking."

Daddy laughed. "That's what you said to him?"

"I did."

Mom groaned. "Baby, you can't say stuff like that to Parliament.

"That explains why your father was on the phone to DeWitt for hours the other night—"

"Why not? I'm the future queen, aren't I? Why can't I say things like that to the men and women *my* people voted in?" I shrugged. "Mom, seriously, you should have been there for the session.

"Father wants me to learn, and I do, but I also recognize that the people in power are morons."

"They often are," Sawyer sniped.

"DeWitt was going on and on about how we needed to shore up our nuclear weapons because of our proximity to the Middle East." My eyes bugged out. "Our *proximity*. I mean, for God's sake, we're nowhere near Turkey, so how can we be in the Middle East when we're in Europe? The man has no concept of geography."

Mom's lips twitched. "I know, but he's who the people wanted."

"Democracy is stupid. In fact, it's democrazy. Father would have picked a much better politician to lead the government."

"He would, but then he'd get more shit for being an autocrat," Daddy reminded me. "Then, when you eventually took over, you'd have three times as much responsibility as you do now." He arched a brow at me. "I don't think you want that, do you?"

"No." I winced then admitted, "I hate thinking about the takeover."

'Takeover' was the unofficial code for when a reigning monarch passed on and the heir to the throne ascended.

The Guard Elect called it Operation: Unicorn because of the unicorn on the family crest.

It was discomfiting that an operation that represented my father's death was given a title worthy of a kid's cartoon.

Mom reached forward and squeezed my hand to comfort me.

"Edward won't be going anywhere for a good long while," Daddy reassured me. "Maybe you'll be like King Charles was: a timeless heir to the throne."

"I wouldn't complain." A thought occurred to me, and guilt hit shortly after—I should have asked this sooner. "Are Christel and Victoria safe?"

"Of course. They were on lockdown the second the shooting happened and are flying in as we speak."

That it was taking them so long to return home told me something had happened behind the scenes before they could fly to Veronia.

Anxiety riding me, I reasoned, "If the UnReals were targeting me, then we have to assume they'll target my sisters next."

"We're working on that premise," Daddy intoned smoothly. "Christel should be arriving shortly. Victoria's still inbound from Sydney."

He shot me one of the patented smiles that made the female population in the country swoon.

Of the description, 'tall, dark, and handsome,' he fulfilled only two of those categories—he was blond—but that didn't stop him from being adored by every woman between eighteen and eighty.

I wasn't just *any* female however.

Focusing on him, I queried, "What did the UnReals want?"

"What do they usually want?"

"To abolish the monarchy."

He shrugged. "No change there."

"Aside from the fact, of course, that you dropped the ball security wise," Devon pointed out.

There wasn't an ounce of malice to his voice, just... well, he was being Devon.

"He has a point, mon," Sawyer agreed. "If Tin hadnae come and saved yer lassie, then who the feck knows what'd have happened."

Daddy's smile turned tense.

Devon had hit the nail on the head.

"The security breach has been resolved," was all he said.

"Yes, by my son," Devon retorted, and for the first time, he sounded heated.

"Darling," Sascha soothed.

"I don't need soothing," Devon immediately dismissed. "I'm stating it as a fact."

Mom, being her diplomatic self, murmured, "I'm surprised you haven't spoken to your sisters."

"I didn't have any energy to talk with them. When I did, I couldn't get through."

"Because they were flying," Daddy reasoned.

I didn't believe him. Not unless it suddenly took three days to fly from London to Veronia.

I nodded, but what I didn't say was that I didn't feel like being lectured either.

Neither of my sisters were like me.

Christel and Victoria were both studious, with the former being at LSE—London School of Economics—and Victoria studying in Sydney.

Though neither of them shit gold, and they had made many faux pas along the way which they were forgiven for, they tended to lecture me too.

Unlike them, I wasn't allowed to make any mistakes.

"Do Christel and Victoria have husbands waiting in the wings to save them too?" Devon remarked.

"Devon," Sascha warned.

Sawyer shrugged. "Cannae disagree with him. Yer security folks really dropped the feckin' ball, George."

"As I've already stated, the situation is under control. As it stands, Tin's a hero now. Considering the situation, that's the kind of PR we desperately need."

PR.

What sucked the most was knowing he was right.

Being Crown Princess had made me incredibly cynical.

A rustling in the sheets had me seeking Tin out, and I saw he was stirring.

His face was puckered with pain as he awoke, and when his eyes opened, the lashes fluttered like tiny butterflies against his strong cheekbones—they were the most feminine thing about him—I knew the second he was aware.

He saw me.

Me.

It was like he pierced me straight through to my soul.

He didn't see the hospital room or the monitors. Didn't notice our families or what was happening.

He just saw me.

And I basked in it. Basked in him. His focus. His attention. His awareness.

God, I'd missed this so much.

Never having realized how lonely I was until he'd left me, I knew that he was the only person who saw the real *me.*

Someone cleared their throat, and I wasn't altogether surprised it was Daddy when he muttered, amusement lacing his tone, "Nice to see you awake, Tin."

Tin didn't break eye contact with me. "It's nice to be awake, Uncle George."

I squeezed his hand, relieved when he returned the gesture. My grip was stronger than his, but that made sense.

He looked weak. Everything about him was unlike the Tin I knew.

Sascha leaned forward, and her hand sought out his. "God, Tin, you gave us such a scare."

His nose wrinkled as he turned to look at his mother. "Sorry, Mom."

"I don't like seeing you like this," Devon commented from his place on the floor.

With his gaze still on his documents, it would be easy to think he was unaffected. But I'd never heard Devon raise his voice before... It made sense that his son lying in a hospital bed would be a breaking point for him.

"You're always snowboarding and swimming and cycling," Devon grumbled.

"Aye," Sawyer agreed, but there was a somber twinkle in his eye. "We're used tae ye doin' all three at once as well."

My lips curved. "Do you play the drums and sing at the same time?"

"Yeah," Tin said sleepily. "I'm famous for it."

Devon grunted.

"I'm sorry I scared you all. I really didn't mean to."

Devon stunned the hell out of me by stating, "I don't believe you."

Then, I stunned the hell out myself—because, I realized, I didn't believe him either.

"What?" Even Tin's sputter seemed ingenuous. "Why don't you believe me?"

"You called us to warn us."

I zoomed in on Tin's expression, trying to read every nuance of a face I knew as well as I did my own.

"No," he countered, "I called you so you'd understand why I was in Veronia. That's all."

While he sounded sincere, Devon's statement was like he'd thrown a bucket of cold water over Tin.

My husband sounded and looked more awake as I studied him. Because of that, however, more unease filtered through me.

"You went straight to Alice's college," Devon continued. "You were waiting for the shooting to happen."

Tin flashed his dad a look, then his gaze shuttered. "It was time for me to come here."

"I don't doubt it, but why?" Devon countered, his focus on his notepad. "Why now?"

A heavy silence filled the room, and it was clear that both his parents and mine wanted answers because Sascha and Sawyer didn't rush to defend him, and my folks didn't break the silence to change the subject either.

They weren't alone.

Devon was right.

Tin hadn't just come to me.

He'd come to Casterby.

He'd been there *before* the shooting.

Minutes before.

As if he'd known it would happen.

"I'm tired," Tin muttered, and my brows rose at that.

He'd just lied.

He'd just lied to *Devon.*

He shuffled around the mattress like he was trying to get comfortable but physically couldn't because he'd just lied.

To Devon.

What the hell was even happening here?

"The timing was too strange, son," Devon murmured, but his tone had changed. It had morphed into a pleasant one, like he was discussing the weather or asking a neighbor to borrow a cup of sugar. "I don't think you should start married life on a lie."

Tin's eyes flared wide, and I saw his temper stir. But, again, this was Devon who was chiding him. Had it been Andrei or Sean, I had no doubt that they'd have argued. But Devon, and usually Kurt and Sawyer too, he was pretty calm around.

His free hand moved to rub at his forehead, and he swept his hair off his face before he cast me a glance. I sensed that he was measuring my response to what I was hearing.

If I were anyone else, if we'd married any other way, then I'd be angry.

As it was, I had no right to be.

I'd started our married life on a lie, after all. It wasn't like I could take the moral high ground here.

"There was some news I wasn't supposed to hear," Tin eventually told me.

Not his fathers. Or his mom. Not my folks either.

Me.

Christ, this didn't bode well.

"What kind of news?" Mom queried, enunciating each word.

His gaze remained on mine. "It was just a trickle of information." He fell silent a second. "It concerned me."

"You knew the UnReals were going to attack?" Daddy demanded, no longer sounding his regular smooth, unruffled self. "Why the hell didn't you say something?"

"What could I say?" he retorted, his eyes flashing hotter now. "Dammit, I shouldn't have seen the report I read. It was only because I can read shit upside down that I happened to see it on my superior's desk. I could have been wrong. It might have been a falsehood.

"You more than anyone know how intelligence works, dammit. Sometimes there's more bullshit to wade through than in a cow field."

"You believed it enough to come here," Sascha snapped, her shoulders bunching as she glared at Tin. "You believed it enough to tell us the truth about your marriage—"

"Of course I did. I wasn't going to risk Etta. Whether or not it was BS, I had to make sure she was safe.

"I came as soon as I could. They didn't let me out of the clinic until the morning before I arrived, and even then, they bitched at me for discharging myself—"

"I wonder why," Sascha sniped, eying the many bandages that were wrapped around Tin's torso.

"I got the first flight I could out of there. Made it to Etta's school and did a check of the perimeter. I thought the information was wrong, so I went to meet with Etta."

"But the information *wasn't* wrong," Devon pointed out. "There was a sniper."

Tin winced. "Yeah. There was."

I shook my head. "Why didn't you tell my parents? Contact Andrea, even."

"I couldn't." There was guilt in his eyes. "It was just chance that I saw it. Even more of a chance that I could read it—it was in Russian of all things.

"It would have been treason to share that kind of news, and I wasn't about to get strung up when I'd just decided to start living."

Daddy argued, "What the hell does that mean?"

"I mean I'd decided that I was coming home anyway."

"Home? You didn't come to the estate," Sascha said with some confusion.

"No, not that home. *My* home." Tin peeked at me through white gold lashes. "Etta's my home. She always has been."

I damned myself for a fool because my heart started to pound like crazy.

Those were words I needed to hear. All those years of his rejection couldn't be wiped away with just that one remark, but it went a small way to making me realize that he loved me just as much as I loved him.

He'd just been punishing me.

And while it sucked, I'd done a shitty thing.

Choices... if anyone knew how important it was to have choices, it was me.

I had so few of them really. I was forced down one path every day, guided down another every other day.

I pretty much had to stay in Veronia all the time, unlike my sisters who could travel the world. I had to go to college. I had to attend Parliament. I had to open libraries and attend fêtes.

I had to, I had to, I had to...

If anyone should know how it felt to be forced into a situation, it was me.

Yet I'd done it anyway.

But that he'd forgiven me was etched on his features. Written into his eyes. More guilt was there too. While I was grateful he felt bad, I didn't need that shadowing the early days of our new relationship, however.

Because his words touched me, I inquired, "You came here for me?"

"Of course I did, Etta," he rasped. "Do you know how much butt fluff I've sifted through over the years? Intelligence isn't always intelligent. Most of the time, it's all false leads and nuisance tips.

"I knew your guards. I figured you were safe, but I wasn't going to risk you. I wanted to be there, just in case, but I wanted to be with you period." He wafted a hand at his stomach. "This stirred me into action. I *did* almost die. It was my catalyst.

"I was in the hospital, staring up at the ceiling, wondering what the hell I was doing with my life." He sighed. "All I've wanted for years was to be with you, and I might not have—"

Tears burned my eyes. "You might not have come back to me."

His gaze was averted as he nodded. "So, the second I was released, I handed in my resignation—which they weren't happy about. Dad—"

"I'll deal with them," Devon mumbled, his focus still on his notepad where he was now sketching something with a pencil.

"Thanks." He blew out a breath. "I handed in my notice and just happened to read something I shouldn't have. Veronia was never where I was based. Central Europe wasn't my scene."

And I knew why.

Me.

"You could have given us a heads-up," Daddy ground out. "We lost good people because of your silence."

"In hindsight, I know I should have. I genuinely just thought it was chatter," he answered, and I knew he meant it.

Tin, even at his most furious with me, would never want me to be hurt.

Or, worse, dead.

But Andrea *had* died because I shouldn't have gone into school that day. I should have stayed at the palace, safe in my pretty prison.

"Poor Andrea." It was all I could think to say.

He flinched. "I'm so sorry, love."

I shot him a weary smile. "Me too."

While Devon was right to have outed the truth, it left me facing Andrea's parents, the rest of her family, and the Guard Elect, knowing that it could have been avoided.

Guilt... it was a royal's stock-in-trade.

So-called ordinary people leveraged their lives for us on a daily basis, when the divine right of kings was eighteenth century propaganda.

"Is there any other chatter you should have told us about?" Daddy snapped.

I understood his anger. He was going to be mad at Tin for a good long while, and Father and Papa probably would be too. In a sense, Tin deserved it. Even if he'd done what he believed to be the right thing.

"No," Tin replied earnestly. Then, he winced and his gaze shuttered. "Maybe watch your allies in Russia."

Daddy jerked back at that. "What the hell does that mean?"

Tin's mouth just firmed. "You know what I'm talking about. I worked for my government. I worked for my king. You can't ask me to break my oath—"

"And he won't," Mom intoned darkly, shooting Daddy a warning look. Appreciation for her back-up filled me. "Tin is right. We'd string him up by his balls if he gave away state secrets too."

"This is different—"

"No, it isn't," she snarled. "Don't you dare push him on this, George."

He ground his teeth. "Edward won't be happy about this."

Mom sniffed. "That stick has been up his ass for quite a while. I'm sure it gets uncomfortable from time to time—now is one of those occasions for him to have to grin and bear it."

Nothing about this situation was funny, but the imagery was enough to have my lips curving, and when I squeezed the hand I was still holding, Tin squeezed back.

He'd compromised, and I was grateful for that. I just wished...

God, I just wished Andrea hadn't paid the price of Tin's honor.

THIRTEEN

TIN

A glance around the graveyard revealed enough Guard Elect to fill a football stadium.

And I wasn't just talking about Andrea's team who were attending the actual service.

Experience and a weather eye enabled me to see the royal guards in the distance—near and far—something that the grim day enabled because not an ounce of sunlight disturbed the view.

The weather mourned Andrea's loss as much as her friends, family, and charge did.

"What are you looking at?" Etta questioned. "Do you see something?"

I heard her worry and could have kicked myself for upping her concern.

"No, nothing aside from what I should be seeing."

She released a relieved breath but commented, "Mom shouldn't be here. She's in danger."

"The same could be said for you," I argued.

She was the reason I was here today.

I should still be in my hospital bed, but Etta insisted on attending, just like her mom did.

And her parents wondered where she got her stubbornness from.

"I wish…" Etta sighed. "It doesn't matter."

"I'm sorry," I replied, knowing what she was about to say without her having to utter a word.

Not because I was a mind reader or an Etta-whisperer, either. But because I was human.

Even if MI6 liked for us to forget that fact.

"You don't have to be." Her smile was weak. Somber. "I get it."

And I sensed she did.

Her parents and mine didn't. Well, aside from Perry. I was getting the cold shoulder all round, and I'd take it.

I deserved it.

"I was only a pencil pusher."

She shot me a glance as we walked down the black carpet, through the gravesites of the men and women who'd fallen for their country.

"You got stabbed," she said flatly.

"I did, but it was accidental." I sucked in a breath. "Even if the only thing you handle is information, you have to sign the Official Secrets Act—"

"Tin, you don't have to explain."

"No, I do," I rasped, and this was the first time I was able to do so when it was just Etta and me.

Mom had been hovering around me since I'd awoken, and Dad was always on the floor, working on those interminable notes of his.

"We have a similar law, Tin," she reasoned. "I understand why you held your tongue."

The grim day, the bleak sky, the haunting cry of a red jay that sent shivers up my spine, the dew on the grass that brushed the hems of my pants, making them damp. The hole in the ground fifty feet away. The coffin that was being carried into the graveyard, just waiting to be buried.

It was all my fault.

"All I knew was that I had to get to you. I knew I had to keep you safe."

She cast me a frown that was visible even beneath the black veil she wore. The jaunty hat she pinned to her crown held the cascading fabric in place, shielding her expression from everyone but me at this distance.

"Would you have taken the bullet meant for me?"

"In a moment."

Her jaw worked a second before she demanded, "And what kind of life would you have left me with?"

My brow puckered. "What do you mean?"

"What do I mean?" she repeated in a tone that didn't bode well for me. "I mean that I love you, Tin."

"I know you do."

"Well, then? Why would you do that?"

"Because I couldn't do a damn thing else. I could only come here, make sure I was with you and that you weren't the one who got hurt." My jaw clenched. "How else could I show you how much I love you, Etta?"

She froze in her tracks. Which triggered a change in the parade behind her.

People braked so they didn't rush into her, but she had to be aware she was causing a stir.

Regardless, it didn't stop her from hissing under her breath, "You live with me, Tin. You show me. You make me goddamn breakfast in bed when it's my birthday and you deal with me shoving my cold feet against your legs on winter mornings." Her hand grabbed my lapels, and she jerked on them then got in my face. "That's how you show me you love me. You do *not* die for me."

With that, she relinquished her hold on me and started to walk again.

Because people were already whispering about what had made

her break protocol, I shuffled after her, not stopping until we reached the graveside.

As I hurried along, every bruise in my body made itself known. I felt like one big broken bone and it rammed home that the only place I should be was in bed. Not here.

But I wasn't about to let Etta handle this on her own.

I reached for her hand, half certain she'd shrug it off, but she didn't. She allowed me to clasp her fingers.

That caused more whispers, of course.

I knew the public had learned about our 'status' as a married couple so curiosity was at an all-time high about us.

"You're only here because you want to protect me."

I blinked, surprised by her remark. "You say that like it's a bad thing."

"It is when that means you're willing to die for me." A soft choked sound escaped her and I knew she was holding back tears. "I want us to live, Tin. Not to die."

I knew her gaze was on Andrea's casket as her team carried her toward us. Knew it because mine was too.

Andrea was only in there because I'd let duty run over everything else. Duty to a country over my woman.

It hurt.

It hurt because my loyalties should always lay with Etta, but the stuff I'd done, the stuff I'd seen and heard in my years with MI6 could only be described as heavy shit.

Even though my work had mostly been administrative, and I hadn't been a younger Daniel Craig roaming around the world with a gun constantly half-cocked, my position, my own security had rested in the ability of other people like me being able to keep their goddamn mouth shut.

There was a unit assigned to the UnReals, a British unit, and if I'd said something, I'd have been potentially bringing them into the light.

I knew what that felt like.

Knew how the shit could hit the fan when your cover was blown —that was what had happened to me.

It was why my stomach was shredded like I'd been through a blender: because someone had dropped the ball.

While I'd been trying to save *many* people's lives by being there for Etta, by hoping to be the one who could keep her safe, Andrea had died as a result, and there was nothing I could do to take that back.

As guilt hit me, I watched Andrea's team continue their march toward us, outfitted in their dress blues—well, their uniforms were black and red—her casket on their shoulders.

Today, they'd lost one of their own but you wouldn't know it. They were stoic and silent in their grief.

As the men and women settled beside the grave, and they placed the casket on the stand, they stepped back and waited.

I'd never attended a service like this before, but I knew Etta had.

She snapped to attention the same time as Perry did and, releasing my clasp on her hand, she saluted the Guard Elect almost at the same time as her mother did.

It was a moving moment, and I wasn't surprised by the intense flash of cameras as reporters covered the tragic event.

When the lone call of a trumpet pierced the air, she strode over to the coffin.

I made a move to follow her, but Perry was there, her hand on my arm, holding me back and keeping me in place.

Shooting her a questioning look, she responded with, "Leave it, Valentin."

Irritated and worried, I watched as Etta stood beside the grave. I felt as if I could see the actual crosshairs on her, because she was a clear target.

Not even when, in a voice as clear as a robin's, she sang the national anthem did I calm down any.

"For my country, I will bleed. For my country, I will perish. For my country, my family, I'll stand. Veronia, the land I call my own."

Clearly affected, Perry raised a hand and maneuvered a handkerchief beneath her own veil to dry her wet eyes.

As Etta sang the Veronian anthem, living up to my nickname for her, the Guard Elect bowed their heads at her tribute.

When the last few notes filtered through the air, pure and beautiful, she began to tug on the Veronian flag that draped the coffin.

I'd seen soldiers make this move before but there was usually someone to help them fold the large flag. Etta did it on her own.

That was when I shrugged off Perry's hold and limped over to Etta. Her startled gaze clashed with mine, but her eyes were drenched with tears, and just when I thought she'd argue, she didn't. She handed me one corner of the flag, and together, we folded the rectangle of fabric into a perfect triangle.

That done, I followed her as she returned to her mother's side, bowing when she curtsied and watching as she handed Perry the flag. The queen pressed her fingers to her daughter's cheek in thanks, then as Etta and I returned to our earlier position, Perry moved over to Andrea's family.

There, she graced them with a second salute before she passed the flag to Andrea's weeping mother.

The service moved fast after that.

The unit in attendance saluted the coffin as the prime minister gave his final words. The reverend passed Andrea into the Lord's care, and then her team lowered the coffin into the ground as the congregation, on the whole, sang the national anthem.

All the while, I stood there, feeling helpless and useless and guilty.

Etta's hand sought mine once more, and she tightened her fingers around mine, simultaneously seeking and giving comfort.

The strength in that hold gave me some too. It was like she knew I was faltering, but then she'd always known how to read me.

Seemed all these years apart hadn't changed that.

"What's wrong?"

Her whisper had me flicking a glance her way. "Nothing."

"Why do you keep huffing then? People will notice."

"I feel..." I sighed, well aware the word didn't convey my emotions at all but I settled on it nonetheless, "...bad."

"She died for me, Tin, not you."

"Only because I didn't pass on the information."

"Because you couldn't. If anyone could understand duty, it was Andrea."

She sounded calmer, as if the service had given her some closure.

I wished I could have some of that.

My makeshift plan had made sense back at HQ in London. Now, with the consequences of that decision right in front of me, I felt like a traitor. Torn between loyalties to too many people and to too many countries.

The service had taken no more than forty minutes, and I stood throughout it even though my doctor had insisted I leave the royal clinic in a wheelchair.

Perhaps it was masochistic, but the least I could do was honor Andrea properly by standing, but that didn't stop my entire body from aching like I'd been whipped.

I gritted my teeth throughout, and remained in place behind Etta as she shook hands and murmured condolences to Andrea's family, and proceeded to greet each guard who walked in a procession past Perry and Etta.

"Antoni," she greeted one, her hands clasping both of his. "How's your husband?"

He shot her a weary smile. "Not well, Your Highness. The cancer's returned."

Etta's distress was clear. "I'm so sorry to hear that, Toni. Have you arranged for some leave?"

"Davide doesn't want me to make a fuss."

"Nonsense," she chided, squeezing his hands gently. "You must. Time is precious. Haven't we learned that today?"

Antoni tensed and slowly nodded. "Thank you for your kindness, Your Highness."

He hovered in place, clearly unsure of what to do next. Ordinarily, I knew, he'd salute her then head away from the ceremony. Today, however, was different.

Etta extracted her hands from his then saluted him. He snapped to attention, turned to his left, then departed, his boots squelching in the mud that had dared grace the green lawn.

I learned that one of her guards was breeding Labradoodles, discovered that one had recently adopted a little girl from Africa, and that another's wife was due to go into labor soon.

Did how much she knew about her guards surprise me?

No.

She was anal about that.

Still, seeing it was believing, and it was impressive.

Pride filled me.

Etta was a modern royal. Her mother's laxer ways were inbred into her, meaning she had the *noblesse oblige* of her father and Perry's tactility. Her ability to blend in with her people was a strength that her family didn't value enough.

Even from a distance, I'd noticed how much crap they gave her for being so friendly with her people. That was something that'd be changing under my watch.

It'd taken two brushes with death to realize that I was *nothing* without Etta. I'd underappreciated her for too long, and I was about to make sure her family stopped doing the same.

"Where now?" I rasped as Perry finally led the procession toward the fleet of cars. I was aching like a bitch, and the cold wasn't helping. Christmas was almost upon us, and I was feeling every inch of the shorter, chillier days in my bones. Still, I asked, "To the wake?"

"No," Etta told me, shaking her head. "The DeSauviers pay for the wake, but it's only for the Guard Elect and her family and friends."

"That's unusual, isn't it?"

"No. It's a gift. It's actually set down in the constitution of the

Guard Elect. It's our way of giving thanks and honoring the fallen member of the team."

"They're only young, aren't they?" I asked.

"The Guard Elect?" At my nod, she hummed. "Yeah. They were created after my mom became Queen, and, well, you know what happened to my grandmother."

She'd been assassinated.

By UnReals.

DeWitt, the prime minister, muttered something to Etta that dragged her attention away from me, and I took a moment to catch my breath.

But as I tracked the grief in the cemetery, as well as the thousands of graves of military servicemen and women who'd died for this chunk of land on the European continent, my temper stirred, and rage followed at the waste of life.

That was when I made these poor souls a vow—those fucking bastard UnReals needed eradicating, and Etta and I were man enough for the job.

FOURTEEN

TIN

Thoughts whirring, I was quiet on the ride back to the palace.

As we passed the cemetery, we moved onto the famous road that was pure coastline, and I let Perry and Etta chat among themselves as I kept my head tilted to the window.

In the summer, this stretch of tarmac was majestic, with unrelieved and unsurpassable views of the Mediterranean Sea.

This road was in every guidebook known to man on the bucket list of things to do before you died.

Up there with driving down Route 66 or going to the top of the Eiffel Tower.

Even on a miserable day like today, it was magnificent. A reminder of how timeless nature was and how *we* weren't.

I might have missed seeing this again.

Could have missed out on so fucking much by being an obstinate piece of shit—

"You're in pain, aren't you?"

The words were more of a statement than a question, and I recognized that Etta had stopped talking with her mom because Perry had received a call.

I blinked, surprised I hadn't heard her phone ring. "I've dealt with worse."

She sniffed. "Lies."

"I'm ready for bed," was all I'd admit to.

"The doctors say you should stay in the ward."

"I don't want to," I replied, and it wasn't just because I was like my daw—hated doctors and hospitals and clinics. It was because ever since I'd awoken from my initial surgery, Etta refused to leave my side to sleep.

The bed was large enough for me, but not for her, not with all the wires on there, so she often slept at my side, making a pretzel look like it was bent straight. She was getting shadows under her eyes, and I knew she had to be exhausted.

I reached for her hand. "I don't want to be in there."

She sighed. "It's for your sake. What if there's a complication?"

"Then you can put me in the damn wheelchair and guide me to the ward, can't you?"

She snickered. "You'd let me push you, would you?"

My lips curved. "Who else?"

"I dunno, I thought you'd be a prick and insist on wheeling yourself."

My nose crinkled at that. "Okay. Maybe. But I'd imagine I'd have to be in crippling pain to want to go to the ward."

She huffed. "It isn't even like a hospital. It's pretty."

"I don't care. All the monitors give me the creeps." I shrugged. "Plus, I need space. Your bed will do nicely."

Her chin dropped, almost butting her chest. "I don't know if—"

Because I knew exactly where she was going with that sentence, I cut her off. "Etta?"

"Yes?"

"Are you over the age of eighteen?"

"Yes."

"Am I?"

"Yes."

"Are we married?"

"Yes, but—"

"Do you really think they're going to keep us apart?"

She bit her lip. "Father won't like it."

"I don't care," I rumbled. "I really don't. Lie about my presence in there, hide me, I don't give a shit. I know things can't be official until we get married in front of your father, but until then, I refuse to be without you any longer than I already have."

"It's about time you fought for her."

Auntie Perry's grumble had my eyes widening, and I shot her a surprised look. "Pardon?"

"I was mad at you before, Valentin, for dumping my daughter like a hot potato. But she never complained, so I didn't think I had a right to meddle. Your friendship was between the pair of you, and I assumed you'd had a falling out that would untangle itself over the years.

"But to think you let her wallow for—"

I could feel my left eye start to twitch.

The peevish desire to share the truth of our wedding hit me, but I shoved it aside. I wasn't in the habit of trying to score points, and it was only the fact my control was as shredded as my torso that the words had almost tripped off my tongue.

On top of that, Perry was right about one thing—I *had* let Etta down.

Because I didn't want to say a word, and because Etta's cheeks had turned pale as if she expected me to set Auntie Perry straight, I turned away from her and, staring out the window once more, murmured, "Behind closed doors, we never know what's happening."

Perry sniffed. "You can use that with someone else, but not your *wife's* mom. Now, I know something funky went down between you two. I know you refuse to tell Edward what that is, and to be frank, I don't particularly blame you.

"He can be a stuffed shirt sometimes, for all that I adore him. I wouldn't want him to know either, and I'm not asking you to tell him, but I will say this—if you let Alice down again, I will make your life hell, Valentin Dubois, do you understand me?"

I nodded stiffly. "It happened for a reason. I wasn't being cruel or mean. It's not something that will happen again."

"He *wasn't* being cruel, Mama," Etta whispered, and the tremor in her voice had me squeezing her fingers.

"It's in the past," I told her. "I won't let her down again."

Etta was clearly in self-destruct mode because, miserably, she confessed, "I let *him* down, Mom. I deserved—"

"You *didn't*, Alice." Perry shook her head. "Decades of friendship can't be swept away by a single act. Unless she cheated on you— which I know my daughter wouldn't—that's the only reason I could use to justify what you did to her.

"Tin, Alice and you have been friends since you were babies. Dammit, you used to have baths together! I never suspected that something would develop between the pair of you. I thought you were more like brother and sister. But now that I know things are serious, I want you to understand that you've not only let her down, you've let me down.

"I understand about the issue with MI6. I really do. I'm not happy about it, but I get it. It's this other stuff I can't get behind."

"You don't have to," I retorted, uncaring that I was being an ass. "Things happened like they did for a reason. I was young, Etta was young, and I couldn't cope with what went down."

I sucked in a breath, trying to seek patience because Perry's only crime was giving a shit about her kid. That was something I could support, especially when Etta was in the crosshairs of her momma bear mode.

"We're still young," I continued. "I made mistakes, she did too. All you need to know is that I love your daughter, and while we've had a shakier start than most, I will do my damnedest to make sure she's happy."

Perry narrowed her eyes at me. "You promise that?"

"I promise to do my best." I shrugged. "I'm stubborn, she's stubborn too. We're going to butt heads."

"I don't mind you butting heads. I just mind you getting into an argument and thinking you can run back to the UK every time something doesn't go your way—"

My eyes flared wide at that. "When have I ever given you the impression that I was flighty, Auntie Perry? Jesus. I'm not a kid anymore. Neither is Etta.

"I have no doubt that we'll argue, and if I'm mad enough to need some space, I can go into another room. As far as I'm aware, the palace has a ton of them. But I'm done with distance, all right?

"I'm also done with this conversation. I'm in pain, I'm tired, and your daughter is exhausted from sleeping beside me. I want to get back to the palace and sleep too. With her. Because she's my wife.

"Maybe she isn't in the eyes of the Veronian King, but in the eyes of the law, she's mine and I'm hers." I didn't give a damn that I was talking smack to a queen. "You won't take her away from me, not when we're just finding each other again."

"You're only finding each other because you left—"

"Mom!" Etta butted in, midway through Perry's snipe. "Thank you, thank you so much for caring about this but please, don't give Tin a hard time. It was my fault. I deserved this... I broke his trust."

"You're not like that, love. Never think you deserve to be treated badly."

"I don't think I do," she whispered, her voice a low rasp. Then she ducked her head. "I got him drunk—"

"You don't have to tell her anything, Etta," I said quickly, needing her to know that I didn't want the truth to come out.

This was our past. Not her parents'. It wasn't ideal but it was ours.

"She needs to know. I don't want her treating you badly or holding a grudge when you weren't in the wrong."

Reaching over even though it hurt my midriff, I smiled as I tapped her chin with my finger. "Always so honorable, Etta."

She bit her lip. "Just not when I was nineteen." Because I couldn't argue with that, I merely sighed. And seeing that, with her eyes on me, she confessed, "When we were in Vegas, Mom, I-I encouraged him to drink.

"He didn't know what he was doing. The chapel didn't care, not when I gave them a couple hundred extra to look the other way. I was the one who came up with this plan."

"You mean you got him drunk so he'd marry you?" Perry sputtered.

She licked her lips. "I-I'd heard Father talking to Lawrence Fortsythe, and then... I heard you two discussing him as well."

Breaking my stare with Etta, I cast a look at her mother and found that Perry's cheeks had blanched, but as stark as her reaction was, it was nothing to how the wind fell from her sails as she mumbled, "Oh."

At Etta's confession, Perry's umbrage had switched from me to her, but at her dropping that name, a name I didn't recognize, something clicked on in my head. It seemed to do the same for her mom.

I'd never understood why she'd done what she'd done, and to be frank, waking up with the hangover from hell, my 'wife' still sleeping beside me, a ring on my finger and a wedding certificate perched between two empty bottles of vodka, and memories of a rotund Elvis in my not so distant past, I hadn't exactly been in the frame of mind to ask questions first.

All I'd known was that she'd used me.

And suddenly, all my fucking insecurities had risen to the surface.

"I always felt like I was waiting for the other shoe to drop," I rasped. "Like you were going to wake up one morning and realize that I wasn't worthy of you—"

Her mouth gaped at that. "What?!"

I shrugged. "You're a future queen, and I'm... Hell, I don't even know what I am."

People weren't defined by their families, but I was.

Bagged and tagged in infamy.

Rosie, Bethan, and Jack all wore it well, but I didn't.

Never had.

"You were dating before the wedding stunt?"

"It wasn't a stunt, Mom. I was desperate."

I winced as those three words hit home.

Maybe she knew because she told me, "Tin, not like that! God, I wanted you to ask me to marry you so badly. I was waiting and waiting, but I knew you wouldn't without asking Father for my hand first."

I'd never have done that.

Her gaze was miserable as it settled on mine, and her misery only increased when she saw the truth in her words reflected in them.

"You needed a nobleman, some politician or statesman as a consort. Not someone like me."

"You're the only person I ever wanted," she immediately countered. "Why do you think I forced the situation?"

"Because of this Lawrence Fortsythe?"

"Yes. I needed the security of knowing I was tied to the one man I wanted—you."

My jaw worked at that. "Not just any man would do?"

Her brow furrowed. "You're being obtuse. You fell out with me for forcing your hand down a path you didn't want. You can't also be upset with me because 'any man would do.'"

"I think you'll find I can be upset."

"No. You can't. Not anymore. I'm telling you the only man I've ever bloody loved is you, Tin. What more do you want? My heart on a stick tattooed with your name on it so you can see I'm not lying?"

"Don't be melodramatic, darling," Perry chided, earning a huff from Etta.

Obtuse or not, I demanded, "Who the fuck is Lawrence Fortsythe?"

"He's a jerk who wanted to marry me, and Father actually agreed to it!" She shook her head. "I wasn't about to let that happen."

"He offered for Alice's hand." Perry sighed, her eyes on her lap. "Years ago, before he, well, he overdosed, didn't he? Edward accepted at the time though."

"On her behalf?" I snarled.

Perry reached up and rubbed her brow. "You know how Edward is. He's so set in his ways sometimes. H-He wouldn't have made you marry him. I wouldn't have let him."

"Edward's an asshole. I swear to fuck," I growled under my breath. "I love him like he's my uncle, and as an uncle and as a dad, he rocks, but when he's in king mode? He sucks. He sucks fucking hard."

"And that's treason," Perry hissed, outraged color flooding into her cheeks. "I convinced him that this wasn't nineteen fifteen," she continued, glaring at me. "All he's ever wanted is what's best for her! And Alice never helped him do that." She cut Etta a look. "And you didn't, love, you know you didn't. You were never like Christel or Victoria. You never wanted to study, never showed an interest in anything really."

"Because I wasn't allowed to have an interest," Etta snapped. "What was the point?

"I couldn't do what Christel or Victoria could. I wasn't granted the liberties they were permitted. I had to toe the line at all times." Her shoulders straightened. "You can't have an interest in the Crown. It's not like a hobby, is it? It's all-consuming. I've played my part because that's all Father's allowed—"

"That's nonsense."

"It isn't," came the sharp reply. "You want to shove me down a certain path but maybe I'm not like that.

"Maybe I don't want to go to college. That isn't a crime! Maybe I just wanted to be allowed to be me. To find my path on my own merits. To be allowed to learn how to be a better leader without being shoved into Art History.

"My people like me, but that's not enough for the privy council. 'Don't be so friendly,'" she mocked in a fake baritone. "'Don't be so curt.' 'Be more open.' 'Don't wear that dress.' 'Visit this hospital.' 'Don't care about politics.' 'You're not interested enough in the government...' I can't win. I've never been able to win.

"I love Veronia. I want to be her queen, but I'm not and have never been a willing sacrifice to what the government wants of me." Her words waned, and she heaved a sigh. "What's the point in arguing? It never gets me anywhere. I'm never good enough.

"If I'd done what Christel had done last year, they'd have drawn and quartered me. Christel just got sent to London and was told to toe the line. That's it."

Perry sucked in a breath but steadfastly defended Edward with, "I think your father believed you wanted to be a homemaker, and Lawrence was as good a candidate as any."

Etta's voice was flat. "Not for me. Never for me. So I made sure that couldn't happen.

"I always wanted Tin, and I knew, a few years down the line, he'd want me too if he could build up the courage to overcome whatever it was holding him back. But I couldn't wait... I knew I needed to make sure that Father couldn't force a marriage between Lawrence and me."

"He wouldn't have done that! I would never have let him. He gave the Fortsythe boy permission to ask you to marry him—you misunderstood. It was just an idea he got stuck in his head. He will always do what's in your best interest, love. Always."

"It doesn't feel like that."

"No. It doesn't," I retorted. "More like it's in Veronia's best interests, not Etta's."

Perry bit her lip, and that alone told me that, at least partially, she agreed. "Edward has more responsibility than you'll ever know. And when you do know, he won't be around to guide you anymore, Alice.

"I dread the day you take his place, not because you aren't worthy of the throne, because you are.

"You'll rule in your own style, and that will be very different than how your father does, but that's a day when he won't be around.

"Yes, he's intractable and stubborn. Yes, he's set in his ways, but he's the finest man. He loves you. Hell, he adores you. He wants only what's best for you, and if he could, I know he'd live forever to spare you the duties you'll have when he passes." Perry paused, seemed to seek patience, then, in a calmer voice, asked, "How many hours do you spend serving the Crown, Alice?"

She frowned. "I-I don't know. Maybe thirty hours a week. It depends on my classes."

"When he was Crown Prince, he worked sixty. Sixty hours. He worked the equivalent of two full-time jobs just keeping things afloat. Of those thirty hours that *you* don't work, who do you think picks up the slack for you?"

Etta frowned for a second, but I saw her cheek turn concave as she nipped it. "Father?"

"Yes. Father. He works every hour to give you more freedom than he had. It might not be the freedom you want, but you're as tied to this nation as he is.

"He makes mistakes, I know he does. He doesn't always make the right decisions, and I'm there to guide him the right way.

"Do you think I'd have allowed him to force you to marry the Fortsythe boy? Of course not. He takes the bit between his teeth sometimes. Decides you need to settle down, decides that he knows how to make you happy, but it's all from a good place.

"He's king second, always father first. Whether you believe that or not, it's down to you. But there's many an hour where I sit with him in his damn office when he's doing work that should be on your shoulders—"

Etta gulped then reached for Perry's hand. "I'm sorry, Mom."

Sun beamed in through the window, revealing a glint in Perry's eyes that couldn't be denied.

"Don't be. Just don't judge him too hard."

"I won't, but there's a miserable irony to the fact he's working himself to death, and I'd gladly take some of the load."

Perry sighed. "You need the experience of college—"

"Says who?" she demanded grimly. "We're arguing in circles. All you need to know is that Tin was my ultimate rebellion. He's all I've ever wanted, Mama."

She probably didn't realize how badly I'd needed to hear that.

Though this was a mother-daughter moment, I rubbed my chin and said, "Etta, you probably can't understand how what you did fucked me up."

She jerked back like I'd slapped her. "What? I—"

I stalled her. "I'm not saying that to make you feel like a piece of crap. I'm saying that because I was wet behind the ears in Vegas. I was finding my feet.

"You know what school was like for me. I was ahead of everyone, and graduated early, and I was out on the road by myself for the first time ever. I'd just been headhunted, and everything was up in the air. You were the one person I trusted, and you betrayed me."

Her eyes turned watery. "I'm so sorry, Tin."

"I know you are, baby," I rasped. "But this isn't a regular marriage we're going to have. I had a queen breathing down my neck a couple minutes ago, and we're going to be living under the same roof even if that roof is massive.

"She needs to know why I reacted the way that I did so she can get your dads off my back. And she needs to know what to say because I don't want your fathers to know what happened."

Perry studied me. "You don't want them to know Etta forced your hand?"

"No. I don't. I think they're already hard on her, and I don't want our marriage to make them harder on her still.

"Four years ago, I was not ready for what being Etta's husband meant. I was a kid," I repeated. "Etta's never been allowed to be that, but that wasn't how I was raised."

Perry flinched. "That's not true!"

My brow puckered. "I'm not saying this to hurt you, Auntie Perry; I'm saying it because it's the truth. Whatever fuckups Christel and Victoria make, sure, it's like someone dropped a bomb, but if Etta makes even a fraction of a mistake that they do, it's like the start of World War Three."

When her gaze darted away, I knew she was aware I was speaking the truth.

"Now, I get it. She has a massive responsibility looming overhead, and from what you just said, Uncle Edward's tried to protect her and shelter her from what's coming, but I'm here now. Once things are official, I can help. We can take some of Edward's workload. He doesn't need to do it all."

We were quiet a second, the tension in the limo growing, and I was grateful for the privacy screen that was shielding us from the driver's ears.

No one needed to hear this conversation.

No one.

"You mean that?" she questioned after a few moments.

"I do."

And I did.

God help me, I really did.

It was time to step up.

She bit her lip. "Thank you for that."

"You're welcome. It's only through distance and the passage of time that I can see what happened with clear eyes. She did wrong, she shouldn't have forced my hand, *but* she felt backed into a corner.

"I was bitter when I realized what had happened. I was nervous and anxious, so I dove into work and found solace there. I guess I did a Devon," I admitted rawly, "but the truth is, what I felt that morning, the fear of the expectation and the duty ahead of me as her husband, was what she feels every day.

"I could run away; she couldn't. The only option she had open to her was to run *to me*. But, I let her down too. I see that now."

Etta shook her head. "I should never have done what I did."

"You were placed in that situation because you know that sometimes your wants and wishes are never taken into consideration. You know that the Crown comes first, and that was how you reacted.

"Your flight-or-fight responses kicked in, and because you're Etta, and because you can do nothing the easy way, you chose both. You flew to me, and you fought what you thought was coming with fire." I raised her knuckles to my lips. "I just wish I'd been half the man you needed back then, to be worthy of all the woman you were."

A shocked breath escaped her, and her misty eyes clashed with mine as gratitude and love blossomed to life inside them.

I kissed her fingers then shot Perry a look. I could tell she didn't like what I had to say but knew she couldn't argue.

And that, I figured, said *everything*.

"Will you please not share the circumstances of our wedding with her fathers?" I requested politely.

At that moment, where displeasure and disagreement had sowed their dissent, I saw the respect for me in her eyes increase tenfold.

"I won't tell them," she agreed. "I don't want them to know either."

I nodded, then to Etta, I asked, "We'll deal with the future together, won't we?"

Her eyes were bright with hope, but guilt shadowed that too.

"Won't we?" I repeated, not allowing her to stay quiet.

My woman had a voice, and it was time she started to use it. I'd noticed that she was more outspoken than before with her family, but I knew she held back.

Only with me, did she let loose, and it was time her family saw her for the powerhouse that she was.

Her eyes still on mine, she told me—not her mom—*me*, "We will."

FIFTEEN

"I can feel you looking at me."

Though my cheeks burned at Tin's sleepy mumble, I replied, "Then you shouldn't have come to bed without a shirt on."

Snickering with his eyes closed, he drawled, "So it's my fault?"

"Of course."

"Bandages are your weakness, huh?"

He rolled his head to the side and finally opened his eyes. They were drowsy, and there was a hint of pain in the lines about his mouth, but I knew, probably better than he did, that he wasn't allowed any more meds for at least another hour.

I hated seeing him in pain, so I figured the best thing to do was to distract him.

"I'm pretty sure you could wear a sack and I'd think you were hot."

A laugh escaped him. "You haven't seen me in a sack. I might not look hot in it."

"It's what's underneath it I'm interested in."

Even as a kid, he'd been toned and strong. I supposed that was what happened when you had Sawyer for a father.

Post-cancer, he hadn't let his diagnosis get him down. He'd forged full steam ahead back into being a health nut. Tin, in the same house, probably couldn't help being swept along for the ride.

"I guess I understand," he murmured, his tone faux demure.

"Big head," I teased, even if he totally deserved to have a bigger head than he did. Thinking about Sawyer made me say, "You shouldn't compare yourself to your fathers."

His brows rose. "That's out of the blue." But he grunted. "I don't compare myself to them."

Not much. Ha.

"You do." I reached over and pressed my hand to his cheek. "You can't call out my mom the way you did and then not take a look at your own relationship with your parents."

"Can't I? Says who?"

I grinned. "Me. And don't try to allay it either."

"Who's allaying? I'm just *lying* here."

"You need to go on stage with that act," I said with a groan. "You're lucky you're sick. If you weren't, I'd have whacked you with a pillow."

He grinned. "Pillow fights. How very sleepover."

"Those days are long gone."

"You know how a sleepover would end, don't you?"

"Why, with sleep of course," I joked, loving when he laughed.

Loving that even though four years separated us, the past few days were like a bridge between the past and the present.

"Sleep. Sure." He snorted. "And I don't compare myself to my dads. Much."

"Much. Huh." I arched a brow. "You tell me this..."

"I'm all ears."

"You're all something," I grumbled before I quickly said, "Would you consider yourself as smart as your fathers?"

He blinked. "No."

"Thought not."

"I'm not though."

"Maybe not as clever as Devon," I conceded. "But the rest?"

"With what they've achieved, no."

"So, you're super-duper smart, just not super-duper pooper scooper smart, right?"

Tin rolled his eyes. "I'm sure Mensa has been classifying their members like that since its inception."

"They should. Everyone would know what's what if they did." I laughed at his second eye-roll in as many minutes. "Would you prefer to have a bigger IQ than a bigger cock?"

"What kind of a question is that?" he huffed, for the first time rolling onto his back.

Though I saw the strain on his face, it didn't make me let up any. Mostly because I already knew the answer.

"Well? Would you?"

"Why? Do you need a bigger dick?" he sniped.

"Nope. Got one hole, and you've already molded it to your specifications."

A shocked laugh escaped him. "You did not just say that."

Pleased I surprised him, I smirked. "You want me to lie?"

"No." His brow furrowed. "You know what my family is like."

"I do. Very well."

"Health and smarts..." He shrugged. "Jack and I both struggle with our places. Rosie and Bethan less so."

"That's because they're girls. It's different."

"Is it?"

"I think so. Men have massive egos that constantly need stroking."

"When I'm better, I have something that constantly needs stroking," he mumbled.

"Those are fighting words, and you aren't ready to fight."

"True," he conceded with a grimace. "Even my cock agrees." He peered at me, taking in the satin and lace I was wearing, mumbling, "You've been wearing that torture device all night, and normally, I'd have it off and on the floor before you could slip between the sheets, but I'm just too fucking tired right now."

I winced, and my arousal disappeared with his words. "I'm sorry—"

"Don't be. I didn't mean it that way, love. I just meant that even if I wanted to, and trust me, I *want*, I couldn't do anything right now." He scowled. "Which sucks."

"It does," I rasped, even as my heart was reeling at his casual use of the word 'love.'

It wasn't the first time he'd said it, but it was still music to my ears.

"So to make up for torturing me, you can tell me what you were thinking when you were perving on me as I slept."

"I wasn't perving on you. I just woke up," I argued. "What was I supposed to look at?"

"Aphrodite's tits up there are nice."

Casting a glance at the mural overhead, I grunted. "Only if you bat for the other team, which I don't. And don't make me get someone to paint a bra on her."

"As if the palace would let you."

"You can tell how criminally few crown princesses there have been in our lineage because only guys want to wake up to that mural above them."

Snickering, he said, "You may have a point."

"You wouldn't like it if Aphrodite and Ares were getting it on and I compared his dick to yours, would you?"

"They were adulterous."

I blinked. "So?"

"So? They were cheaters."

"What do you want me to do? Rewrite history? She was more likely to be boning Ares than Hephaestus."

His brow puckered. "Someone's been catching up on their Classics."

"Why does that come as a surprise? I have to sit through a ton of lectures on that stuff."

"You hate school."

"I do." I blew out a breath. "Wanna know a secret?"

"Always."

"They found out I have ADHD."

He cocked a brow at me. "So, we're twinsies?"

I hid a smile. "I guess."

"That makes sense, actually. Now that I think about it."

I didn't take offense. "Yeah."

"You were always too smart for your own good—"

"Hey!" I argued.

"You were, but in class, you never did better than Bs or Cs, right?"

"I'd shove you off the bed if you weren't injured."

"We've already established there are many things we'd be doing if I wasn't punching above my weight right now," he said wryly.

I huffed. "I never thought about having anything like ADHD because I'm not like you."

"It never manifests in the same way," he pointed out.

"No, I know, but I just compared myself to you and how you were without meds. Then my issues in class got worse. The privy council thought my grades were atrocious, so they made me see this specialist.

"I think they're happy I have it because then they can make me look more like the people's princess when I don't graduate college."

He sniffed. "Jackasses."

"You won't hear me disagreeing." Because I didn't want to talk about them anymore, I murmured, "It was nice, wasn't it?"

"What was? Five minutes without us arguing? Missed me?"

The twinkle in his eyes almost made me melt into the bed.

It had been *years* since I'd seen that twinkle, and those twelve hundred-plus days felt more like twelve thousand.

"I did miss you."

He sighed, muttered, "I'm a dumbass."

"You are. But so am I."

"What smart kids we'll have."

I laughed. "Christel and Victoria's brats can take the throne."

"You mean that?"

My nose crinkled. "I'm teasing. We won't have a choice, I don't think. After it's all official and the people get their royal wedding, they'll probably be up in my business about when I'm getting pregnant."

"Who's 'they?'"

"The palace." I wafted a hand. "The household."

He scowled. "Your ovaries have nothing to do with the 'household.'"

"Everything's their business," I said gruffly, but because I didn't want to think about the level of control a non-existent 'body' had over me, I continued, "It was nice waking up with you. Sleeping with you."

He blinked at the change in topic, but nodded, and said, "Not another night apart. Not a single one."

My eyes flared wide. "You can't say that."

"Sure I can," he countered. "Where I go, you go. And vice versa."

"That's..." I tried to settle on a word. "...impractical."

But I was here for it.

Totally.

"Impractical? Maybe. But you're forgetting, Etta, I'm not a boy anymore." He shot me a smile that could only be described as danger-ous. It sent shivers down my spine and made everything feminine in me stand to attention in response. "I'm not about to be led around by the palace. I'm not about to let *anyone* treat you disrespectfully."

"Would you have before?" I questioned, aware that I sounded breathless.

"Honestly?"

"I always want honesty between us."

His gaze was measured as it settled on mine. "Before, I wouldn't have been confident enough to stop it. I don't like that this is the truth, but I know myself well enough to recognize that I'd have been swept along in the tide.

"Let's face it, Etta. That's what this incorporeal 'palace' is—an ocean. Everyone's just swimming along, trying not to drown."

"That's a good analogy," I whispered, sadness filling me because it was *too* good. How damn depressing was that? "I'm sorry you—"

A soft laugh escaped him. "You don't have to say sorry. You didn't ask for this life. You didn't ask to be who you are."

"I didn't," I agreed.

"And, right or wrong, it *is* who you are, Etta. Your parents can tell you off for whatever it is you've done on such and such day, and the privy council can give you shit about saying too much or too little or wearing too low a neckline or too high a hemline, but you *are* a queen, Etta."

My cheeks blazoned with heat. "I'm not."

"You are." His lips twitched. "Don't be coy. It's true.

"Have you ever thought that your interests are so wide and varied because that's what you need for the role ahead?

"Because you're *supposed* to be interested in everything and nothing?

"People like me, like your sisters, we specialize. Because that's what ordinary folk do. And for all that they're princesses, they're ordinary. Their roles won't be defined by the palace.

"But you, sweetheart," he breathed as he shook his head, "there's nothing ordinary about you..."

SIXTEEN

ETTA

"There's nothing ordinary about you..."

For a second, his words seemed to echo around the bedroom.

I'd often been told I was difficult, flighty, a pain, even, but Tin's words held no criticism.

Only appreciation.

For me.

I swallowed. "That... I'm... Is that a good thing?"

"Good or bad, you can't fight who you are. Your father's the same. Born for the job.

"If it weren't so annoying, it'd be amusing that he can't see how alike you are.

"And let me tell you something, Etta, if you *were* like your sisters, if you weren't born for this godforsaken job, the second I was better, I'd sneak you out of Masonbrook one day and never let you come back."

His words resonated with me on an atavistic level.

My inner cavewoman preened at what he was saying because, in any given situation, there were two people in the whole world who ranked above me.

My mother and father.

That was it.

And technically, according to the law of inheritance in Veronia, it was only my father who truly ranked above me.

I was his next-in-line, whereas Mom was his consort.

I was *destined* for this role.

Just as he'd been.

So for Tin to tell me that he'd steal me away, that he'd throw the rulebook at the authorities, that he'd take charge of *me*, every female bone in my body quivered in reaction.

Tin had never been a submissive man.

He was not born to stand behind me.

He was born to stand at my side.

He might not have seen that in himself when he was younger, but I had.

I'd known he was my future consort even if he didn't.

As a million thoughts raced through my mind, I said the first thing that tripped from my tongue, "Remember when we measured your dick?"

He groaned, raised a hand to cover his eyes, and muttered, "You can change the subject, just don't make me laugh."

I couldn't stop myself from snickering, even as I allowed his earlier words, his resolve to settle inside me.

They were an affirmation, proof of a level of confidence in *me* that I'd never known I needed to hear.

"Every time I touched it to hold it against the ruler," I said, continuing to snicker, "it would twitch, then I'd drop it in surprise and—"

"Yeah, I blew my wad in the shortest time imaginable." Another groan escaped him. "I was mortified." He peeped at me from under his hand. "Trust you not to have forgotten that. Memory of an elephant, that's you."

Smirking at him, I guesstimated, "You were only..." My eyes widened as I tried to think back to that day. I whistled. "Fourteen?"

"If we do have kids, then we're locking them down from thirteen."

"Our parents were definitely too trusting, but..." I shrugged. "We were, I guess, childhood sweethearts, and we waited until we were old enough that first time so their faith in us didn't go to waste."

"We did, and waiting was fucking hard." He groaned as he raised a hand and scraped it over his jaw. His fingers rubbed against the scruff, making a scratching noise. "I can still remember how you looked when I came on your face."

I chuckled. "I didn't expect it to explode!"

"Yeah, well, you got what you were asking for even if you didn't expect it." He pinched the bridge of his nose. "I can still remember your wide eyes, and then, you scooped some cum up on your finger and sucked it off..."

"At least I got a chance to measure it again," I rasped, amused and turned on by the memory of his second hard-on.

Which had lasted about as long as his first one.

Only this time he hadn't come on my face.

Just my chest.

I snorted at the memory.

Knowing what I was laughing at, he grumbled, "You deserved the double blast. It was your suggestion to measure it! What's a guy to do when he gets that kind of challenge from his best girl?"

I stuck out my tongue. "You were curious too. I don't know why you hadn't measured it yourself. You're all about the math. I thought you'd have it mapped out and everything."

"Know the angle of the curve of it? Yeah, I'm not that interested in my junk."

"Said no man ever," I retorted, deadpan, then, softer, I told him, "I missed this, Tin."

"Me too." His lips twisted. "Punished myself as much as I punished you, but, Etta, I need you to know this—I'm here because I missed you. I got hurt, and I needed to come home. Then shit went down. It happened in that order. I was always coming back to you. Do you get that?"

I knew him. Knew the man.

Tin didn't do anything unless he wanted to, and he wanted me.

"I get that," I said softly, watching the relief crease his expression, sensing that had been a huge concern of his.

Tucking my hands under the side of my face, I rolled my legs toward my belly to get more comfortable.

There was far too much distance between us on the bed, and for the first time in my life, I resented how big it was.

He was so yummy. All pale, creamy skin that was golden on his forearms, throat, and face. His pecs were defined, his belly rippled with muscle, and his biceps were much more delineated than they'd been before.

The last time I'd seen him like this, he'd been skinnier, younger. He'd been a kid, just like me. But now, we were adults. We were both grown-ups, and we had the bodies to prove it.

I'd had a bit of puppy fat on me that years of being glum had slimmed down, my boobs were bigger though, and my hips were rounder. I had a butt that wasn't going anywhere, and I hated how I resembled a ruler because I had zero waist, just went up and down, but for all that, I knew he liked what he saw.

There was no way he didn't.

It was there, in the fiery heat in his eyes that was only banked because of pain. It was there, in the interest he showed me as he touched me with his gaze.

I knew, just as much as I wanted to touch him, as much as I wanted to pull the sheets down and throw myself at him, he wanted to hurl himself at me too.

And fuck, what a ride it would be.

I nibbled my bottom lip as my heart began to pound.

This wasn't a girl's nervous need but a woman's. It was like the difference between a full-bodied glass of red wine and a spritzer that had been left out to sit in the sun.

I was full of need and none of it was PG.

"Stop looking at me like that," he rumbled, his voice low and deep, sending shivers into my core.

"Not doing anything wrong by looking."

He grunted and turned to stare up at the ceiling. "You totally are." Another grunt. "I can't believe you're still in this room."

"It's where the crown princess sleeps."

His nose crinkled. "It's like a museum."

I glanced around the room that *was* like a museum. "I quite like it."

"You hated it when you were younger."

I huffed. "Of course I did. I was fourteen when I moved in here, and I hated everything but you."

"True."

He sounded smug, so I retorted, "I couldn't put posters up, couldn't get speakers installed. I had to preserve everything. It sucked.

"Now I'm used to it. I guess, more than anything, I just like the space. Plus, because it's a suite, I don't have to leave it if I don't want to see anyone."

He rolled his head on the pillow again, no longer looking at the gilt moldings and the frescos that decorated the ceiling—Aphrodite in her bath as cherubs washed her. It was weird going to sleep looking at a Michelangelo, but that was how the cards fell sometimes.

"How do you feel about yesterday?"

"About what Mom said?" I shrugged. "I feel bad."

"Why?"

"I guess, in my head, I always give Father a hard time—"

"Understandable. They've always been hard on you."

A breath whistled out of me. "Yeah."

"You should have told me about Fortsythe," he grumbled.

"I was scared, Tin. Terrified. I could see my life changing all around me. I could—" I reached up and rubbed my eyes. "I made stupid decisions, but they were out of fear and panic, not malice. I didn't do what I did to trap you; I did it to trap *me*. To make *me* inaccessible."

"I can see that." He sighed. "I just wish you'd told me."

"I do too. It might have saved us a lot of misery, but, also, it might not have. Back then, I wasn't as strong as I am now."

"Weren't you?" He smiled. "As far as I know, you've always had a mouth on you."

"Yeah," I agreed, not even bothering to get sniffy about his less than charming compliment, "but there's being all mouth and then not having the balls to stand up for yourself. You gave me that, Tin.

"Being married to you changed me and liberated me in ways that you don't get because, to you, it just tied you down. It didn't free you."

Guilt creased his expression, but he didn't reply. In fact, for a few silent moments, we just watched each other.

"Things are going to change now," he rasped after a couple minutes. "I'm ready."

"Ready for what?"

"To be the man you want by your side. To become the consort you need.

"I missed you, Etta. I missed you so fucking much, but I was such a stubborn asshole that I couldn't admit it.

"Not a goddamn day passed where I didn't want to call you. Where I didn't want to tell you about some prick I was dealing with, or laugh about some shit one of my dads pulled." A breath whistled from him. "In the future, if I'm ever that stubborn, feel free to kick me in the balls."

Though I snickered, I countered, "That wouldn't be much fun for me though. We have a lot of time to make up for."

His nose wrinkled as he stared back up at the ceiling. "This is my punishment. Not being able to have all the sex I've been missing out on—"

"What?" I shrieked, leaning toward him slightly.

He blew out a breath but didn't look at me. Just carried on staring at the ceiling.

Fucking Aphrodite.

I was going to get jealous if he didn't stop studying her conical tits.

Softly, hope loading the words, I whispered, "You haven't—"

He finally cut me a look. "I tried. Fuck, I tried." When I winced, he shrugged, utterly unapologetic. The asshole. "But I could never do it. You're mine and I'm yours. And I knew, no matter what, no matter how long it took, you'd never betray me that way, so I couldn't do the same to you because I knew, deep down, you'd never forgive me. You'd forgive me of many things, but never that."

I'd always imagined he'd have a girlfriend or some kind of fuck buddy, and I'd tortured myself over it. Had died inside when I thought of him with someone else.

Now?

I knew the truth, and I didn't know what to say. I just sat there, gaping at him. My nightdress was rucked up, the strap half slipping down my arm revealing God knew what, but I didn't care.

All I could see was him.

All that mattered was him.

"Thank you," I whispered shakily.

It was too small a reply, too unworthy of the sacrifice he'd made.

And yeah, it was a sacrifice.

He'd been faithful to me, even in the aftermath of what I'd done to him.

He'd stayed true to us even though he was a young man.

A *hot* young man who traveled all over the world, had a face like an angel, the body of a sinner, and was *kind* to boot.

My mind was frazzled. More so than it had been yesterday when Mom had told me how much work Father shouldered on my behalf.

The concept of Tin not sleeping around was enough to have my elbows blowing out from under me and I sank back onto the bed, uncaring if I plopped down ungracefully, and just stared at Aphrodite's tits.

"Etta?"

"Yes?" My voice was low, quiet.

Unlike me.

"I thought you'd be pleased."

I closed my eyes.

Pleased?

Everything inside me was ablaze with need and want and love and desire.

I didn't know how to show him how he'd made me feel by telling me that.

Because Tin and me?

We were made for each other.

And he'd just confirmed that.

He could have used other women to get back at me. He could have done whatever he'd wanted and I'd never have been able to say anything, even if the knowledge *would* hurt, because I'd been the one to start our life together atop a bed of lies.

I released a shaky breath and whispered, "I love you." It wasn't enough, but it was all I had.

"Ah." He hummed. "I love you too."

And I knew he understood. I knew he *got* why I was speechless. Knew he wasn't worried about my reaction anymore because, deep inside me, there was a war going on.

A war of feelings and emotions and...

God, too many things.

I wanted to kiss him, to fuck him, to make love to him, to caress him and hold him.

I wanted to be in his arms, to have him touch me, caress *me*. So many damn things, and we couldn't do any of them.

Not a single one.

"If I promise to lay still, can I come closer?"

"Of course. You don't have to ask," he rumbled, so I carefully twisted onto my side and half crawled across the wide mattress, only stopping when I was about a foot from him.

I wasn't touching him, but I could feel his heat, and that heat warmed me right through.

"I missed you," I said again, knowing this would be something we said often in the coming days.

"I missed you."

I tilted my head to the side and pressed it, carefully, to his shoulder.

"I won't break," he rasped.

"Not going to risk it. Not now."

He sighed. "I know." He reached for my hand and tucked it in his. "The first night we were in bed together, I never imagined it would be with you on the other side of the mattress."

"Our blue balls are mutual."

"You've grown a pair since the last time we did it, huh?"

Chortling, I told him, "I've grown something."

"I'll bet." He snorted, then I felt his lips brush my temple. "All in good time, yeah?"

I hummed. "Definitely."

SEVENTEEN

TIN

From the balcony of the Madelan Parliament, I stood as tall as I could, well aware that there was a nurse on standby in case I collapsed.

My ego was pricked, but I did feel faint as hell.

"This is a disaster waiting to happen," Christel murmured beside me.

I didn't necessarily agree or disagree.

"Security is heightened. If the UnReals get through, I'd be surprised."

She turned to me. "I guess you'd know," she said snidely.

Etta frowned. "Christel, watch your mouth. Don't talk to him that way."

"You almost died because of him."

"No, I lived because of him," Etta retorted.

I didn't need her to come to my defense, but that she did, *immediately,* made me wish I wasn't still on bed rest.

That was what being a royal meant, however. Getting up and putting on your best suit despite the fact you should be in bed, resting.

"Tin shouldn't even be here," Victoria hissed.

"He's my husband," she spat. "He stays with me. God, the doctors advised he shouldn't come, but he's here, isn't he? Standing for Veronia as much as we are."

Well, that was a lie.

I was standing for her.

I didn't believe her parents were in danger, but I wanted my eyes on Etta.

I wanted to know where she was and what she did, just until this edgy feeling inside me faded.

Tucked up in a padded, oversized jacket to offset the windchill, with a *ushanka* on her head, she looked as cold as I felt.

Snow was on the horizon, and had been threatening to drift down for the past few days, but for the moment, it was just frigid cold.

A roar of cheers waved through the crowd as the royal open-top carriage surged onto the courtyard in front of us, breaking into the girls' argument.

I didn't care if her sisters were pissed at me. Etta wasn't. That was all that mattered.

I spied Perry tucked up in an oversized coat, a simple gold circlet on her head—I knew it was a crown that was worn in times of war— and Edward, sporting a circlet as well, but this time of carved wood, and carrying a scepter and a lance, were inside the carriage. Prince George and the Duke of Ansían, the girls' fathers, were on horseback behind them.

The imagery was unlike usual processions, that I knew.

They weren't wearing ornate clothes, just outerwear necessary for these temperatures, but the royal jewels that were worn in wartime were a declaration of intent.

Having attended this procession before, but always from the ground, never from this balcony where the royal children waited on their parents to meet them so they could wave to the crowds, I well knew what the next hour and a half looked like.

The notion that, one day, I'd be in the carriage with Etta made me want to puke, but that was definitely tomorrow's problem.

Yorke Abbey was at their side, a grandiose building that had seen more weddings and funerals than any place in Europe, even Westminster.

The palazzos of a few Veronian nobles and even a military barrack all surrounded the massive courtyard that had been made famous by these oversized parades which took place four days to Christmas.

Come hell or high water.

Or a shooting that had almost killed the crown princess.

Yes, I disapproved.

The carriage began to make its way toward Parliament. A feat that ordinarily lasted five minutes would, today, take ninety as troops on foot and horseback performed a highly choreographed military march.

Cannons exploded every fifteen minutes, guns also went off in tandem with fleets of aircraft zooming overhead, and in the distance, the naval fleet took part in the war symphony.

Eventually, with marching bands serenading them, the carriage moved toward the front steps of the Parliament building.

Nerves hit me because I knew, before Etta's birth, there'd been a terrorist attack on this day. It was why this balcony was shielded by bulletproof glass.

Scars from the damage were still visible on the walls surrounding the courtyard, and the visible reminder was exactly what I didn't need.

My heart was in my throat as the royal procession finally made it to the bottom steps of Parliament.

Cheers and cries from the thousands of spectators who refused to be deterred by the recent terror attack serenaded the king and queen as they made a journey that dozens of their line had completed hundreds of times in the four centuries of the DeSauvier family's reign.

When they were safe, I sagged against Etta, relief making me stagger because I hadn't realized it was tension that was keeping me upright.

"Tin! Are you okay?" she cried, stabilizing me. "Christel! Help me!"

I felt like a fool with the entire country watching on because I could almost sense the cameras zooming in on me and my weakness, but it couldn't be helped.

"Fuck! He's bleeding," Victoria rasped, and she did me a solid by moving in front of me.

"You must have burst one of your stitches. Where's the damn nurse?" Etta growled as we began a slow retreat off the balcony and into the interior of Parliament.

The nurse popped up, and that was when Edward, Perry, Xavier, and George ascended the stairs.

Edward frowned at the sight of me and ordered one of his guards, "Get them home."

"No. It's tradition—" I bit off, uncaring that people gasped around me at my tone. "I won't be blamed for Etta missing this—"

Edward peered down his nose at me. "If I have to give you a royal command to stay in bed, Valentin, I will."

"He will," Etta concurred with a grimace.

I pulled a face when the nurse tugged my shirt aside.

"He's pulled a stitch," she soothed. "It looks worse than it is."

"You can't stand on the balcony bleeding," Perry said waspishly. "Go home, Tin. All will be well here."

"I'm sorry," I told them all, hating that I was being a nuisance.

"You have nothing to be sorry for," Etta countered, glaring at her family before they could disagree with her. "Let's get you to bed."

As the family fussed around me, the crowd outside growing noisy as the DeSauviers hadn't rushed onto the balcony for the customary salutation, I muttered in her ear, "The next time you say that, I want my dick inside you as soon as the door's closed."

Her lips quirked before she firmed them. "Don't even joke. I told you it was too early for you to be up and about."

I shrugged. "I don't know how I pulled a stitch."

"You're in pain anyway. You shouldn't be here."

"I wanted to make sure everything was okay," I told her as I was guided toward the exit we'd used to get here.

Interestingly enough, I'd learned there were tunnels beneath the Madelan Parliament that connected with Masonbrook, the royal residence in Veronia's capital.

They were there for the royal family to escape a siege, but now they were used as secure channels for the DeSauviers to reach their government without having to use roads.

As I was settled on a golf cart, Mika, one of Etta's guards, jumped behind the wheel and drove us back to the palace.

Now that we were on our way, Etta told me, "What would you have done if everything *wasn't* okay?"

I blinked at her. "I don't know."

"You're not G.I. Joe," she retorted.

"I never said I was."

"You should have been in bed."

"Yes, I know."

My agreement stopped the wind in her sails. "Really?"

"Really. I just... if you'd have been able to stay with me, I'd have remained behind." I stared at her sheepishly. "I don't want my eyes off you."

"Oh, Tin," she whispered, her hand moving from my lap to my chest as she twisted to look at me. "I love you."

"I love you too. I almost lost you, Etta." I wasn't sure if she knew how that was going to fuck me up for a long time to come.

"I almost lost you," she countered. "You were in more danger of leaving me than I was of leaving you."

I complained, "That's ass-backward logic."

"I'm the queen of that."

My lips twitched. "You're the queen of something."

"Your heart?" she joked with a laugh, patting my chest. "Anyway, if you keep pulling your stitches, we're never going to be able to have sex. So that should be encouragement enough for you to get better."

"You horny, baby?" I teased, pressing my lips to her temple.

"For you? Always."

I groaned. "You're right."

"I know I am," she countered, but deep in her eyes, I sensed her concern.

Reaching up, even though it hurt, I cupped her chin and rasped, "I've never told you how lucky I am that you love me, have I?"

She blinked. "No. But why would you?"

"Because I am."

She kissed me gently on the lips. "I'm lucky too."

EIGHTEEN

Yule was in full swing by now.

By tradition, Christmas trees weren't decorated in Masonbrook Castle until Christmas Eve, but Mom had changed all that in her time as Queen.

Now, on Thanksgiving, trees popped up, one at a time, gradually filling all the spaces in the palace. They'd be there until Epiphany.

The tunnels were handy because they transported us home quickly but it meant Tin had to walk a large portion of the way, and the trees dotted the path he took.

We passed a thirty-foot fir that was brought to us every year from a special forest in the North, one that soared past the mezzanine floors and which was tipped with a star that was encrusted with actual diamonds.

That was when Tin remarked, "I'm sure this wasn't here when we left."

He hadn't said anything before which told me how anxious he'd been about today's events.

I'd been nervous. The lives of my family were at stake, after all, but that he'd been so concerned made me wonder if there were other official secrets he didn't feel he could share.

"It was here. It's been up since Thanksgiving," I said wryly. "You were too out of it to notice."

He cast me a look but didn't say anything, just tugged me to a halt and stared up at the tree.

There were thousands of ornaments and lights that decorated the massive fir. He reached out and brushed one of the Swarovski stars that Mom had been collecting every year since I was born.

"Mom said she bought that when I was one, because I was her star."

Tin turned to me with a smile. "That's sweet."

I nodded. "She liked me back then."

"You're being hard on yourself. She likes you now," he argued.

Shrugging, I mumbled, "I make a lot of mistakes."

"You're human."

"I'm royal. I'm not allowed to be human." My throat choked a little. "Didn't mean to make that into a pity party."

"I don't pity you. And you *are* human. I mean, you're my princess too, but you're human, sweetheart."

He slipped his arm around my waist which prompted me to mutter, "We don't have time to dawdle. You're bleeding," I pointed out.

"I wanted to look at the tree."

"The stars are for me," I said softly, "the crackers are for Christel, and Victoria's are the little dogs."

"They make them specially for her, don't they?" he asked.

"Perks of being a queen," I drawled. "Now, come on, let's go."

He heaved a sigh but let me help him down the many corridors of Masonbrook until we reached my apartments.

Well, *our* apartments now.

As we stepped inside, he muttered, "I really was out of it, wasn't I?"

I had to smile because in here there were two trees as well. One either side of the fireplace which had a massive stone crest at the peak.

With the fire roaring, it was a cozy scene. Two cream armchairs were settled on either side of the trees, and between them was a large navy sofa with more pillows on it than I knew what to do with.

It was high-backed with a long body so that I could slump against the cushions and kick my legs up, free to be myself, and not a princess, by slouching and actually being allowed to be comfortable.

Beside the sofa, there was a stand with my current book perched on it and a cozy light to read by.

"This is more your style," he declared, and he wasn't wrong.

My bedroom belonged in a historical novel with its grand four-poster bed that matched the cabinet, armoire, and dresser.

Crafted by a master carpenter, they were protected pieces and would be there in my son or daughter's time—if I were to have a kid—and their great-great grandson or daughter's time too.

It wasn't my style, but I appreciated the heritage. Whereas the living room *was* to my taste.

"Can't see you sitting on those armchairs though," he muttered as we headed into the bedroom.

"No, they're for guests. Not that I get many. We all respect each other's privacy here and congregate in the family room if we want to talk."

"Best way. You live in a goldfish bowl. You'd go crazy otherwise."

I hummed my agreement, then finally managed to settle him on the bed, and dragged off the layers that were needed for a bitter Veronian winter's day.

A second later, a knock sounded, and I called out, "Come in."

The doctor bustled in, the nurse from Parliament too, and together, they worked on stitching Tin back up amid the splendor of the carved pine four-poster that had more details on it than mantilla lace.

As Tin cursed under his breath with every stitch, Aphrodite perved over the scene from the mural overhead.

Trying not to hover, I leaned against the dresser, pretending I wasn't watching every move the doctor and nurse made when I really was.

Whether it made them nervous or not, I didn't particularly care.

Tin was my everything.

If they broke him, I'd break them.

When a low, pained grunt escaped him, I surged forward, on the brink of shouting at them, but Tin rasped, "Calm down, Etta. It's okay."

I gritted my teeth until they were done, and as they walked out after gracing me with a bow and a curtsey between them, I stormed over to him and demanded, "Are you okay?"

"Been better. Been worse," he mumbled.

"They should have put you under," I chided.

He blinked. "Etta, you don't do things like that for stitches. They put local anesthetic on it."

"You're my husband. They should knock you out for it."

His lips curved as I headed over to the closet to find him a replacement T-shirt. "You're being irrational. I like it. It looks good on you."

I scowled at him, but he grinned as I helped him change.

Huffing, I asked, "Do you want anything before you get some rest?"

"I don't want to lie in here. It's like a mausoleum."

My nose crinkled because I couldn't disagree. "Want to sit in the living room?"

"Yeah. Help me up?"

I let him put as much weight on me as he wanted, tensing whenever he hissed beneath his breath as he tugged on his wounds, then we clambered into the living room.

I swore I was sweating like I'd been working out by the time I deposited him on the sofa. I backed off when he awkwardly knelt on it, climbing up and crawling onto it then twisting around and plunking himself back on the cushions with a tired grunt.

"That was elegant," I said, trying to tease because I wanted to cry.

I knew he'd prefer teasing to tears.

He didn't bother raising his head, just lifted his hand and gave me the finger.

"Will we have to live here?" he asked after a couple minutes of him just staring up at the ceiling.

"It's where the heir to the throne lives," I said softly. "Sometimes, upon marriage, they're granted a palace."

He snickered. "Let's hope your fathers are generous, eh?" As my lips twitched, he pointed at the fireplace. "Is that a Monet?"

I cast a look at the watercolor that hung over the hearth. "It is."

"Pass me the photo of your ascension?"

I moved over to the mantelpiece and reached for the photo he was talking about.

Stacked amid six or seven frames, mostly of us throughout our childhood, including the one he'd given me in Vegas of us sharing a bath and sporting soapsud hair and a beard, I was surprised he'd noticed the ascension.

Glancing at the picture, I smiled, taking in my ballgown and the surcoat of my new station, hair loose about my shoulders and beaming with happiness because my parents had surprised me by having Tin attend.

We'd danced my first dance at the celebratory ball, and there he was, all skinny and young, standing in a tailored tux.

As I passed it over to him, he rasped, "Why this one?"

"I was happy. You were too."

He cast me a look. "We were happy after that."

"Yeah, but those were my secret times. This wasn't. The whole world saw how happy I was." I shot him a soft smile. "That's the real me."

His eyes narrowed. "When you're with me?"

"Always. You're the only one who knows the real Etta."

His nostrils flared. "Say that when I'm better."

"We're going to have to write these down."

"Stop saying things that make me want to eat you out, then."

His raw words had me blinking.

"I'm already thinking of ways we could get each other off—"

"The doctor said bedrest. Not orgasms," I pointed out, even though I was definitely running hotter than before.

"Orgasms are good for the soul. My soul took a battering too."

"Bullshit."

"Are you going to stand over there all day?"

"No. I'm just waiting for you to get comfortable. It hasn't happened yet."

He grunted. "I'll be glad when this is healed. I hate being incapacitated."

"You're just like your daw."

His nose crinkled. "I am." He waved a hand at the bookshelf in the corner. "Bring me your favorite book."

"I don't have to. It's on the stand." I walked over to the table that held an old favorite.

"You haven't changed," he said, shaking his head as he read the author name—Lisa Kleypas. "I tried one of these once."

I laughed. "Wouldn't have thought they were your style."

"No," he concurred, "It wasn't. Told me a lot about you though."

More laughter pealed from me. "What?"

"You're a romantic."

"We both knew that already."

"Maybe. Maybe not. I doubt your family knows." His eyes gleamed. "I'm going to take full advantage of that side of you."

"Is that a challenge?" I mocked.

"If it is, it's at myself. But... I *won't* be wearing breeches."

I snickered. "Shame. You have the legs for it."

"Yes, I do."

His teasing had me smiling at him, and as our gazes connected, the flames from the fireplace flickering in each of our eyes, I had to admit that it didn't feel like it had been months and years since we'd sat this close. It was like time had never stopped rolling on without us being this way.

"How are you feeling?" I inquired softly as, sensing he was comfortable, I climbed onto the sofa.

Sitting opposite him, there were still three or so feet between us, so I was in no danger of doing anything that could hurt him.

He heaved a sigh. "Better for being in here and not in that clinic. Better for being with you. Better for knowing that you're safe."

"They should be on the journey home by now." I peered at my watch. "Tin?"

He tipped his head forward. "Yeah?"

"Did you..." My mouth worked. "It's not that I don't trust you. It's that... You were so anxious."

"Did I read about another attack that might have happened today?"

Slowly, I nodded.

"I didn't."

"Then why were you so nervous?"

"Because I don't need to have read any intelligence reports to know that these kinds of things tend to be clustered."

"Even if security is heightened?"

"They're whack jobs. They don't care about heightened security. They have specific ideologies and goals. It's like bashing your head against a wall and expecting not to get brain damage. Expecting, in fact, to get smarter. That's the UnReals."

Pondering what he said, I nodded. "Thank you."

"For what?"

"Telling me the truth."

"I will always tell you the truth, Etta. I'll even answer things about the last four years if you ask."

"Doesn't that break your Official Secrets Act?"

"It does. But I'm going to ask that you don't put me in a position where I have to tell you details... details that could endanger people whom I worked with. People whom I came to care about."

A flash of jealousy whipped through me as I pursed my lips. "Nice save," was all I said.

"It's about trust," he soothed.

"It is," I agreed. And if my family's safety didn't revolve around those secrets, I wouldn't think anything of it. Deciding that we'd better change the subject, I cleared my throat. "You know there'll be a ceremony, don't you?"

"Of course. I knew that before I even made the decision to come back here."

I arched a brow. "You did?"

"I did," he confirmed. "Our marriage is legal and binding—but not enough for Veronia."

My cheeks blanched at the memory of how exactly I'd made sure of the legal and binding part of the ceremony. "I'm sorry, Tin. What I did was terrible."

He grunted. "Hardly."

I winced. "You wanted it?"

"I did. I always wanted you. Still do." He blew out his cheeks. "I mean, I guess I wasn't complaining at the time about you consummating our marriage on my behalf, so I can't complain about it now either, can I?"

"If you say so," I rasped.

"Well, I do. I'm not going to cry over spilled milk anymore, Etta. You made a lot of mistakes. So did I. I think we need to work together as a unit to make sure that neither of us does anything that can irreparably damage our relationship again."

Though it wasn't a question, more of a statement, I whispered, "I'll never do anything that heinous—"

"Let's stop referring to the ceremony that almost made Edward have a fit as heinous, hmm? At least you're mine now. Otherwise, there'd be issues.

"I know my family is a problem, and this way, it's a *fait accompli.* I prefer it like that."

Me too.

But I didn't say that.

"You'll rest tomorrow, won't you?"

"I don't have a choice," he groaned. "It hurts like a bitch."

"There'll be things I have to do, but we're going to start arranging the ceremony. The Yule Guard Procession triggers the start of the holiday. We're on a break now until the fifth. That'll give us time to get things underway."

"Good. I don't want to have to wait to make us official."

"It's going to be crazy," I warned.

"Like you're going to have much to do," he said, laughing. "Mom and Auntie Perry will take over. Make no mistake about it."

"True." I shrugged. "I'm not that interested anyway."

He arched a brow at me. "Should I be offended that my bride isn't blushing and eager?"

"Oh, I'm eager, and I'll blush, just not about having to go through the whole ceremony. It's going to be a lot of pomp and no glory." I cringed. "You'll have to be crowned, Tin. You know that, don't you?"

"I do."

I peeped at him from the corner of my eye. "Are you okay with that?"

"It's going to make you my wife for real, Etta." He arched a brow at me. "Of course I'm okay with it."

"I hope they do take over, to be honest. It's never been my thing."

"I'm not even sure how that's possible considering you love the books you do."

"Yeah, but in books they never go on about the weddings."

"Just the good stuff, like sex," he teased.

I smiled at him. "Not the books I read."

He snorted at my pious comment and started flicking through the pages of the one in his hand. "Do I spy the word 'cock?'"

My grin widened as I admitted, "So, some sex is had."

"They'd have bluer balls than me if they didn't," he drawled with a wink.

"I'm kind of turned on by your blue balls."

"Sadist."

"No. I just know what it represents."

His gaze softened. "I've only ever seen you, Etta. You have to know that."

My cheeks turned pink as I reached for his hand. As we bridged our fingers, I whispered, "If it were down to me, I'd be happy going back to Elvis. I can't go to the bathroom without there being some formality I have to complete sometimes. This is going to be a thousand times worse."

"I'm sure your bathroom habits are of interest to no one."

"Ha!" I exclaimed. "Just you wait until it's official. I bet we have problems with people trying to figure out if I'm pregnant."

He twisted his head to gape at me. "You can't be serious."

"Bet your non-royal-soon-to-be-royal ass I'm being serious." I grazed my bottom lip with my teeth then mumbled, "You don't want kids right away, do you?"

He cut me a look. "Do you?"

"I mean, there'll be pressure from the privy council. But there always is." I hitched my shoulder. "You know me. I hate kids."

"Do you want a family?"

"I want a family with you. I assume I won't hate our kid or kids."

He laughed. "No, I'd hope not. But I don't want you to want a kid just because of the line of succession, babe. There's more to having a child than that."

"Yeah, I know," I murmured drolly. "Honestly, I do. But it's different with you. Anyone else, and I probably wouldn't. I dunno, I'd pretend I was sterile or something. Which would be really awkward because I bet they'd make me go and get tested." I heaved a sigh, not seeing his horrified glance. "But I want your child. Just, like, not for another six or so years."

"They'd make you get tested?"

"The council? Hell, yeah. They're all about the line of succession."

"The UnReals should just be a fly on the wall for this conversation and then they'd realize it sucks to be you."

"Thanks."

He shook his head. "I can't believe they'd make you get tested."

"The line has to stand true, even if my sisters and their kids would ascend if anything happened to me."

He clenched his fingers around mine then growled, "Nothing's going to happen to you."

"I know. But nothing had better happen to you either."

"It won't. I don't intend on us finding each other again only for things to end with me taking a bullet."

"Good."

"Anyway, I'm down for six years. There's no need for us to have a family so young."

"It's weird that we're talking about this. I'm sorry," I said earnestly.

"Stop saying sorry."

When he winked, I beamed a smile at him, one he returned.

My heart, beating fast from the conversation, began to slow down as we stared at one another, and everything just fell into place.

He passed me my book, pointed at the word 'cock' and smirked, before he reached for his phone.

I ordered us some hot chocolate and a dish of *jun*—traditional spiced Christmas sugar cookies—and as we both relaxed, my eyes burned as I looked around the room which seemed to be brimming with life now he was here.

This was my present but, even better, it was going to be my future.

TIN

CHRISTMAS EVE

"What the hell?"

I heard her surprise from behind the fir tree I *shouldn't* have been carrying, but Christ, I couldn't spend another minute in bed without losing my damn mind.

"Tin?" she sputtered. "You shouldn't be carrying anything heavy!"

Even as a branch prodded me in the face, I had to grin at her chiding.

She really was a nag when she chose to be.

"Hush," I countered, then I shoved a bag at her. "Here. Take this."

It was snatched from my hand, but she grumbled, "We already have two trees. Where's this one going?"

Ignoring her, I shuffled forward, feeling the spray of needles cascade around my feet every time it collided with my legs.

Heading for the bedroom, I didn't stop until I'd plunked it down in the corner, beside the godawful dresser.

Huffing, red-cheeked, I held it upright and found her standing in the doorway, blinking at me.

"I didn't pull a stitch," I argued before she could chide me further.

But she didn't. Instead, her gaze darted to the tree, to the bag, and then to me.

Understanding her silence, I smiled and held out my hand as I proudly told her, "Our first Christmas tree."

She rushed over to me and entangled our fingers.

It was a smaller tree, nothing like the ones in the living room or out in the common areas of the palace. But it was ours.

I snagged the bag from her grasp and said, "New traditions." Then I delved into the carrier for one box in particular. Passing it over to her, I said, "Open this first."

She peeped a look at me, but nodded, and then opened the case to reveal a transparent glass bauble that was empty apart from a crystal Christmas tree in the center.

Raising it to the light, after she stared at it for a couple seconds, Etta asked breathlessly, "Is that what I think it is?" Her bottom lip wobbled. "You kept it?"

My wedding ring.

"Of course I did," I told her gruffly.

She reached for my arm and tucked herself into me. "Thank you."

"There's room for yours on the tree too, unless... do you want to use them after the wedding?"

Swallowing, Etta whispered, "Would you mind?"

"Wouldn't have suggested it if I did." As her eyes glistened, I pressed a kiss to her temple then teased her, "You never used to cry this much."

Etta shoved me in the side. "Oh, shush." But she was smiling as she did so.

Her smiles, I thought, were going to be *my* new Christmas tradition.

TWENTY

Amused, I watched as Tin peered around the formal dining room.

He'd never eaten here before.

We didn't use this dining room all that often.

"In my grandfather's day, we used to dine here every week," I told him, staring up at the grand fresco overhead of frolicking cherubs dropping grapes into the mouths of nubile nymphs.

Definitely wasn't my style, but it had floated someone's boat back in the day.

"For special occasions?"

"Sometimes, not always though."

"It's massive."

"It's eighty-feet-long," I agreed with a grin.

"There are two fireplaces."

Outright laughing, I said, "I know."

"There are eight chandeliers in here."

"I have eyes, Tin, and this isn't the first time I've used it."

He snorted. "I knew this place was fancy. I just didn't realize *how* fancy."

It was a testament to the ludicrous elegance of Masonbrook that a man as wealthy as Tin could be surprised by the splendor here.

With a wall of windows overlooking the infamous waterspout that was currently frozen over, we could see Saren, a small town that bordered the Ansian mountain range.

The view was unsurpassable, amid the prestigious old world glamor of the dining hall that was only exacerbated by a massive Christmas tree that made the one in the hall look small.

"Are all the presents for the family?"

"No. They're for staff."

"The staff?"

"Mom hands them out at the end of the day."

"Why not in the morning?"

I shrugged. "Tradition."

"Not thanks for working their asses off on Christmas Day?"

My lips curved. "They get paid four times the going rate, and they don't *have* to work. It's their choice."

He hummed. "Okay, so what's going to happen then?"

"Brunch first, then we'll head to Yorke Abbey."

"Why?"

"To sing carols and for the Christmas service. Then we return here for dinner, and afterward, we exchange gifts, and toward the end of the evening, Mom hands out the presents to the staff." I stared around the table. "I don't think we've had a Christmas this big in forever."

"The joys of having lots of fathers," he drawled with a laugh.

"On both sides." I smirked at him. "Don't you think it's funny how neither of us want what they have?"

"I think we do want what they have."

My eyes widened. "I don't want more than one guy."

"Good, seeing as I'd have to convince you otherwise."

Relief settled inside me. "One of you is more than enough. Mom is always having to juggle the dads. I don't need that kind of stress in my life."

Tin laughed. "And there was me thinking you were being romantic."

"Well, I am. In a sense. Just not in a way that's appeasing your alpha streak." I peered down my nose at him as we took a seat at the table. "You've gotten bossier since before…"

"Before we married?" He arched a brow. "You can say it out loud, Etta."

"I know I can," I grumbled.

"Say it then."

I huffed. "You've gotten bossier since before we married."

"I know. I had to do a lot of growing up before I was worthy of you. I still don't know if I am."

Touched, my hand shot out to grab his. "I didn't need you to grow up. I just needed you."

He shook his head. "Thank you for that, but I was insecure and dumb and young and too stupid to live. Right now, if you did what you'd done back then, I'd have spanked the hell out of you and we'd have argued and then we'd have fucked and we'd have gotten on with our lives—"

A gasp escaped me at his cavalier mentioning of him spanking me. "No way you'd do that!"

His eyes gleamed. "Why not? Wouldn't that have solved things faster?"

"Than four years of you sulking with me?" I sniped.

"Yes," he said simply, but his hand reached out to trail across the butt of my chin. "And when I said we want what our parents have… I meant the connection. Our connection is like theirs. Timeless."

Feeling oddly choked up, I clasped his wrist in mine and held it in place as I settled my chin against his palm.

"I love you, Etta. Merry Christmas."

I shot him a shaky smile. "Merry Christmas, Tin. I love you."

"The first of many together," he rasped.

"Hear, hear."

We both jumped when Devon's face appeared between the chairs, his words booming between us.

"Dad!" he snapped, clearly as surprised as me by the interruption.

I heard laughter and saw that almost our entire family had joined us in the dining room, and neither of us had even registered that particular fact.

Cheeks burning, I shot them all a sheepish smile and said, "Happy holidays, everyone."

There were a few chuckles, but other than that, attention soon drifted to brunch.

As we ate *pankeks*, an oat and nut biscuit that dripped with honey, as well as *kenfe*, a type of donut that was stuffed with ricotta cheese and blackberry jam, and *bele*, buns packed with bacon and caramelized vine tomatoes, the atmosphere around the table turned festive.

Tin and his family dove into the fayre with gusto, and my own merely took the time to relax because this was the one holiday where we didn't have a timetable.

Brunch lasted as long as we wanted because the carol service was at four in the afternoon.

Large mugs of hot chocolate were served, as well as steaming flagons of spiced cider for those who wanted it.

We feasted, and we enjoyed each other's company.

For all that I relaxed, I still noticed how my fathers studied Tin. Their gazes fixed on him from time to time as he bickered with Rosie and Bethan. But while I wasn't sure if they approved of him or not, I found that I didn't care.

Tin was mine.

I was his.

And if he'd ever worried about what Christmas present to give me, he'd given me the best one of all this year—himself.

TIN

THREE KINGS' DAY

Three Kings' Day for Veronians was Christmas Day for Anglophiles.

That was why I handed Etta her gift on the sixth of January.

Her smile was gleeful as she unwrapped the present, but I wasn't as excited as she was.

I was nervous.

Unsure.

What did you buy the woman who had everything?

Before, I'd known exactly what she wanted. Now, though, we were learning each other again.

Christ, I hoped I didn't miss the mark.

But when she pulled out the picture frame, one that gleamed in the light because it was made of crystals, her eyes sparkled with emotion in a way that outshone the crystal. That would outshine a diamond.

"Oh, Tin," she whispered. "I love it."

I shot her a rueful grin. "You do?"

Her fingers traced the lines of my face, an expression that was forever immortalized. "How couldn't they know?"

Aware of what she meant, I plunked my ass on the bed and stared at a face I saw in the mirror every day. But it was younger.

More hopeful.

Less world-weary.

No lines of stress or pain on my brow.

And I was clearly in love with Etta.

When I'd seen the photo she had of us on the mantelpiece, of us at her coronation ball, I was reminded of the table full of pictures we had at home.

The second you walked through the doors, you were greeted with them. Dozens of photos in mix-and-match frames. Of us as kids, of the parents before they'd had us and after. This picture was amid the bunch.

I knew she had to have it.

Knew she needed to see it.

"They probably thought it was puppy love." A belief that had likely been perpetuated by our falling out for four years.

She pressed the photo to her chest and held it there. "It's going on the mantelpiece."

"Not in the bedroom?" I queried, nose crinkling at the bridge.

"Nope. I want to see it whenever I'm on the sofa."

My lips twitched. "You just want guests to see my moon eyes."

A laugh escaped her. "That as well," she teased, but her smile turned soft. "I love it, Tin. Thank you."

I tapped the face of the watch she'd gifted me earlier—her grandfather's vintage Longines that had been crafted for him and sported the DeSauvier crest at the hour marker.

"You're welcome. I love my gift too. Thank you, sweetheart. Happy holidays."

She reached forward and pressed a kiss to my lips. One that boded well for later, and it *had* to be later too. I was ready, but she still had to dress for the feast day, and I knew from experience that Auntie Perry made a communist dictator look relaxed where these festive holidays were concerned.

That was why I left Etta to prepare herself, as if she were attending a red-carpet event, and decided to head to the sitting room to decompress with family.

My family.

I couldn't say that the DeSauviers had welcomed me with open arms, not that I blamed them.

The rest of the fam were treated as the old friends we were, but I was definitely being watched.

Inspected.

I could almost see the cogs churning in Etta's fathers' heads as they tried to calculate what it would take to turn me into a man worthy of being their daughter's consort.

I'd take their lessons on the chin, accept that I needed to grow, but for the most part, I avoided being with them so my end destination was the suite of rooms where *my* family was holed up.

As I walked, I noticed the number of Guard Elect on duty had increased, but I shoved thoughts of security aside for the moment, especially when I opened the door and found Jack scowling at his phone.

"What's with the scowl?" I asked as I headed into the grandiose living room and plunked my ass on one of the sofas that made me feel like it was about to crash whenever I sat down heavily on it.

There were many like that in Masonbrook.

And my core control was shot to hell thanks to my wounds.

Fun.

"Beau's pissed at me."

I frowned. "Best friend Beau?"

"How many other Beaus do you know?" he grumbled.

"BASH!" The screech had me wincing. "Give it back."

"How long have they been arguing?" I questioned, unsurprised by the yelling.

Whenever Rosie and Bash were together, they were always yelling at each other.

Well, Rosie yelled. Bash was his usual quiet self.

"About twenty minutes. Rosie found out that it's a tradition on the grounds to go hunting on this day..." He shot me a glum look. "You can imagine how that went down."

"Is she threatening to castrate the hunters?"

"Yup."

"What did Bash take away from her?"

"Something sharp," he said with a quick grin.

I rolled my eyes at him then frowned when Rosie let loose a shriek as Bash laughed.

Jack and I shared a look.

"It's weird how she's the only one who can make him laugh, right?"

I nodded. "It's very weird. Especially as she hates him, and I don't think he particularly likes her." When the argument continued, ignoring it, I asked him, "What's going on with you and Beau?"

Jack muttered, "She's got a girlfriend."

"So?"

"I don't like her."

"Why not?"

"She's a bitch? And she's called Penelope."

"Is that a crime?" I laughed.

"It is in my book." Grumbling under his breath, he said, "She always wants to hang out with her."

"Not like you can hang out with *her* when you're here."

"And whose fault is that?" he sniped.

"I'll make sure I get stabbed on English soil in the future," I retorted.

"That would be better than having to be here." He cast a displeased look around the living room.

"Jesus, you'd think you were staying in a shithole."

"I'd prefer to be home."

Ignoring him, I asked, "How was the drive down?"

"Fine."

A sniff sounded from the doorway. "Fine? You crashed."

Twisting around, he glowered at Bash. "I did not. It was dark."

"I saw it."

"You would."

"You're just pissy because Beau's started calling you Jackass."

I grinned. "You live up to the name."

"Thanks for the vote of confidence."

"My pleasure." To Bash, I asked, "Where did he crash?"

"In a parking garage. Slammed into one of the columns." That was Bash. Always speaking in short sentences. Brisk and to the point.

Smirking, I glanced at a scowling Jack and asked, "Which pisses you off the most? The nickname or the crash?"

"The crash, of course," he said with a huff before he exploded onto his feet and said, "You can both fuck off."

"Nowhere to fuck off to," I shouted at him as he stormed toward the inner corridor that led to their rooms.

"I hope Edward didn't hear that."

With anyone else, I'd have jumped.

But I was used to Dad sitting on the floor, keeping out of conversations, not exactly hiding but keeping a low profile.

The biggest question was—where he'd sheltered himself?

Bash pointed to the near wall, and I straightened a little and found Dad sitting there, his ubiquitous notepad on his knee, but he was wearing a suit for once, no necktie, and his hands were covered in ink from his pen.

"Edward shouldn't be listening in to private conversations," I eventually said once I'd found him.

"Why shouldn't he? Isn't that how you learn the information you need in a place like this?"

"If you live in an Orwellian dystopia."

Dad laughed, and unnervingly enough, so did Bash. "Good one, Tin."

Grumbling under my breath, I muttered, "Cynics."

"Realists," Bash countered. "Anyway, do I have your permission to restrain Rosie if she tries to attack a hunter?"

Dad pondered that. "Who's the hunter hunting?"

Bash knew Dad well enough that he didn't frown. "Foxes."

Sniffing his disapproval, he said, "Let her at them."

"No, don't," I grumbled. "Keep her under control. I have enough problems with the in-laws without my baby sister making my life a whole hell of a lot harder."

Bash's smile lit up his eyes but didn't move his lips at all.

Yes, he was odd.

As he drifted away, I watched him go while Dad asked me, "Are you ready for today?"

"To eat too much, go to church, sing songs I can't understand, then eat some more? Sure."

Dad tipped his head to the side. "I always knew you loved her, you know?"

Thinking about the photo I'd gifted Etta, I drawled, "No offense, Dad, but you wouldn't have to be a genius for that."

"I just didn't think you loved her enough to put up with this rigmarole."

His words stung. It wasn't only that they came out of the blue, but that they hurt.

Because he wasn't wrong.

"I let her down," I said stiffly.

"You let each other down," he corrected calmly. "But I wasn't criticizing you."

"No? Feels like it."

"You shouldn't be so sensitive," he chided before reiterating, "I'm not being critical. I have no place to judge you, Tin. I have let your mother down so many times, but she always forgives me—"

Curious, I asked, "How? You've never let her down as far as I know."

"Children see one side of a relationship. They don't see everything."

Because that made sense, I queried, "When? When did you let her down?"

"You didn't let me down, Devon," Mom said, her voice gentle as she stepped into the room, head cocked to the side as she put on an earring.

"I did," he argued, the obstinacy I'd inherited shooting to the fore.

"You don't have to be so mutinous about it," she chided, turning to me with a soft smile. "It was the first time your daw got sick. He collapsed; Devon shut down and couldn't speak to anyone for two months."

"Two whole months?" I repeated as I got to my feet so I could press a kiss to her cheek.

"The worst time was here, in Veronia. Well, it started here.

"If you remember, we moved over to Madela for a time so Andrei, Sawyer, and Devon could fix the little problem they were having—"

Dad sniffed. "Little problem? They were about to be dealing with a financial crisis as dire as the Wall Street Crash!"

Mom ignored him, continuing, "He froze everyone out. Worked incessantly on the Hodge Conjecture."

I cast Dad a look. "You were scared."

"Yes, I was. Fear ate me up, so it was safer to focus on the math. It became my reason for waking up in the morning. It shielded my terror, let me hide from the prospect of losing Sawyer.

"Work that should have taken me years, took me months. I was eighty percent of the way through when I realized I was allowing a mathematical theory to steal me away from your mother." He shook his head. "I'll die with that shame."

Mom clucked her tongue. "Stop it, Devon. There's no need for this."

"There is," he countered.

"Didn't you solve the Hodge Conjecture?" I questioned.

He dipped his chin. "I was eighty percent into proving the theory but it was correct. I'll never publish anything on it though. That Conjecture stole me away... I deserve no credit.

"Anyway, that isn't my point here. Tin, *you* were scared when Alice forced your hand."

I studied him a second before slowly verbalizing, "She did what I wasn't brave enough to do."

"What do you mean, Tin?" Mom questioned, her hand on my shoulder as I slumped against the sofa.

"I've changed."

"The work you've done has hardened you," Dad agreed before he warned, "That isn't necessarily a good thing, either."

I ignored his statement. "Back then, I was chicken shit. I wanted her but I was afraid to have her. She just had bigger balls than me. She forced my hand in the sense that she led me to the altar, but if she'd been just regular Alice DeSauvier, and not the future queen of Veronia, I wouldn't have needed to be led."

Dad nodded. "I'm glad you recognize that."

"Was this your way of telling me to forgive her? Because I already have."

"No. It's my way of telling you that we all make mistakes. Crucial ones.

"Do you think your mother ever brings up the time I let her down? No. Do you think it haunts me to this day? Yes. Do you think I strive to never let her down again? Yes."

"What are you saying? That I should never bring it up?" My brow furrowed. "Why would I?"

He smiled. "You haven't had your first major argument yet."

I blinked. Sensed what he meant.

"He has a point, Tin," Mom murmured.

"In the heat of the moment, resentment and bitterness surfaces and the desire to win takes over everything else.

"Alice has handed you a large piece of ammunition, but if you use it, you'll damage everything you have together. Even worse, you'll damage everything you *could have had* together."

Because this was Dad, I fell silent as I processed his words, and I didn't feel bad about it.

I just sat there, allowing them to resonate, even letting so much time pass that Rosie and Bash drifted in arguing about burdizzos, Mom left to go and find a pair of shoes, and the rest of my fathers congregated in here too.

Just as my phone buzzed with a message from Etta asking where I was, I cast a look at Dad and found he was making eye contact with me.

That was beyond unusual because he buried his head in his notes.

Nodding, I watched as his smile grew before he returned to his books.

Lesson imparted; lesson learned.

ETTA

"God, it's cold," I rasped as Tin lifted his arm and sheltered me beneath it.

He tugged on my cream knitted beanie and made sure that it covered my ears. "It's not that bad."

"It's snowing," I pointed out.

"That doesn't mean it's cold."

"What kind of logic is that?" I grumbled, shoving my face beneath the lapels of my coat.

He grinned at my querulous retort. "This isn't a wet cold. This is dry."

"Are you going to give me a lesson on meteorology?"

"Do you want a lesson?" he countered, and his eyes gleamed. "It's been a learning kind of day."

"It has? What did you learn?"

"That your voice is even better in an abbey."

My cheeks burned with heat. "Really?"

"Really. You're not supposed to give me a boner in church, babe."

"You got a boner from me singing?" I countered with wide eyes.

"I did. Awkward too."

Snickering, I said, "I'll bet."

For Three Kings', the family had pews at the altar, beyond where the choir was positioned. We weren't seated along the sides, however, but facing the congregation.

"You're lucky you're wearing a heavy jacket," I told him with a laugh. "Otherwise the world would know you get a boner for my singing voice."

"Why is everyone so loved up right now?"

I arched a brow at the complaint and found Tin's younger brother, Jack, stomping behind us through the snow.

Every other step, he kicked his foot out, sending an arc of white powder drifting over his path.

"Who's loved up?" I questioned.

"Everyone. Mom and Dads are always like that. I expect that of them, Tin," he grumbled. "But I had higher hopes for you."

Laughing, Tin reached over and scrubbed a hand over his head. Jack hissed and backed off.

"Higher hopes for your older brother than him being with the girl of his dreams?"

Inside, I definitely preened.

Jack, on the other hand, was less impressed.

He gagged.

Bash, striding along like a looming shadow, clipped him behind the head. "You're talking to a future queen."

"She's not a future queen here," Jack argued. "She's Alice."

Because Jack looked like he was about to ram his head into Bash's stomach in one of those stupid moves boys made in fights, I appeased, "It's okay, Bash. Thank you for defending my honor."

He dipped his head in calm assent.

Bash was strange.

Oddly peaceful, with a serene nature that had a habit of making me feel riled up.

Being around someone who was so centered exposed how off-kilter *you* were.

That wasn't Bash's fault, of course. Just mine.

When Jack hung back, we carried on walking toward Masonbrook.

After returning from Yorke Abbey, Mom had declared that we needed to walk before we ate another massive meal, so here we were —walking to build up an appetite for supper.

A couple minutes later, I heard a roar as Jack leaped on Bash's shoulders before both of them started fighting in the snow.

Neither of us commented.

This was par for the course with them.

Rosie and Bash argued, Jack and Bash fought, only Bethan and Tin had a regular relationship with Bash.

"I wonder why he riles them up so much," I mused.

Tin, who'd been reading something on his phone, asked, "Hmm?"

"Bash. Why does he piss Jack and Rosie off so much?"

He pulled a face. "You should have heard him and Rosie arguing before we headed to the church."

"See?"

"He rubs them the wrong way."

"Why?"

Shrugging, he said, "Who knows? He and Jack get along well usually. They just bicker.

"Today, Jack's in a bad mood because of Beau, though."

"His best friend at home?"

"Yeah. I think he has a crush on her but isn't willing to admit it."

I winced. "Isn't she the gay one?"

"Well, I don't think she's officially come out. She just got a girlfriend and he's pissed."

"Isn't the girlfriend the clue?"

He shrugged.

"That's got to suck."

"I'm thinking he's jealous."

Twisting around to watch Jack and Bash messing about, I saw Rosie and Bethan stomp over to adjudicate and had to smile.

"Never thought you guys would be here for Yule," I whispered, oddly happy even though Jack already had a bloodied nose.

Tin squeezed me against his chest. "Even though we bring chaos with us wherever we go?"

I smiled at him. "I love your brand of chaos."

His eyes twinkled. "Good thing. It's yours now. You're a part of the melee."

Patting his chest, I told him, "Bring it on."

TWENTY-THREE

ETTA

TWO DAYS LATER

"You look as sick as a dog."

Certain I'd misunderstood what I'd just heard, I peered at Tin's father and asked, "Sorry, Uncle Sean?"

His smile hit his eyes, but not his mouth.

Sean was the most serious of all Tin's fathers, and that was really saying something.

I often felt as if he were the backbone of the family: the strength and the glue.

I liked how calm he was under pressure. It always made me feel better.

"I said you look as sick as a dog."

"Um, thank you?"

He snorted as he took a seat beside me. "Your mother and Sascha are waffling on about red velvet cake—" When my nose crinkled with distaste, he hummed. "A woman after my own heart. Cakes shouldn't be red."

I smiled. "They should if you're from North America."

"Now, the tradition makes sense to me. Dutch chocolate that

reacts with the heat of the oven? What's not to like? But throwing in a bunch of chemicals to mimic it? And when it doesn't taste of chocolate at all? What's the point?"

My own father took a seat opposite me. He'd been on the phone a second ago, and though his focus was on his cellphone, he agreed, "I don't like it either. I prefer Veronian cakes. Shouldn't we be spotlighting traditional Veronian recipes at the wedding?"

Sean shrugged. "Not when you have two mothers from North America who miss their roots."

Father said dismissively, "Perry visits every year."

"She says she misses Sam's Club," I confided to Sean.

"I doubt she misses the store, per se," he reasoned, clearly settling into 'shrink' mode. "More like what it represents."

"What does it represent? Badly dressed customers?"

I frowned at Father. "Stop being dismissive. They're not all bad dressers. Anyway, that's in Walmart. Not Sam's Club."

"If you say so."

"I do. And you can't judge. You've never stepped foot in a supermarket in your life."

Father smirked. "You do the weekly grocery shopping, I suppose?"

I popped my nose in the air. "I've run errands before."

"When?"

"Infrequently," I conceded. "But it's happened."

"When?" he repeated, his eyes gleaming with amusement.

Much like Sean, Father tended to show his humor in his gaze.

I thought it was to do with how both men had been given more responsibilities to handle than any one person should ever bear.

Sean had dealt with consequences that could mean life and death to someone, solving cases and trying to find murderers before they could strike again. And Father, who had to rule over a country despite constant civil unrest...

"Last year," I retorted. "I had to stop at a grocery store—"

He stalled me. "Did one of your guards go in for you?"

I huffed.

His smirk made another reappearance. "Thought as much."

"Before you two start bickering," Sean intoned, "I feel I should point out there's nothing wrong with wanting to do a simple task like that."

Father shuddered.

"Elitist," I hissed.

"Pot. Kettle. Black," he countered, surprising me by grinning.

It was so unexpected that I blinked.

Mouth rounding, I almost spluttered, but Sean saved me by saying, "The next time she's in the US, you should make a point of taking her to Sam's Club, Edward."

Father frowned. "George takes her."

"Why?"

He shrugged. "I'm busy."

"All the more reason to take her. I'm sure there's a state visit you could use as an excuse."

"I don't need an excuse."

I snorted, my equilibrium reset. "You do. Your inner workaholic cringes whenever a vacation is mentioned."

Father squinted at me. "You're particularly argumentative today."

"I'm always argumentative, but Mom's just rotted half my teeth with all these confections." I grimaced. "I don't understand why we can't have a cheese cake."

Sean nodded. "I like cheesecake."

"You can't serve cheesecake at a wedding. Never mind a royal one," Father scoffed.

"No. A *cheese* cake. Cheese wheels are stacked on top of each other to make a cake."

"I'm not sure I could imagine anything more disgusting," Sean admitted.

"I like the sound of it." Father wagged a finger. "Do you know where to get one, Alice?"

"I'm sure I could find one," I said somewhat eagerly.

"If no one else wants it, we can keep it to ourselves."

Because that perked me up, I grinned at him. "I like the way you think."

TWENTY-FOUR

TIN

"Hope you're proud of her," I muttered, my gaze on Xavier as he watched Etta on his phone.

The country's main news channel had decided to cover Etta and her comportment over the past few weeks.

Someone had managed to grab a picture of her bowing over Andrea's body at Casterby, then there were more of her with some of the victims who'd been caught in the crossfire.

There were a couple shots of me at the Parliamentary balcony, looking like a wimp, but the cameras were mostly focused on Princess Alexandra, as the world knew her.

On her tigress stance over her injured husband who'd been hurt protecting the princess.

Not his wife.

The princess.

Because to Veronia, she was that first.

Not to me, however. Never to me.

There was even footage of her singing at Andrea's funeral, and I knew, for damn sure, that there wouldn't have been a dry eye in any household who'd seen that on the nine o'clock news.

It had to be a PR stunt by the palace, but it was damn effective. Mostly because, PR or not, every scene was reality.

None of this was staged.

This was *our* life.

"Yes," Xavier rumbled simply, breaking into my thoughts enough that I almost forgot what I'd asked him.

Realizing he was saying that he *was* proud of her, I left him to it because he was looking every bit as impressed as Veronia was with his daughter.

The tailor tugged and pulled, getting me into a position to be measured, but damn, it hurt. Enough that I groaned.

When he didn't give me a breather, I spat, "You do know I have injuries, don't you?"

The guy, a little mouse with a bald pate that gleamed more than a mirror and with an honest to God toothbrush moustache that made him look like a rotund Hitler, glared at me.

"The suit must be tailored to you to perfection."

"I'm not going to be walking down the aisle any time soon if you're tugging and pulling at my stitches."

Daw, standing at my back, snorted, but Xavier, who was still watching Etta on his phone a few feet away, intoned without looking up, "He has a point, Jean Luc. Try not to cause too many injuries with your poking and prodding."

Daw wandered over to a stand that was like a wooden kitchen island. It had dozens of drawers on either side with tiny handles. I'd seen Jean Luc pull out all kinds of shit from within, but atop it were fabric swatches, and Daw started to flip through them with an idleness that didn't suit him.

None of my fathers were idle. Mom wasn't either, not really. I mean, she could slob around the house in her PJs all day, but she was usually yelling at someone on her phone to do some shit or other so she didn't have to go out.

My fathers, on the other hand, were workaholics, so, to see Daw dawdling was definitely an unusual sight.

I cocked a brow at him. "What's up with you?"

His lips twitched, but *Papa*, in the other corner, opposite George, mumbled, "Insolent boy," in Russian.

I just grinned. "I try." I'd have bowed, but I didn't. It wouldn't have been worth being stuck in the balls with a pin by Jean Luc.

Papa sniffed, but Daw muttered, "Just cannae believe it. That's all."

"Yeah, I know."

My brow puckered as I stared around the tailor's shop that had been dressing men of the DeSauvier line for over two hundred years.

There were the ceremonial robes of two kings in here, encased in glass, and there were countless other memorabilia that would have boggled my mind on an ordinary day.

Today?

I was just over it already.

"I don't know why you don't believe it, Sawyer. I knew it would happen."

Daw rolled his eyes at the voice that chimed in from a corner of the tailor's.

Dad was sitting somewhere out of my line of sight, but I knew he was on the floor somewhere because, otherwise, I'd have been able to see him.

"You're a regular feckin' psychic, ain't ye?" Daw grumbled.

"No, I just know my son." Dad sniffed.

The irony was, Dad *did* know me.

For all that he appeared as if his attention were elsewhere, I knew, whenever I was in the room, Dad always knew where I was, his attention splintering in a way he should patent.

And it wasn't just with me but with the twins and Jack too.

I didn't want to say that Etta had shitty fathers, because she didn't. They were just hard on her because of who she was. But me? I had the best dads in the world.

I knew I was lucky. Not just that they were awesome, or that they encouraged me to follow my dreams whatever they may be, but that I had five of them.

If one was busy, there'd always been another one to play with or to talk to.

Five fathers, one mother, four kids... well, five, if you included Bash, but he hadn't come along until later.

How was I supposed to cope when I was just one person?

The memory of Etta telling me that the second we were married, she'd have people sniffing around her trying to figure out if she was pregnant, surfaced.

It prompted me to mutter, "You guys can't die for like eighty years."

"That would make us older than the records indicate as being possible, Tin," Dad intoned, sounding like he was reading the *Guinness World Records* book there and then.

"I don't care. Break records. If I have to have kids, you guys need to be around to help me."

Daw laughed, so did *Papa*. "Aye, ye were lucky."

Jean Luc tutted under his breath which had me narrowing my eyes at him.

"You have a problem with my family, Jean Luc?"

Silence fell at my declaration, and the tailor froze. The smile he pasted on his face was wholly professional, though, when he tipped his head back to look at me. "No, of course not, sir."

"Well, I heard you tut."

"You moved."

"I didn't," I countered, glaring at him. "If you have a problem with me, then I don't think I want you measuring my inseam."

His nostrils flared, his eyes flashing with outrage. "My family has fitted the coronation robes for—"

"I don't care. Traditions are meant to be broken," I retorted, uncaring that Xavier and George had both tensed at my statement.

But I *didn't* care.

I knew things were precarious with my family. I knew the number of fathers I had raised eyebrows, but I wasn't about to deal with that bullshit, and my fathers-in-law needed to know that right from the start.

I *wasn't* ashamed of my family. I loved my fathers. They'd given me an epic childhood, had made me into the man I was today, and I'd never be without them if I didn't have to be.

No way in fuck was some pompous jackass going to tut at them because they dared to love one woman.

Jean Luc cut panicked looks at George and Xavier, flashing between them like they were going to back him and not me, and to be fair, I almost expected they would.

Veronians were built on tradition.

Just look at Etta.

Her bedroom was like something from a Victorian movie, creepy as fuck, but she dealt with it because it was tradition.

Well, I wouldn't be dealing with that.

She might be willing, but I wasn't a Veronian. Hell, I was a Brit and we were used to the whole stiff upper lip shit, but this went beyond the pale.

"I think you should apologize, Jean Luc," Xavier rasped, his focus off his phone and firmly on the tailor.

"But I didn't say—"

"You didn't have to," Xavier rumbled. "I could feel your disapproval from over here."

His jaw clenched at the dressing down, but stiffly, he muttered, "I apologize."

It wasn't the most gracious of deliveries, but I'd take it. It wasn't like I gave a shit about the man's opinion, but I wasn't about to let his attitude slide. Not when that attitude reflected on the best men I knew.

The rest of the fitting took place in relative silence. It was uncomfortable, but I had zero fucks to give.

All the guys in my family except for Father and Edward were

here, because they were with their wives, sorting out some wedding crap with *mine*.

Mine.

I liked the sound of that.

The others suffered through their fittings, and while ordinarily I'd have been bored as hell watching men getting measured up for penguin suits, I was actually relieved.

It was wonderful to sit down, wonderful to be with my fathers, and wonderful not to be fucking dead.

Plus, if I wasn't here, it wasn't like I could lounge around in bed all day. I'd have to be with Etta, and she was tasting cakes today. Or so she'd grumbled at me earlier.

Etta had to be the only person I knew who didn't like cake.

Give her cheese, a cake made of literal cheese, and she'd be happy. But cake? Nope.

Me, on the other hand, I'd have been happy with the tasting, but having to hang around Edward all day would have left me drained. He'd always had a stick up his ass but it was ten times worse now.

Neither Etta nor me were really that into the ceremony, but I got a kick out of how psyched Mom was.

Last night, she'd barged into our quarters with a binder, and a few minutes later, Perry had appeared with a large bottle of wine, some chocolates, and a bag of chips for Etta because, again, Etta didn't like sweets.

They'd camped out in front of the fire where we'd been chilling and had started discussing things like table settings and venues and how many chairs they'd need.

Apparently, Etta and I were going to have to hand sign over two thousand invitations—three hundred for the wedding ceremony itself, which would be televised—God help me—and then the remainder were for two parties we'd be having in the aftermath.

A further four hundred would be invited to the meal, and then the others would be invited to a night party.

As I thought about having to sign my name two thousand times, Dad gripped my shoulder. "Ye cannae let these pricks get to ye, lad."

I blinked at him, not really online, then I glared at Jean Luc when I figured out what Daw was talking about.

"Yeah, not going to happen."

Daw heaved a sigh. "Since when do we care about what people think of us?"

"You might not, but I do. You're the best fathers a man could ever hope for, and I'm bloody lucky that you're mine. If you think I'm going to let some dickhead start talking shit about you—"

"He tutted, lad. Don't ye think yer being a wee bit melodramatic?"

"Maybe." I shrugged. "I'm going to start as I mean to go on. I refuse to be ashamed, Dad."

"Ye dinnae need to be ashamed, just don't be getting on yer high horse over things that have nae importance in the grand scheme of things."

I grunted under my breath as he hauled me onto my feet. When his arm wrapped around my shoulder, he muttered, "Honestly, lad, it'll only get yer heart rate pumping."

"Isn't that a good thing?"

He snorted. "When it's fer sex and work outs, aye. Stress, no."

"I try not to get stressed," I mumbled.

"I dinnae think ye try hard enough."

"Please don't make me meditate," I half complained.

"I willnae, but only because yer a whiner when it boils down to stuff like that."

I pulled a face at him, but I didn't argue as he hauled me closer to him and, together, we strode out of the backroom of the tailors.

"I'm used to wealth, lad," Daw admitted as we strode into the storefront, "but this is a whole other ball of wax."

I knew what he meant. We were rich. Richer than the DeSauviers, but royalty always did things a little differently.

I'd been to the tailors before, I had a regular tailor who made my suits on Savile Row, for God's sake, but this place was something else.

There were pictures lining the walls of old kings and coronation wear Jean Luc's family had made for centuries, and then there were oil portraits, too, of the royals who'd been tended to within these walls.

"Can ye believe that little prick only works for the family? How many suits do they need cut for them each year?"

"You'd be surprised."

Daw and I both jerked in shock at George's insertion, and I yelped as I twisted around because my entire body ached like a bitch the second I moved.

George winced. "Sorry. Didn't mean to make you jump. I thought you heard me."

"No worries," I panted, holding my side even though that didn't do shit.

"What would we be surprised about?" Daw asked after he glanced at me then took the spotlight off me—thankfully.

"How many suits we need. Don't forget, there are a league of cousins who need outfitting too."

"Seems excessive," I grumbled.

"Jean Luc also maintains a lot of the outfits we have that are hundreds of years old and that go into museums around the country."

"He preserves them?"

"Yes. He's an annoying asshat, but he's damn good at what he does."

As we strolled past a bank of seats that looked mighty fine to me, I was relieved to note that, on the outside step, there was a car waiting on us. Well, several cars.

I almost staggered over to the vehicle and was relieved when the driver was there with the door open for me.

As I began to duck down into the limo, it was only the odd way I had to climb into the car that let me see it.

I couldn't get in, ass first, like usual. My body wouldn't let me. So

I had to put one knee on the seat then kind of climb in. But because of that unusual, and undeniably graceless, positioning, I saw it.

A weird glint in the window opposite me.

I frowned at the sight, unsure why I found it odd.

The sun wasn't shining, *again*, and it was frigid. I was freezing, and mostly focused on getting out of the bitter cold, so the fact I noticed anything untoward at all had me tensing in place.

I'd never had any covert training. I wasn't bullshitting about not being a spy. But I *was* an analyst, and sometimes I was sent overseas to help the James Bonds of my government with sticky situations.

I'd been given the basic defense course—which was anything but basic, but not as intense as what the covert ops agents went through—and I figured it was those instincts that had been drummed into me that had me hollering, "On the ground! Shooter!"

The second I screamed that, I heard it.

That fucking whistle.

That goddamn, motherfucking whistle that was going to plague me until the day I died.

Even as I hurled myself backward, trying to cover my father and Etta's, my body screaming with the movement, I heard someone grunt, heard others fall to the ground at my command, but I knew from the scent of blood in the air that someone had been hit.

Four of my fathers, and two of Etta's, had been walking out behind me...

If any of them were dead, the UnReals were going to wish they'd never been born.

That was more than a fucking promise; it was a goddamn vow.

ETTA

Mom screamed when she saw Daddy being rushed into the private ward.

She ran after him on flip-flop covered feet as the doctors pounded down the hall toward the medical unit, but I didn't watch her go.

No, my focus was on the floor.

Heart racing like I'd been running, I stared at the line of blood on the marble tiles.

My daddy's blood.

He couldn't die.

He couldn't.

My lips trembled as I raised a hand and touched my mouth. A scream was building inside me, a scream that made my very brain rattle.

How was this happening?

How did this threat still exist?

For a second, that white noise reappeared again, and I felt sure I was losing my mind. It overtook everything, all five of my senses, coating each of them until it invaded every part of me.

Then I heard it, a howl of grief. A howl of pain and rage and fury and hurt.

Hurt.

My body shuddered, and then he was there. A hand slipped around my waist as he hurled me into his side. He smelled like mine and home, like warmth and love, and I missed him even as I was grateful to have him again.

His other hand moved to the back of my head, and he cupped it before he pushed me toward him, not stopping until my face was burrowed in his throat.

Another howl.

Like an animal in pain. Raging grief.

No.

No.

No.

It couldn't be.

He couldn't be dead. My daddy couldn't be gone.

My entire body was one big tremor. I felt like I was in the middle of an earthquake, every part of me being torn apart as different emotions tugged at me.

I'd known hurt and I'd known loss—hadn't we all? But I felt like I'd lost more people than most. More death surrounded me as people gave their lives, sacrificed everything to keep me safe.

But here I was, sobbing against the love of my life's chest.

Rage unfurled through me, and I knew I couldn't stay here, listening to my mom's grief. If I did, I'd hurl myself into that abyss too.

I needed to act.

I needed to do something.

The saltwater of tears burned my eyes, but I blinked them back as I tilted my head so I could look into Tin's face.

His expression was grim, and there were spots of blood on his face, splashed on his throat.

My daddy's blood.

My throat tightened. "Help me."

"What do you need?"

The reply was instant.

"I need you to forget your honor," I whispered. "I need you to think of *this* country and not yours."

His eyes flashed. "I acted in both countries' best interests."

"With the scales tipped in the favor of the UK. I got that. *I did.* You were just coming out of active service. It's hard to break ties, harder to sever ties. But you have to act. They're not going to stop."

His mouth worked. "They wanted me."

My entire being tensed. "What makes you say that?"

"The angle of the shot. I only noticed it because of the way I'm climbing into cars at the moment."

"It could have been my fathers—"

"Maybe it was. Call it gut instinct."

"Do you know *anything*, anything at all that might help us?"

"Not about this attack, but..." His eyes shuttered. "I know something that might help."

I grabbed his hand and dragged him down the corridor, out of the private healthcare unit that tended to my family and my family alone, and drew us into the garden. It was cold out here, but I felt like I was burning up. Like I was a fireball let loose on the icicle-strewn garden.

"What do you know?"

"There's a British team stationed here."

"That's not unusual," I retorted. "I bet they have someone everywhere, even if it's not authorized. *Especially* if they're not authorized."

Tin shook his head. "They're here for a reason."

I swallowed. "What reason?"

"It's in Britain's best interests that Veronia's royals stay on the throne."

My brow puckered—but I got that.

In a world where royal families were considered a drain on the economy, we were a dying breed. We only remained on our thrones, continued to rule with power in our hands, by the will of the people.

"So, why's that a bad thing?" I queried.

"It isn't. But their presence here indicates something else."

I reached up and rubbed my temple. "Speak clearly, Tin."

"I only know they're here by accident. I heard some chatter, and I knew a couple of sharpshooters who were redirected suddenly—"

"Wait, you can't think they're the ones who did this today?"

His head slashed to the side. "No, of course not. I'm saying that, like on a chessboard, pieces have been mobilized."

"And if they haven't come out to play, then what? They're waiting for something bigger?"

"Maybe." Tin's mouth firmed, his top lip flatlining and, behind his eyes, I could see the cogs working. Could see his brain flushing through strategies as he did what he did best.

We were far enough away from the ward not to hear anything, but Mom's grief ricocheted in my ears like it was on a constant echo.

I still refused to believe.

I wouldn't.

Not until I saw him with my own eyes. Not until I held his hand and felt his lifelessness.

So I had to stay away. I couldn't deal with that yet.

We needed to act.

"Why now?" Tin muttered, raking a hand through his hair.

"Why do they ever decide to do anything?" I demanded bitterly. "The UnReals just strike whenever they feel like it."

"No, we may believe that, but they act for a reason," he argued, gripping his nape and pushing back from me.

When he started to pace, I noticed his gait was wooden, wondered at it, wanted to tell him to sit down, but didn't.

Couldn't.

I needed him to think this through, to figure out what the fuck was going on.

"There's a reason for everything. Why they targeted the

economy the way they did, why they drained it dry for a good solid few years—let's face it, they gained enough to fund themselves for a lifetime."

"That's bad news," I ground out.

"They were quiet for a while, weren't they? Maybe five years?"

I nodded. "We had a few threats but nothing enacted. A bomb in a shopping mall we were opening, but it turned out to be a hoax."

His pace quickened, like he needed to expend the effort to form the answers.

Then he stopped.

Then he turned to me.

"*Two* groups."

My brow puckered. "What do you mean?"

"I mean, there are two opposing forces here. One was cerebral. Smart. It takes brains to be able to create sieves in the economy like what they made back in the day.

"It took someone of Dad's capacity to find it, for fuck's sake. You plugged in the leaks, and figured out ways to regenerate, but even so, that takes brains.

"This is brawn. This is thoughtless. This is action but with no gain. All they're doing is pissing people off, shooting in public areas, making the general population unsafe in their own homes."

"Since when have they cared about the ordinary folk they hurt to get to us—"

He ignored my snarl. "They always act to get public gain. It's the only real way they can topple royalty. Nothing happens without stirring the masses, and this is doing the opposite."

My head was starting to ache. "Tin, then—"

His mouth firmed. "These shootings, they're making people hate the UnReals. That must be unintentional. They're so focused on their hatred, they forget the majority of the population loves your family..."

"It can't be a coincidence," I rasped when his voice waned. "It can't be that sharpshooters have been brought here—"

He raised a hand. "No. It can't be." He rubbed his head. "I must be wrong."

"You don't sound like you think you're wrong," I whispered. "You sound like you *hope* you are."

"Of course I do. I don't want to think my country is capable of this."

"All countries are capable of this. Even Veronia. Who the fuck knows what the Guard Elect really does? We have security services of our own. You think they don't do stuff that most people would disapprove of?" I released a shaky breath. "You know how dark and grimy geopolitics can be."

"Conspiracy theories aren't real—"

"Now you really are clutching at straws."

He'd been a conspiracy buff back as a kid, looking for answers where there were none to be found, asking questions where he shouldn't.

"I can't believe that—" He swallowed. "I just can't."

He looked at me with entreaty in his eyes, like a little boy who had been told Santa Claus wasn't real.

I sucked in a breath, and because I loved him and didn't want him to hurt, I murmured, "Maybe you're wrong. Maybe you should call up some people you know and see what's happening?"

He shook his head. "No one will talk to me now. Not only because I quit, but because it's hit the news about us.

"Why would they give me information? They have to know it will bounce back to the DeSauviers."

My shoulders slumped. "True."

"This is all speculation."

"More than we had to begin with."

He winced. "Yeah." Tin turned to me. "All I know is that there are two different methods here. Maybe my people are behind the economy drain?"

I snorted at that and his hopeful tone. "Will that make you feel better?"

"What? Than thinking my government is willing to kill members of the Veronian royal family, or at least put them in serious danger, just to shore up public opinion? Damn straight."

His words had me frowning. "It doesn't make sense."

"Doesn't it?" he snapped. "Seems like it does to me."

"No, look, why would they do things on our soil to protect us when the family is popular? We have no need for help in gaining public support. For over a century, we've been popular! Even in dark times, people look to us for strength, and we always give it.

"Since Mama became queen, people love us even more. You know what she's like. She's always doing something to help the country, more so than my grandmother did."

Tin rubbed the back of his neck again. "Follow the money."

"Huh? Didn't Devon already do that?"

Tin shook his head. "No. He didn't. He had a breakdown—I didn't even know about it until—"

I frowned. "Until when?"

"It was when I was a kid. He'd just figured out the money was being systematically drained out of the economy, then Daw collapsed." He blew out a breath. "Dad had a complete meltdown. Didn't talk to anyone for two months."

I'd sat through enough boring history lessons on this subject to know the facts.

"But pretty soon after, we had issues with the UnReals because the truth came out. Mom took me and we stayed with you, didn't we?"

Trying to remember was difficult. I'd been, what? Two, maybe, at the time?

I'd seen the pictures though.

Tin and me in the bath. With his puppies. No pictures of my dads around because they'd been here, while we'd been safely tucked away on Sascha's estate in Surrey.

"I know for a fact that Dad was working on other stuff when he was in the middle of that meltdown. The Hodge Conjecture, to be precise.

"He'd pretty much done eighty percent of his theoretical work on it by the time Mom got him to break out of it."

"So, he was working on other stuff in the aftermath?"

"Yeah. I have to guess that someone, probably *Papa*, gave Veronia Dad's findings."

"Then they dealt with the leak, plugged it up, and, what? Never looked for the culprits?"

"Maybe they didn't." He shrugged. "Seems stupid to me, too, but maybe it isn't. I know you guys had a lot of issues back then, and it looked like you were on the brink of civil war—"

"We're popular with the majority. You know we have issues in the North," was all I could think to say.

It was to our nation's great shame that we'd almost had a civil war, and so close to the new Millennium.

"Doesn't matter. What I'm trying to say is that priorities have a way of pushing things to the background."

I pondered that then blurted out, "You think if we find who was behind the original embezzling scheme, we'll figure out what's happening today? But you said you see two motives."

"I do," he rumbled. "Just thinking it was the UnReals—"

"Surely the security services looked into it," I ground out. "They're not incompetent."

"They had bigger fish to fry."

"Why are you two arguing?"

Was it fate or chance that it was Devon who wandered out into the garden?

He stared at us like we'd just landed in the yard from a trip to Venus, his head tilted to the side as he took me in in a glance then studied Tin with a laser-like stare.

Tin, quite used to that, didn't flinch.

Devon seemed to take everything in.

The blood spatters, the slight fleck of blood on his belly where I knew he'd started to bleed through his bandages—fuck, he'd split his stitches again and hadn't realized it. Then, he took in the lines of strain, the tension in Tin's body—it was weird knowing what Devon was assessing, but it didn't take a rocket scientist.

Devon knew everything about Tin.

Whatever there was to know.

I doubted Tin had many, if any, secrets from him.

I was probably the biggest one, and even then, Devon claimed he'd known how Tin felt about me.

"You're bleeding," Devon said flatly.

"It's nothing. It's from—"

"Yes. George. He's asking for you, Alice."

My heart stopped. "He isn't dead?"

Devon blinked. "Would he have asked for you if he were?"

Hope filled me. "I-I thought—"

"You thought wrong." His mouth firmed. "I believe he'd like to see you before they operate. You have approximately two minutes. They're setting up the surgery as we speak."

I didn't stick around to talk more conspiracies, didn't wait for Tin. I got the hell out of there.

Racing down corridors that, since I was small, I'd been forced to walk down otherwise I'd be scolded, I ran as fast as I could.

By the time I made it to the medical wing, I was half-sure that I'd be too late, but as I burst inside the room, I found Mom standing with Father, her face turned into his chest as she bawled her eyes out. Then I saw Christel and Victoria huddled into Papa's embrace.

That was when I was certain he'd died.

That Devon had lied to me.

That my daddy *had* passed away—

"Alice?"

The soft croak, half-Veronian accent, quarter-British, and quarter-American, might as well have been an angel singing in my ear.

The relief that hit me was worse than a two-by-four to the temple.

I staggered like he *had* hit me, then I rushed over to the bed.

Grabbing his hand, I pressed it to my cheek then whispered, "Daddy, oh—"

But he didn't let me finish.

In a face as bloodless as could be, with spatters of red everywhere, lines and IVs and all kinds of equipment sprouting from his body, he somehow managed to grasp a firm hold of my hand and tug me closer.

"Never forget, my darling, Alice, that you are my daughter." I heard Mom's sobs turn into soft wails. "*Mine.* No matter whose blood —" He swallowed, pain creasing his expression. "Love—"

"Don't speak, Daddy, conserve your energy!"

"Love you," he managed to grate out, as if it were a race he was determined to win.

But I didn't have time to whisper the words back to him.

Because as if that were the only reason he'd stayed awake, he closed his eyes.

TWENTY-SIX

TIN

"You're bleeding."

I sighed at his repeated comment. "I know, Dad."

"If you know then why aren't you trying to stop it?" Dad tipped his head to the other side. "Mom won't be happy if you need another blood transfusion."

"No, I think she'd be the opposite of happy," I groused, peering down at my stomach. "It's nothing. Only small. I just pulled some stitches." Again, damn it.

"That was insane what you did today." His tone was flatter still. "I saw it from the window in the tailors."

"What was I going to do? Let them get hit?"

He narrowed his eyes on me. "Since when do you carry a gun?"

"You don't know everything about me, Dad," I rasped, but I twisted away and stared out at the garden.

The palace was famed for a fountain that, even though they'd had issues with water conservation—issues that stemmed from another round with the UnReals—they hadn't shut down.

It worked, if memory served, thanks to high water pressure. It had a geyser spouting dozens of feet into the air and had been a feat of engineering back in the day—hell, it was pretty impressive now.

Especially when you realized that not an ounce of electricity powered it.

"There were guards there. You should have let them handle the situation."

"He was in my line of sight. The second the glass shattered from the shot, I knew where he was. I was faster than him."

"You killed a man, Valentin."

"Some man. A traitor." Then, jaw working, I twisted around, ignoring the ache in my side, and demanded, "You know who was behind the embezzling, don't you?"

His eyes shuttered. "Not personally, no."

My nostrils flared—but once again, I was reminded of the importance of patience with Dad.

He'd never hurt the Veronians. Would never hurt anyone. Especially not people Mom or I cared about.

"Don't be pedantic. I don't care if you know them personally. I want to know if you know their identities."

"Of course I do." He eyed my belly. "You're bleeding more."

"I'll get stitches when you answer my questions."

"I'm not under trial, Valentin," he rumbled, folding his arms across his chest.

"No, I don't think you are, but I want answers, and I'm not going to stop until you give them to me. What happened?"

His gaze darted around the courtyard and his shoulders hunched. "You know what happened."

He was embarrassed?

"You had nothing to be ashamed of," I tacked on, hoping it would encourage him to talk. "We all have moments where we can't cope."

"Do we?" His lips formed a thin line. "Even you?"

"Of course. Why do you think I ignored the love of my life for a few years? I didn't want this." I lifted my hand and waved it, encompassing the palace and all it represented. "I wanted a quiet life, like you have with Mom and the dads."

"You think we have a quiet life?" His smile was small. "It's anything but."

"You know what I mean." Running a hand over my head where a headache was blossoming, I couldn't deny that I felt no guilt for what I'd done today. I'd probably saved my fathers from being shot... "Is George okay?"

"He died. Twice." Dad shrugged. "They brought him back."

That was why Perry had been howling like she had.

I knew how that felt. My grandmother, Jacinta, had passed like that. Two heart attacks, she'd been dead twice, then they'd brought her back only for her to be brain dead.

The memory of her was still strong enough to make me weep.

Such fire and sass in one so frail, but she'd have been happy, I knew, to be back with her Hamish.

My lip quivered at the memory, and I whispered, "What's going on, Dad?"

"I don't know."

And Dad would have told me if he *did* know. Unless I hadn't asked the right question.

With that in mind, I queried, "Do you know why Etta was targeted? Why someone was targeted today?"

"No." He hesitated for a second. "I can postulate."

"Postulate away," I rasped, fascinated, as always, by the way his mind worked.

"Someone knows that Etta is Edward's daughter."

I frowned. "Of course someone knows that—everyone does."

He shook his head. "You're my son, but your blood is Andrei's."

My heart thudded in my chest, and I thought about Etta and Christel and Victoria. Victoria with her auburn hair like Xavier, Christel with her blonde like George, and Etta with her dark chestnut locks...

Like the king.

"Someone knows," I whispered.

"I'd hazard a guess, and you know I don't like to guess," Dad said with a sniff.

"No, you prefer to *postulate*," I ground out, trying to think of the implications. "Why target me today?"

"They were targeting George." He tutted. "Use your common sense, son."

"He's the third in line if someone can reveal the paternity—"

He raised a hand to his lips. "Hush. Loose lips sink ships."

"So, the Brits aren't involved?"

"Of course not," he scoffed. "They're helping."

"How?"

"I told Edward a long time ago that if someone had the capacity to infiltrate as many of Veronia's ministries as they did back when you were a baby, then they had the power to find out other things... things he'd never want people to know." Dad shrugged. "I didn't think he took me seriously, so I set my own traps."

"What kind of traps?"

"I have people who are useful in these situations."

"MI6."

He smiled. "Yes. MI5 too. Very handy."

"Handy?" I echoed.

I knew my father was powerful, even if he didn't appear to be, but thinking that he might have the run of Military Intelligence when he forgot to tie his shoelaces some days was pretty fucking terrifying.

"You're the reason there's a team here?"

"Of course." He tapped his nose. "Russia."

"The Big Bad Wolf of Europe," I rumbled.

"Indeed," Dad replied with a smile. "Although Putin was very friendly when I met him."

"You met him?"

"Just once. When Vasily was alive."

I hadn't thought of Jacinta, Hamish, or Vasily in too long, but today, I'd thought or heard their names in the space of five minutes.

God, I missed my grandparents something fierce.

"He was very shrewd," was all Dad said. "Russia gave the hackers who infiltrated the ministries a home."

"They back a lot of people," I muttered.

He hummed. "These were Veronian."

"UnReals."

"Definitely."

"What about this situation?"

"More UnReals. There's no conspiracy," he surmised. "Just someone in possession of a secret they shouldn't know, and by killing those in line to the throne, they can alter history."

"Who told them?"

"I have no idea. Loose lips sink ships," he repeated. "There's a reason that's been floating around for a long time, and they have a lot of staff here. Someone could have mentioned how the king's brother has a tendency to drift into the queen's private rooms. It's probably a badly kept secret."

"I don't like this. I'd prefer to think there was one clear enemy."

He snorted. "Don't be so facile, son. Life is never cut and dry like that." His eyes were alight with excitement. "Did you know Andrei and I managed to get every single euro back?"

"From the embezzlement scheme?" That had my brows rising. "Wow, Dad. No, I didn't know that."

"Well, to be fair, you weren't supposed to." He raised a hand to his lips in the universal sign of silence, to which I just nodded. "And we had the Russians toss them out."

I smirked. "You mean *Papa* did."

His eyes gleamed. "Handy to have the Bratva on your side, isn't it?"

"That means they have no resources now."

"Nope."

"They must have found a home somewhere."

"Undoubtedly. We didn't have them killed."

He uttered those words so easily that it was a reminder of *who* my dad actually was.

Capable of burning water in a pot on the stove, yet the brightest mathematical brain in the Western World.

"I don't understand these UnReals," I grated out. "It's not like the DeSauviers are bad for the country."

"There's money to be made from civil unrest, Tin."

"You just said there was no conspiracy."

"There isn't. Just a nice, old-fashioned plot." He rubbed his hands together. "What do you reckon an arms dealer is behind these shootings?"

Stunned, I gaped at him. "You can't be serious." He stared at me, and I stared at him. "Stupid question."

ETTA

THREE WEEKS LATER

"Mom?"

She peered up at me through teary red eyes. "Yes, sweetheart?"

"Do you think you should go shower?"

Blinking, she whispered, "When he wakes up."

I shook my head. "You need to go freshen up. You'll feel so much better. I'll sit with him."

Though I knew what she was going through because Tin had been in this position barely seven weeks ago, it didn't stop me from trying to take care of her like she had with me.

She bit her lip. "Five more minutes."

Though I sighed, I nodded and headed over to the door where one of the sitting rooms had been turned into a makeshift office.

Father was there, his brow furrowed as he pored over papers, while Papa was sitting in an armchair, reading something on his tablet.

There was an unofficial separation of duties going on, and while my feminist core bristled at being left to shelter the family, in this, I was mostly grateful that Father and Papa were working to identify the threats to our nation.

To *us*.

Their experience outweighed mine, and while I had to learn, where our security was concerned, now was not the time for lessons. Not with Daddy...

I tapped on the door. "Any news?"

Father peered up from the desk, blinking from exhaustion. "No."

Quickly realizing Papa had fallen asleep, I strolled over to Father, and in a softer voice, asked, "Is that good or bad?"

"It's unusual. No chatter? Your Tin will tell you how rare that is." He rubbed his eyes. "How's Daddy?"

The wound had suppurated, and there'd been a scramble to find effective antibiotics. That was why he was still unconscious.

He knew all that though, so I murmured, "The antibiotics have finally kicked in. The fever's close to breaking."

He blew out a relieved breath. "Mom?"

"As exhausted as you." I hesitated. "You might need to put her to bed. I'm not sure she'll go otherwise, and you both need to sleep." I cast a look at Papa. "You all do."

"She won't, but I'll go sit with her."

"I've tried to get her to shower, but she's scared he'll wake up without her."

Father blinked. "You're a good girl, Alice."

I blinked back, uncertain of what to say.

His mouth firmed, a wry twist pulling at the corners as he said, "Valentin is right. I am too hard on you."

"Not exactly. I know you're preparing me for..." I hesitated. "*This*."

"I am. But there's more to life than that." He scrubbed a hand over his face. "This is proof of that. I never imagined—" His voice broke. "I know George will be fine."

"Daddy *will* be fine, Father. The doctors are monitoring him. Everything's on track now."

It hadn't been, though.

And that was why Mom was refusing to leave his side.

We shared a glance which silently encapsulated that.

Father got to his feet, groaning as he straightened.

I watched him as he approached me and found myself surprised when he tugged me into a hug.

Melting into him, I sighed as I tucked my arms around his waist. A small smile curved my lips as he pressed a kiss to my head.

"Thank you, darling, for all you're doing." He squeezed me. "You need rest too."

"Christel will be awake soon. I'll get some rest then."

He nodded, his chin digging into my head as he did so. The scent of his aftershave was fading, but it was the same as always—oud. Strong and pungent, but Mom loved it for some reason, and I always associated it with him.

"How's Tin?"

"Been busy, but his wounds are healing."

"Good." Another squeeze. "I'll see to your mother." Another kiss to the crown of my head before he pulled back and moved away to care for Mom.

Shuffling around the desk, I stared at the papers on there. The font was so small that it was no wonder he'd been rubbing his eyes.

Peering down at them, I saw intelligence reports from two of our military agencies: one that detailed the UnReals' leadership and another that discussed how a rifle was confiscated on parade day.

Interested, I almost sat down but the door creaked open and I saw Tin standing there.

Smiling, relieved to see him because he'd been working with his fathers the last time I'd checked on him and I hadn't wanted to disturb them, I headed over, gently closing the door behind me so that Papa could continue napping.

As Tin pulled me into his arms, I caught sight of Christel who was peering at us from the corner of her eye, and I noticed that Mom and Father had pulled a disappearing act which meant he'd convinced her to take a nap.

"Time for you to get some rest," Tin rumbled in my ear, and

because I wasn't about to disagree when I felt like I was living on my nerves, I just nodded.

As I stepped away, I caught my sister's gaze and mouthed, "You going to be okay?"

She cast a look at Daddy then shrugged.

I got that.

If he was fine, she was.

Same with me.

Tin's fingers slipped through mine as he tugged me out of the bedroom and deeper into the private wing of the palace.

Mom had insisted that he not stay in the medical ward, that he be brought home even if it was only a wing away, and Daddy had been in there ever since. In the bed that, officially, the king and queen slept in.

"The staff must be wondering what the hell is going on up here," Tin mused as we caught sight of some housemaids whispering a way down the hall as they dusted a console table that housed a seventeenth century clock—one of the first timepieces ever made.

As they curtsied at us, I murmured, "You called it the Official Secrets Act in the UK. We have something similar. Plus, to work here involves jumping through so many hoops, Michael Jordan would struggle."

"Really?"

"Really. You gossip about *anything* you saw in the palace and you're not only fined more than the average person earns in a lifetime, but you're sent to jail too.

"And, depending on what you share, be it official or family secrets, you can be tried for espionage which comes with the tag of execution at the end of it.

"So, yeah, people tend to keep their mouths shut."

Until they didn't.

When Tin tugged me into our suite, I sighed when he deposited me in the armchair beside the fire, and rather than taking a seat in the one opposite, he moved behind me and began to rub my shoulders.

"You're tense."

"I am." No point in denying it.

"He'll be fine."

"Almost lost him, almost lost you. I'm tired of losing people—"

"You're tired of 'almost' losing people," he corrected. "No one has gone anywhere. You're fortunate. Even if it *is* stressful."

I bit my lip. "Stressful isn't the word, and I'm not even doing anything to help. Papa and Father are doing it all."

"You're keeping the family together. That's just as important."

"I guess."

"How's he doing?"

"Unaware that he triggered a war in the wards."

Tin chuckled softly. "Yes, I heard whispers about the lead surgeon's dismissal."

"Mom blamed him for not knowing Daddy's allergic to cephalexin. I'm not sure if it's rational, but I'm not sure if he's been fired either."

"You think your father shuffled him away for the moment?"

"I think Father's shrewd enough to send him on a vacation rather than pissing off one of the best medical minds Veronia has to offer," I agreed. "The antibiotics have held at least, and he seems to be on the home stretch. Once the fever breaks, we'll all be able to rest easier."

"I'm glad."

The simple words were redolent with emotion.

"Me too," I choked out. "What have you been doing today?"

"Wrangling my parents. Well, most of them. *Vati* is with Mom and the brats, but the rest are with me."

My lips twitched at his name for his sisters which reminded me... "Jack's race went well?"

"Bash said he crashed the car once, but it didn't damage the body. His or the Chevy's," he finished dryly.

"Where did he crash it? Talk about burying the lede, Tin!" I demanded, concerned enough that I twisted around to peer up at him, prompting his hands to still their delicious massage on my shoulders.

"Nah. Not in the race. In a parking garage after the race. Again," he said with a laugh. "You've seen his car. It's one of those stupidly wide ones. He hit one of the columns."

"Idiot."

"That was going to be his new nickname, but his friend... you remember Beau, don't you?"

"Yeah. She lives on the estate, doesn't she?"

He hummed. "Her father's *Papa's* COO. She's calling him Jackass."

"It suits him." I tugged on his hand again. "Any news?"

It didn't take a man of his intellect to figure out what I was discussing.

"We're working on it," was all he'd say.

"Is it bad that I have more faith in you and your fathers than I do in the Guard Elect?"

"No. I don't think it's bad. I think it's smart. You know exactly who you're dealing with, after all. You know they're completely loyal to you because they love you." He hitched a shoulder. "And you'd be correct to have faith in them."

Nodding, I peered into his beautiful eyes and whispered, "Once upon a time, back when I was a baby, Father thought the UnReal threat was no more. Did you know that?"

"I did." He started rubbing my shoulders again. "I've seen his speeches."

"Where?"

"A class I had to take."

"That sounds ominous."

He shrugged. "It was."

"Why?"

"Crowd manipulation tactics."

"Makes sense. He knows how to work an audience." I hadn't

attended a college class on 'Becoming a Queen 101' but I'd had to watch Father's speeches too.

How else would I learn to emulate him?

"Like he was born to do it," Tin agreed.

I wished I'd inherited that gene.

Pulling a face at the back wall, I shuddered a second later, deep inside, when he hit a good spot that made my body want to purr.

"That feel good?"

I could hear the amusement in his voice and didn't even care. "Yeah, that feels good."

He leaned over me, pressing his chin to my crown, and murmured, "Want more?"

I bit my lip. "Depends."

"On what?"

"If you're ready for what it will bring."

"I can deal with the repercussions of a massage," Tin rasped. "Just not sure if you can."

I'd left my father's sickbed ten minutes ago, so, technically, the last thing I wanted was sex, but the connection?

With Tin?

I needed that more than anything.

Reaching up, I let my hand sift through his hair and ruffled through the short waves.

It was spiky thanks to his shade cut, but the top part was long enough to slip my fingers through.

He shivered, and my heart skipped a beat as I contemplated how much power I had over him, and how much I loved it. Because he had that much power over me.

"Are you sure?" he murmured, making me fall for him even more.

"I'm positive."

And I was. I needed to feel him, to be one with him, and God, I needed that so badly my skin ached with the demand to have him on me.

He pulled back, then with our fingers still connected, rounded the armchair so he could tug me onto my feet.

He was beautiful, even if his face was drawn.

Once I was standing, I pressed my hand to where I knew only a small gauze rested on his belly.

"Are you sure?"

"Doctor approved me for exercise." His eyes gleamed.

"Exercise?" I hummed. "Interesting."

He grinned. "Best way to burn off calories, I think."

"I agree."

Snorting, I reached down and cupped him. He was wielding a semi, like he was excited by the prospect of what was about to happen but wasn't expecting much. I figured he thought I was going to cut and run on him at the last moment because of the situation.

He tensed when I cupped him though, and his dick went rock-hard the second I shaped him further.

Letting my hand fall from his, I reached for his zipper and tugged him free.

A shaky breath escaped him as his dick pierced the slit in his briefs, then his fly, and was out in the open.

It boggled my mind to think that he'd stayed true to me, and I could only think of how grateful I was, and how I needed to show him my gratitude.

So I slipped to my knees.

I'd seen this in enough porn movies to know what I was doing. Kind of. Although maybe not.

It was thicker at the tip than I remembered, so I ran my tongue down the underside like I'd seen a porn star do, fluttered it here and there, slickening him from root to tip with my spit.

Every time I touched him, he shuddered where he was standing, but he let me do what I wanted. He let me kiss him and suck him and nip him and nuzzle him, leaving me astonished by his patience.

I could feel his cum leaking onto my cheek every time it bobbed and tapped me there, but he let me play.

Until he didn't. And his hand was in my hair and he rocked my head back so I could see the blue fire in his eyes.

"Suck it," he growled, and his voice sent that fire in him surging through me.

I opened my mouth, even as I let my head fall back, and groaned as, with his free hand, he grabbed his cock and aimed it at my parted lips. I gulped when he pushed the tip onto my tongue and thrust in an inch.

He pulled back, his gaze trained on my face, looking for my discomfort. "Clean the tip."

I shuddered at the order but did as bid, letting my tongue smooth over the little hole, slurping him down even as I cleaned him up as requested.

His hand tightened around my hair to the point of pain, but I didn't complain.

"Gather spit in your mouth," he demanded next, making my heart soar.

I nodded then nearly melted when he rasped, "Show me."

It was strange to open my mouth, to reveal the saliva I'd collected in there—I was a princess. I didn't even sit with my legs crossed, for God's sake, and this... it made butterflies settle in my stomach.

But I did it.

I showed him, and he hummed his approval.

"Open your mouth wider," he commanded, and I did, then his cock was there, inside the haven of my mouth.

Not all of it, maybe not even half, but he rocked his head back on his shoulders like I'd driven him to the edge—like I'd deepthroated him or something.

"Fuck," he growled, his hips pulsing like he was helpless, rocking his cock back and forth, fucking me slightly, even if I got the feeling he wanted to push in deeper.

If I were being honest, I wanted that too, even if I didn't know if I'd gag.

Could you spew around a dick if they thrust in too far?

That was not something I wanted in my memory banks.

Or Tin's.

Every time I gave him a blowjob in the future, he'd tease me, and then I'd have to kill him.

But I couldn't stop myself from giving him what he needed. When I thought of all the women he could have had, I wanted to thank him. And sure, I could have had a hundred different men too—equal rights, sista—but my life was different.

I couldn't date, and getting any man near my bedroom, or near *a* bedroom, was harder than planning a war.

Tin had freedom, he'd had opportunities, and he hadn't taken them.

Not a single one.

So I reached up and cupped his hips even as, carefully, I pushed myself onto him, taking more of him, accepting what I could, breathing through what I couldn't.

I closed my eyes so he couldn't see me panic, and I forced myself to focus on breathing first, even as I moved my head, letting him into me, letting him claim what belonged to him, what he could have always had had he not been so angry with me.

I shuddered when I opened my eyes next. I looked straight at his fly and suddenly realized that the reason I couldn't breathe so well through my nose was because I'd pushed into his pants-covered belly.

I swallowed which had Tin groaning like I'd done tongue acrobatics, then I pulled back some so I could breathe again.

It was uncomfortable and big and awkward, but I kind of liked it.

Kind of because it was Tin.

But I *did* like how he was shaking, his body trembling, and I knew why—he didn't want to come yet.

Sure, the poor guy hadn't exploded in anything other than his fist for years, so I was proud of him for not having busted his wad the second I licked him, but also, I knew he liked what I was doing and didn't want it to end.

I wore an A-line skirt and a simple strappy tee, and I'd never been more grateful for the comfortable clothes I'd put on this morning.

As I reveled in the feel of him against my tongue, I dropped my hands, reached behind me, and unsnapped my bra.

Slipping out of it, I pushed the neckline down so that my breasts were supported by the fabric hammock I'd created.

When I pulled back, I surged up onto my knees, and as I grabbed my tits, I cupped him with them, wriggling the flesh around him, wanting him to feel all my curves.

I needed him to come now, needed it because otherwise he was going to get inside me and burst, and I really thought I deserved an orgasm after all these years of waiting.

So, it was awkward and definitely wouldn't win an AVN Award, but I sucked the tip of him into my mouth every time I could, and I sucked hard, urging him to explode inside me.

When a gargled groan escaped him as I did this for the fourth time, his knees buckled before he righted himself, and then he came.

My mouth was full of the stuff, and for a second, I didn't know what to do with it.

Spit it out?

It was bitter and salty and really not something I felt like eating, but they always did in porn, didn't they?

So, I looked up at him, saw he was watching me through lash-sheltered eyes, and I gulped.

He shuddered.

And I smiled.

He shuddered again.

I retreated and moved onto the floor so I could let my legs out in front of me.

Within seconds, I had my hands on my hips and was wriggling out of my panties.

The moment I was bare, I fell back against the rug, shoving the skirt I still wore aside, and I could no more stop myself from slipping my hands between my legs than I could stop myself from looking straight at him as I did so.

Tin stood there, panting like he'd been running, his body one big tremor from his first blowjob, but his face, his eyes, they were alight once more.

He stared at my pussy, stared at my fingers, then he rasped, "Did I say you could do that?"

Whatever I'd expected him to tell me, it wasn't that.

My fingers stilled.

"N-No," I whispered, wondering where that timid voice had come from.

He stood there, so self-assured, his cock hanging through his pants but otherwise fully dressed.

He could have headed out the door the second he'd zipped up.

Me?

I was a mess.

My mascara had run whenever my eyes had smarted from taking Tin too deeply into my mouth—I could feel the dampness on my cheeks—and my tits were out, my pussy on display, and I was wet, so wet.

Achingly so.

I felt dirty and filthy and needy.

I felt like he was the prince and I was a nothing, a nobody.

Then he whispered, "Clean your fingers."

And I moaned.

I wiped the tips on my leg, but he shook his head.

"Suck them clean."

Shivering, I reached up and slipped one in, then another, then another, until the three I'd used to touch my clit were, relatively speaking, clean.

He crouched down in front of me, one knee coming to the ground as he moved between my legs, and he gazed at me, his eyes everywhere.

I wasn't sure why he didn't touch me when I needed his touch so badly.

But he just looked.

Studied.

Stared.

Then, he reached up, and with the tip of his pointer finger, rimmed the areola of my left breast.

Instantly, the nipple puckered and my belly rolled. I could smell how wet I was, which was kind of embarrassing, but from how he was looking at me, also kind of hot.

I shivered when that finger moved to the hem of the top I was wearing. It was pulled taut the way I had it supporting my tits. He tapped it, then he dug around in his pocket with his other hand and revealed a pen knife.

My eyes widened as he flicked out the blade that was scarier than any Swiss Army Knife I'd seen before, and he pressed it to my skin, just below the hem, letting me feel the cold chill of the steel, before he plucked the top and cut it straight through without stopping.

The remnants of the—very expensive—shirt fluttered to my sides. And my skirt was next.

He let the pen knife sit on my belly as he plucked the waistband up, then he collected the blade and set it to destroying another expensive item of clothing.

But did I care?

Nope.

I wasn't sure I could breathe, but I didn't give a fuck. He could destroy my entire wardrobe if it meant making me feel like this.

I'd never anticipated this, had never expected this level of intensity. But Tin was a man of depth, many, many depths. I should have known that he'd have changed.

Hell, that I'd change too.

I was trimmed neatly down there, and when he properly looked at me, he turned the blade over to the dull edge and he tutted as he scraped it over me. "I want to see you bare."

I shuddered. "O-Okay."

He hummed, clicked the knife back into its slot, then tossed it on the floor beside him.

"Spread your legs. Wide."

I did as he ordered, aware that his gaze was trained on my pussy, and I bit my lip as I stared up at the ceiling, wondering why I felt so anxious, wondering why—

"Ahhh!" The high cry escaped me as he slipped a finger into me.

"So wet." He shuddered. "So fucking wet."

And then he was there, in between my legs, splayed out on the ground.

No longer distant.

So close I wanted him to crawl into my skin.

His lips were on my clit, then his tongue in my pussy, and he fucked me and sucked me, and in seconds, I was screaming, my legs clamping down on his head as I rocked from side to side, crying and sobbing and shrieking as he carried on, not stopping, not stopping until—

I squealed.

God, I squealed like a pig.

His hand came up to cover my mouth and I bit him, dug deep into his palm to shut me the hell up even as I locked down elsewhere, my body juddering with the power of the orgasm he gave me.

When he finally pulled back, I felt like I'd been given a drug. I stared at him, my body limp and lax, my eyes sleepy and tired, but he was the opposite.

He was incandescent.

So alive with energy that everything inside me craved being nearer to him, to feel that power too.

His mouth was wet with the taste of me, and his face was stern with the need I saw down below—his cock was hard again.

"I want to come home," he rasped, melting my heart even as he set me on fire with need.

I lifted my arms, beckoned him close, and didn't stop until he was on top of me. I curved my arms and legs around him, wrapped him tight in my embrace as he moved between us, grabbed his dick, and slipped it into my gate.

That had been out of sync. In time, I knew we'd get better at this. It would have been much easier for him to slip inside me before I wrapped around him like a pretzel, but it was perfect all the same.

Even if it hurt.

He was big, I was still small, and I closed my eyes because even though I couldn't be wetter, it had been a long while since this had happened, and even then, it had only been a handful of times.

With every inch he reclaimed, I moaned in pain and he groaned in sweet agony.

But I clung to him, pushed my face into the side of his throat, and refused to let go, to let him stop.

I dug my heels into his hips, pushed him on, urged him inside me even if I was the one in pain, and then, he was there.

And it was, as he'd said, like he was home.

At long last.

I shivered; Tin groaned. Then he pulled back, and he showed me how, together, we could reach for the stars.

TWENTY-EIGHT

TIN

"You look better."

I cleared my throat. "Thanks, Dad."

"You do." His brow puckered. "A lot more relaxed. Unusual considering our situation, no?"

Vati snorted, and I damned my pale coloring because I blushed. Fucking blushed.

"Fuck's sake," I muttered under my breath, grateful only Kurt—*Vati*—and Devon—Dad—were here with me after breakfast, otherwise it would be a thousand times worse. "Guess this is as bad and as good as it could be."

Dad blinked. "What do you mean?"

"You have zero boundaries, and *Vati* has all the boundaries."

Vati clapped me on the back, squeezing a little, before he murmured, "There's no need to be embarrassed."

"I just don't want to talk about..." Jesus Christ. Be a man. I cleared my throat. "Having sex."

"Not sex." Dad tutted. "You love her, don't you?"

"Yes."

"Not sex, then."

"I agree," *Vati* said with a nod. "It isn't just sex when you're with the woman you're meant to be with."

"Tin, you're lucky," Dad grumbled. "You didn't waste decades waiting for yours."

I winced. "No, just four years."

"Still doesn't explain why you look so relaxed. Are you well?"

"I'm sure he's never been better," *Vati* retorted, but it sounded like it was a warning.

Which I was grateful for, even if I knew Dad wouldn't understand it.

So, feeling like I was five, I mumbled, "Etta and I are together. Together. You know?"

Dad tipped his head to the side, studying me as was his usual way.

"In a previous life, I'm sure you were an X-ray machine."

He frowned. "Hardly."

But he was.

And not just with me, but with all his kids.

The twins were the apple of his eye, and he had countless hours for them even if he didn't understand what the hell they were talking about.

He'd bought Rosie Starlight, her first horse, and he was the first one she'd told about getting into university.

Bethan argued with him on the phone over human rights just so that she could be prepared for class—I'd been there for that.

It was amusing watching her blow her top over Skype because Dad could talk about the worst things and still remain calm.

War, famine, plague, he was untouchable. Not because he was cruel, but because it was how he was.

Mom cut her finger while she was cooking? It was like WWIII had been declared.

Rosie fell off a horse and bruised her ass? She had a hard time stopping him from calling an ambulance.

The world, while large, was somehow tiny for Dad. We were his everything, and I knew that.

Jack probably had the easiest of it. Dad hated driving, but that hadn't stopped him from teaching Jack when, at six, he'd wanted to know how cars worked.

Of course, Mom had seen them in the driveway and had pitched a fit, but Dad had just said, "He wanted to know."

And in our house, knowledge was power.

Knowledge was never ignored or shied away from. It was embraced.

If I'd wanted to know how to make a bomb, I was sure Dad would find out and teach me. Life was a lesson, a constant one, and Dad was the best teacher imaginable.

"Why are you looking at me like that?"

My lips twitched. "How am I looking at you?"

"Like I'm looking at you," he stated simply, making me laugh outright.

"That's probably because I am." I sighed and decided there was no use in being embarrassed around him. "You were right. I *am* more relaxed. We did..." I cleared my throat. "...make love."

"I should hope so," Dad blustered. "You mean," he paused, "that's the first time since you've been back together?"

"The boy was bleeding out for the first half of his stay here, Devon," *Vati* groused, sitting back in his seat even as his eyes were bright—like he was taking in a show.

"But..." Dad shook his head. "A man has needs."

"I couldn't get into bed without help, Dad, never mind do anything the second I was in it."

He winced. "Do we need to have *the* conversation?"

"No!" I barked the same time *Vati* did. "I already know way too much about your sex lives." My ears turned pink. "Fuck's sake," I repeated. "Those servant corridors serve as a ghostly reminder to never open your doors unless you knock first."

"Well, you're a young man." He frowned. "Maybe I should talk with Alice."

"No!" *Vati* and I barked in unison again.

"You're a young man," he repeated, like that explained it all.

"So? I haven't had sex for years," I rumbled, dipping my chin so I didn't look at either of them. "Not since the first, well, second night we did…it," I finished awkwardly.

Not that I remembered much about those times in Vegas.

Well, I remembered Etta's hair and her smile; I remembered how she'd gleamed in the gold lights of the suite in that Vegas mega hotel I'd reserved for us.

I remembered her skin turning to cream against the black marble in the bathroom as I took her—

Huh.

Maybe I did remember more than I thought I did.

Tugging on my bottom lip, I didn't realize my fathers still hadn't spoken.

"You've never been with another?" *Vati* asked carefully.

I blinked. "No."

"You waited all those years for her?" Dad's question had me staring at him.

"Yes. If you'd known Mom—"

He raised a hand to stop me. "Fair point."

I smiled, as always, appreciating his devotion. "I think I'm like you," I rasped. "I-I just need her."

Dad frowned at me then muttered, "Does she feel the same?"

Vati clucked his tongue. "Of course she does. She looks at him like he made the world for her. Stupid question, Devon."

"It was a fair question." He smiled. "I knew I liked her."

"Why doesn't Mom?"

Dad shrugged, but *Vati* answered, "I think she always knew Alice would take you away to Veronia."

That had me frowning. "That makes no sense when you all spend a couple of months here a year anyway."

"You're her baby." *Vati* laughed. "Nothing has to be rational where you're concerned."

I gnawed on my bottom lip. "Can you talk to her? Etta has enough crap to deal with without Mom giving her crap too."

"Your mother's hard time isn't—"

"Isn't what?" I interrupted. "Etta gets enough crap from her parents about always being perfect, then there's the government, and did you know that if we don't get pregnant right away, the privy council might make us go see a fertility specialist?"

Vati's brows rose. "I doubt it."

"Etta doesn't," I stated grimly.

Vati frowned, and he shared a look with Dad, but he was quick enough in saying, "I'll talk to her."

"Thank you."

My mind flittered onto more pressing matters than whether or not Mom liked the love of my life. I released a worried breath because I was exactly that.

My wife and her family were in danger, and I felt like there was nothing I could do to help.

My contacts were useless.

I'd burned them by quitting.

I shoved away the eggs I'd been eating and muttered, "I'm scared for them."

"You don't have to be."

"I do."

Dad reached over and scrubbed a hand over my head. "It'll be okay, Tin. You know that, don't you?"

"You can't promise that, Dad."

His eyes turned stony. "Yes, I can."

When he got up, leaving the dining table where we were sitting without another word, I eyed *Vati* blankly. "What was that about?"

"Your dad just turned into Robocop."

My lips twitched before I let out a chuckle. "Not funny."

"*Was* funny."

The twinkle in *Vati's* eyes made me grin wider. "What do you think he's doing?"

"Being Devon?" *Vati* ran his finger around the golden rim of his coffee cup. "You know he and Sawyer have friends in high places. I think he pulled a few favors and was hoping things would be sorted by now."

"Things being the unseen threat against the Veronian royal family?"

"*Ja*, those kinds of things." *Vati* tilted his head to the side. "Will you be happy, son?"

"As long as Etta's by my side, yes."

The simplicity of my answer seemed to settle him, and he rocked back. "You're a lucky man."

"I know."

"I wish I'd met your mother at your age. Of course, we might not have lived the lifestyle we do if that had happened, but like Devon said, she would be worth waiting for."

"Etta's..." I blew out a breath. "She's always been a part of me."

"But the life put you off?"

"Can you blame me?"

Even now, we were sitting in an informal breakfast room and it was like being in a museum.

There was a carriage clock the size of my torso that was decorated with flowers and metal and all kinds of crap and a little bird flew out and didn't just cuckoo, it danced around the clock itself on some kind of special mechanism.

The chairs were ornately carved, the wallpaper made of silk, and until a half hour ago, there'd been two footmen lining the back wall waiting to see if we required anything else after our meal.

This kind of life?

No. I didn't want it.

Vati seemed to sense what I was thinking without saying, and he advised, "You'll get used to it. You'll be good for her, and she'll be good for you, and together, you'll be good for the country."

"I don't care if I'm good for the country," I stated firmly. "Don't mean to sound selfish, but I don't. I'll look after her, and that's it. Whatever she needs from me, I'll be there. I'll work with her, do what she needs, but she comes first."

Vati's eyes gleamed. "We raised you well."

My brows lifted at that. "I thought you'd lecture me."

"Why? Because you don't care for a country that isn't even your own?" He snorted. "You are British, American, German, and Russian, Tin. You, by marriage, are now Veronian too. I think that's enough countries to worry about, don't you?

"Your duty is to be honorable, to respect your mother countries but never kowtow to them." He shrugged. "Easy for me to say that, but it's not that difficult. Be impartial, care for the people, not for the land, and you'll do well."

"Thanks, *Vati*," I said, but my voice was low.

"No need. It's the truth. You're a good boy, Valentin. You always were. We were fortunate that you came first and not Jack because he'd have been a hellion as a consort to Etta."

My nose crinkled, but I just inquired, "Do you think Dad will be able to fix things?"

"I'd be surprised if he doesn't. To be honest, I think he expected results before now. He's been in a mood—couldn't you tell?"

I shook my head. "He's been more talkative than usual. That's all."

Vati dipped his chin. "That's how he rolls. Has been ever since you were a baby."

"What do you mean?"

"There was a time when he shut us all out. Locked down."

"Mom told me. After Daw's initial diagnosis."

Vati nodded. "*Ja.* He had a meltdown, and he wouldn't talk or, well, anything. He barely lived. He made your mother a promise, so now, if he talks more than usual, that's his way of keeping that promise."

Despite myself, I had to grin. "He's so literal sometimes. It always amuses me."

"*Ja*," *Vati* agreed, taking a sip from his dainty cup of coffee. "I don't think Sascha anticipated she'd be getting a chatterbox instead of someone who made a ghost look talkative, but that's how the cards fall, I suppose."

"I suppose."

But we shared a grin as we both finished off our coffees.

TWENTY-NINE

ETTA

FIVE DAYS LATER

When I looked up from the paper I was reading my daddy, who was snoring now and fast asleep, I saw Sascha standing in the doorway, eying me like I was a rattlesnake on the brink of attack.

"Is everything okay?" I asked, surprised she was here.

She nodded. "Where's your mom?" Her voice was pitched softer, so I shuffled toward her so I could speak without disturbing Daddy.

"She's catching up on some rest. Now Daddy's out of the woods, she agreed to leave so long as someone stays with him."

"Let's hope she does more than nap this time."

I grimaced. "Yes."

"Your fathers are with her?"

Discomfited by the question, I nodded.

"Walk with me?"

"Of course."

It didn't occur to me that I was the princess here, just that I was this woman's daughter-in-law, and if she wanted to boss me about, she could pretty much tell me to jump and I'd ask how high.

On the brink of stepping outside the room, I hesitated, remembering that, "I promised Mom I wouldn't leave Daddy."

Something softened in her eyes. "Okay." She leaned against the door, deepening her stance as she relaxed, and murmured, "You love my Tinny, don't you?"

"Of course I do," I whispered, knowing full well that my heart was in my eyes.

She sucked her top lip into her mouth as she stared at me then muttered, "You're a good girl, Alice. I can see why he loves you."

Whatever I'd expected her to say, it wasn't that.

"You're not what I'd have wanted for him," she admitted, "but maybe that's why you're perfect.

"Perhaps I knew that you were always going to be together, but I also know the struggles you have here..." Her words waned as she looked at Daddy in his bed, trussed up with bandages and IV lines. "I knew there'd be a fight on his hands, and a mother always wants what's best and what's *easiest* for her children.

"Please, whatever you do, Alice, try to keep him safe. It's quite clear that he can't keep himself out of danger, getting into knife fights and throwing himself at would-be assassins—"

My eyes widened at that. "What?"

She studied me, then a smile curved her lips. "He didn't tell you. Interesting."

"What's interesting?" I snapped.

"He took down the shooter." She huffed. "I didn't even know he could fire a gun. Since when do desk jockeys carry weapons?"

My nostrils flared as outrage filled me. "They don't."

"Exactly." Her eyes gleamed with amusement, not at Tin and the danger he'd put himself in, but at my reaction. She reached up, patted my shoulder. "I'll leave that news with you. He's too old for me to spank, but wives have ways and means of punishing their men, and I think he deserves it."

Before I could say another word, she drifted off, and I was left sputtering at the doorway.

"Ignore Sascha, *carilla*," my daddy rasped from the bed, making me spin around to face him.

He looked pale and gaunt, and I was so tired of sickbeds that I wanted to scream.

"Daddy!" I exclaimed, relief filling me.

He'd woken up so few times since the fever had broken, and I'd yet to speak with him.

George was the father I related to the most; the one I could be most at ease with.

Though he was smart—very, very smart—he was playful. The least scholarly of all my family. It made me feel like I could fit in with him because academia and I definitely didn't get along well together.

I rushed over to the bed and grabbed his hand the second I was sitting down.

"I thought you were going to sleep all day," I chided, but I was smiling because I would have been happy for him to sleep. At least, then, he'd be getting the rest he needed.

"I'm uncomfortable," he divulged. "I drift in and out, but I heard Sascha. Don't punish him for his past, Alice. Be grateful for it. It means he's even better suited as your husband than he was before."

My eyes narrowed on him. "I'm not okay with him being James Bond."

"He wasn't." At my raised brow, he smiled. "All your fathers have seen his file. He truly was a desk jockey, a fine analyst but still an analyst.

"He was trained well because they used to put him into the field where they wouldn't usually, but he was adept at fitting in.

"With all the Middle Eastern languages he speaks, it would be ridiculous *not* to put him out in the field."

I didn't want to admit that I was totally in the dark about what he was saying. And it hurt that Tin could speak Arabic, never mind however many dialects he apparently had in that big brain of his, and I didn't even fucking know.

Blowing out a breath, I muttered, "Sascha said he took out your shooter."

"He did. I was on the brink of consciousness, but I remember that much. He screamed at us to duck then pushed Sawyer back and down, but it was too late for me.

"Before I knew it, he had a gun in his hand and was taking a shot. I didn't know, until now, that he'd hit the target."

Death and I weren't old friends, but I was comfortable enough with it not to wince at the fact Tin had taken a life.

Every day, in my world, there was a warzone at play.

Just because no one else saw it didn't mean it wasn't there. But I resented that Tin hadn't told me.

I told my dad as much.

"Maybe he thought you'd view him differently. And wouldn't he be right? Tin can do many things. It would be silly to punish him for his skills."

"I don't judge him for what he's done. I'm just mad that I could have..." I heaved a sigh.

"That you could have lost him?"

Suddenly teary-eyed, I whispered, "So many lost to us, Daddy, so many people hurt..." I reached for his hand and squeezed it. "Thank you for not leaving us."

"I will always fight for my girls, *carilla*." He shot me a sleepy smile. "It does my heart good, however, to see that you found a man who'll do the same for you."

"You believe that?"

He arched a disbelieving brow. "Don't you?"

Nodding, I whispered, "I do. But I'd fight for him too, so it's only fair."

His lips quirked into a smile. "So feisty. I like to think you get that from me."

Grinning, I pressed his hand to my cheek. "I'm glad you're getting better, Daddy."

"Me too. I've got far too much to do still. Bugging your mother is a full-time job."

"I think she's quite happy at the idea of you bugging her until she's old and gray."

He laughed. "Nice to know."

I closed my eyes. "Everything is changing."

"Yes, but that's not a bad thing. You'll get married to Tin, and you'll settle down. You'll be happy again—I've missed that, love. I've missed seeing you be happy."

My smile wobbled. "I've missed feeling that way."

"He might be an asshat for what he put you through, but, and it's a big but, he came through in the end."

I gnawed on my bottom lip for a second, his words making me wonder... "Did you know?"

Daddy wasn't stupid. "About the wedding?" When I nodded, he smiled. "What do you think?"

I released a shaky breath. "Did Andrea tell you?"

"No. She knew?"

"Yes."

He hummed. "Well, she kept your secret too. I'm the one who reads the security reports. Though you evaded your guards for a few hours, they dragged in CCTV and spotted you at the chapel. It didn't take much to find out more."

I studied him. "Why didn't you say anything?"

"Because it was your secret to tell, and I understood. I'm the father who fled to the US, Alice. How do you think we met your mother?

"I know how much of a prison this castle can be if you don't have the right person by your side."

"I'm surprised you kept it from Father," I whispered, ducking my head so I didn't have to hold his stare.

"Edward forgets we all have our little rebellions. Tin was made for you, and vice versa.

"He was shortsighted if he didn't expect you and him to end up together. Although, in his defense, he knew you were unhappy and he wanted to fix it for you."

"By marrying me off?" I spluttered.

Daddy shrugged. "For a smart man, he can be an idiot sometimes."

"Pot calling kettle springs to mind."

We twisted around to see Mom standing in the doorway looking brighter, but her eyes were narrowed as she stalked in. "You knew? You knew our baby got married and you didn't tell me?"

Well, it was clear Mom definitely hadn't been lying about being in the dark.

"Of course," he murmured calmly, but fire sparked in his eyes. "I helped keep it a secret though, and I'd do it again."

Mom squinted at him. "If you weren't a bag of bones, I'd rattle you."

"If I weren't a bag of bones, I'd let you," he retorted, and I groaned.

"Please, can we wait until I'm out of here for that conversation?"

He laughed, his eyes still glinting with that fire that made him look much more like my daddy. "You're a wife now, Etta. You're as grown up as it gets."

Mom grunted. "She'll always be my baby."

Despite myself, I had to grin. I got to my feet, rounded the bed, and slipped my arm around her waist. "I won't complain about that. I love you, Mama."

She pressed a kiss to the crown of my head and mumbled, "Love you too, baby. But don't think you can keep anything else major from me or I'll lose my shit."

I snorted. "Don't you know? I'm the boring daughter."

She snorted back. "If you believe that, then you're as crazy as your daddy."

I shot him a wink, was glad to see I got one in return, then Mom ordered, "Oh, go and sort Tin out."

Brows lifting, I demanded, "You knew too?"

"Just spoke with Sascha. Don't be too hard on the boy, my love. He did save your daddy."

I nodded, but I was definitely going to give Tin something to think about.

THIRTY

"Fuck," I rasped. "Fuck."

If I could just keep on repeating the litany, I would have, but Etta stole my breath as she dropped her head and kissed me.

I liked bossing her around in bed, but fuck, the feel of her, what she was doing to me? I was quite happy to be ensnared in her net.

And ensnared in other things.

Shuddering, I let her tongue play with mine even as she toyed with me.

She'd climbed on top of me with promises of riding me, but then the second I was inside, the second I was home, she just stayed there and tormented me by twitching muscles I had known about scientifically, but not physically.

She slipped her fingers through mine and pinned our hands on either side of my head as she finally moved, taking forever to release me then to drop back down.

After four more thrusts like that, I was about ready to beg when she pulled her mouth from mine, dropped her lips to my ear, and whispered, "Tin?"

"Y-Yes," I stuttered.

Could a man go blind from this torment? I was pretty sure I was cross-eyed.

"If you ever—" She nipped my ear lobe. "Ever keep something like—" Another nip, followed by her sucking on it with enough force my goddamn eyelashes fluttered. "Shooting an assassin from me—" Suck, suck. "I will make you pay."

If this was the price, then I'd pay it.

Fuck.

"Who told you?" I grated out.

"Never you mind."

She clenched down around me, hard enough to make me throw my head back and for the veins to pop out on my throat.

"Fuck," I whispered.

"That's right. You own me in here," she whispered back, filling me with lust at her statement, "but I own you too."

I shuddered, and though I'd let her have her own way, I was a lot stronger than her. I reared up, making her shriek, grabbed her hands, and didn't stop rolling until she was under me and I was on top of her.

Then I fucked her.

And I fucked her.

I went so deep I knew she'd taste me in the back of her throat. I plowed into her so fast that the bed shook and rocked.

She screamed as she exploded with an orgasm. Her sobs filled my ears, filled me with a white noise that had me seeing stars when, finally, I burst into a thousand of them as I reached my climax.

But still, I carried on, thrusting into her until I was soft and she was moaning, her head rocking from side to side like she couldn't take anymore. Then I pushed down, even though I was soft, ground my pubis into her clit, and her eyes popped open and she let out a groan so guttural, I felt it in my fucking balls.

As she cosseted my cock in another orgasm, I let myself fall against her. Limp as spaghetti, I just flopped, and she let me.

Though she was the same, it didn't stop her from propping her arms and legs on me in a way that proved her muscles evidently had no strength to hold me, but still made me feel like she was hugging me.

After a few minutes, when I felt certain I was probably squashing her, I acted like a gentleman and heaved myself off her. Only she tightened up on me, so when I flopped down on my back, she came with me.

My cum and her juices started to trickle out until I felt the slickness slide onto my skin. I wasn't sure I'd felt anything as fucking sexy in my life, and I muttered that into her throat.

Muffled laughter escaped her, at my expense, but she nipped my chin and wiggled into me like she agreed but didn't have the words to say it.

I sighed as I stared up at a Michelangelo, wondering how this had become my life. How this was now a part of my day.

With one hand sliding up and down her back, I began to relax and she did too.

Maybe I should have expected it, but I didn't. We were all pretty good with privacy, knowing full well that Mom and the dads could get it on in any room they chose so long as the door was shut.

But I never expected Dad to come bursting into the bedroom like the mad genius he was.

Because it *was* Dad, and while we both jerked up and Etta shrieked in surprise, he didn't even notice.

I quickly wrapped her up in the sheet, and she huddled into me as he began pacing, talking about Russia and the UK and some North Koreans, until, finally, I roared, "Dad! What the fuck?"

He blinked at my outrage then turned, looked at me, and did the damnedest thing...

He grinned.

"Good lad," he praised.

"Sawyer says 'lad,'" Etta sniped, "not you."

"You stick around someone long enough, you pick things up here and there," he intoned piously.

"How about you pick up on the fact that I'm with my wife, Dad," I growled, my eyes flashing with anger.

He huffed. "Just thought you'd like to know...the organization behind the shootings—we've taken them down. They'll be in our custody within the hour."

I jolted at that news, but just when I had questions in need of answering, he stormed off and made a distinct show of closing the door and not slamming it.

We both stared at the wide set of doors for a long time, then I mumbled, "Did that really just happen?"

"Did your dad really see me naked?" Etta rasped, burying her face in my throat.

"I doubt it. I don't think he even knew we'd been having sex until I shouted at him."

"Thank God, it was Devon—"

"If it had been anyone else, they'd have knocked," I pointed out.

She pushed her forehead into my chest. "Never going to be able to look him in the eye ever again."

I rubbed her back. "Don't worry. He's on Mom more than butter's on toast. That's how we'll get some revenge."

Her nose wrinkled. "I don't really want to."

"It's the only way to teach him anything," I reasoned. "And you and I both know, now that I'm here, they'll be visiting. A lot."

She sighed. "I'm not too upset about that."

"Me neither," I admitted. "So we'll teach him a lesson that Mom will ram home."

Etta snickered. "Okay, I'm down for that." Then, she whispered, "What was he talking about?"

"You know he always says exactly what he means. His contacts found the organization and they're dismantling it."

"Organization? He didn't say UnReals, did he?"

"No. That means there's a story." I kissed her cheek, then let my tongue trail over to her mouth, not stopping until I was tracing her lips with it. "Want to hear it?"

She peered into my eyes. "If Devon says it's sorted, then, I mean, it's sorted, right?"

I grinned at her. "You know it."

"I mean, I'm supposed to be taking on more responsibility—" She let her words taper off.

"It can wait another day, can't it?"

She laughed. "Yeah. It can."

Eyes flashing, I twisted us both over so that my body was on top of hers once more, then I kissed her, and thoughts of assassins and organizations and espionage disappeared because when I was with her, nothing else in the world mattered.

THIRTY-ONE

TIN

A WEEK LATER

Monitoring the eight Veronians seated on rickety chairs, their hands tied behind their backs, I hummed under my breath at the sight.

When Dad said 'our custody,' I hadn't realized he meant *our* custody.

Not the Veronians.

Papa stepped behind me and said, "You shouldn't be here."

I glanced at him. "Seen worse in my time."

"You shouldn't have."

"Why not?"

"I would protect you from this if I could."

His disapproval was clear. Not just at my presence, but at what was happening behind the two-way mirror.

This was not a raid approved of by Edward.

Nor was it aided by MI6 or MI5.

Dad had decided that both were taking too long and that the Veronians were inept, thus he'd called in the Bratva.

And the Bratva were doing what they were good at—taking out the trash.

Dad had told me that the Russians had kicked out the UnReals who'd messed with the Veronian economy back when I was a baby, but they hadn't.

They'd made them citizens.

Tricksy bastards.

A week ago, the Bratva had picked up seven of these fuckers, but it had taken them until today to find the ringleader.

That was why we were here.

"Because this is on Russian soil, it isn't even an international incident," Dad pointed out, stepping beside me and leaning against the glass as he did so.

"Technically," *Papa* countered.

"They shouldn't have defected to Russia," I said wryly, watching as the ringleader spat out a broken tooth after a Bratva meathead punched him in the face.

"No, indeed," Dad agreed, his tone pleasant as the men were each 'attended to.'

After a while, *Papa* knocked on the glass. The beating immediately stopped.

My great-grandfather had been the head of the Bratva in Moscow. He'd commanded great respect, enough that the current Pakhan, who was not related to *Papa*, afforded my family many favors.

Like this one.

"Do you pay a stipend to them?" Dad asked curiously.

"What?" *Papa* grumbled.

"A stipend. Why do they always rush to do you a favor?"

Papa heaved a sigh. "No reason."

I smiled. "Liar."

He knocked me with his elbow. "Disrespectful."

"Truthful," I countered.

"I help out when money gets tight," he muttered after Dad and I just stared at him, waiting him out.

"You give them money or you make them money?"

"Make." He sniffed. "It's what I do, isn't it?" Clearly wanting to change the subject, he murmured, "Now's your time to shine, Tin."

Dad reached for my arm. "You're not going to torture them, are you, Tin?"

"Concerned for my immortal soul, Dad?"

"No. Your knuckles. Edward will know you were involved in shady business if he sees bruised and battered hands."

"Good thinking. I won't. The Bratva can help me out. None of them speak Veronian, do they, *Papa?*"

He chortled. "They barely speak Russian."

"That's mean."

Papa rolled his eyes. "I meant literally. These are all from Siberia. They speak *Chukchi*. You should be fine, Tin."

"Thanks." I clapped him and Dad on the back, then I stepped out of the old cop station that was in a miserable town an hour out of Moscow.

I didn't have much time to get the answers we needed, and this wasn't my specialty, but I'd done more interrogating than either of my fathers had, and unfortunately, this wasn't something I could leave for the Guard Elect.

This was family business.

As I stepped inside, the eight Bratva meatheads had moved behind each of their captives. The ringleader's head was tipped back, his hair in the foot soldier's fist.

"Who's your hacker?" I asked, tucking my hands into my pockets as I focused my attention on him.

His eyes darted to the right. "There is no hacker, *sliema*."

My lips quirked at the Veronian insult. "You still speak Veronian even though you hate the country?"

"I hate the DeSauviers," he spat, a globule of bloody saliva soaring from his lips and splattering against the floor. "They are not my leaders."

"Think you'll find they are."

I kicked one foot against his knee, darted a look at the meathead in the corner. He moved forward and used leverage to keep the man's legs apart.

As I rested the flat of my foot against the ringleader's dick, I asked, "Now, you're going to tell me everything because if you don't, you'll die choking on your cock instead of with a bullet between the eyes.

"Do you understand?"

A scream escaped him as I ground my foot down, and he squealed, "Harrald is the hacker!"

Well, that wasn't as unpleasant as I feared.

"Tell me more..."

THIRTY-TWO

ETTA

The door opened into the darkness of the room, and I switched the light on, settling myself in its glow.

"Jesus Christ, Etta! You made me jump."

I glowered at him. "I made *you* jump. Where the fuck have you been, Tin?"

He scowled at me. "Out."

"Out? Until midnight?"

"It's been a long day."

Narrowing my eyes at him, I snapped, "You didn't answer your cell. I needed help with the ceremony. I told you I'd be calling—"

"I had bigger fish to fry."

"Than our wedding?" I intoned grimly.

He hissed under his breath. "Etta, I don't want to argue with you."

"Then you should have answered my call." His words about the wedding put my back up. "Do you want to cancel, is that it? You've been acting so strangely—"

"You think I want to cancel the wedding?" he blurted out.

"Well? Do you? I don't ask for much input on the ceremony, Tin, but I do need you for some things. I know it's an inconvenience—"

"Wait," he rumbled, holding up a hand as he stormed toward me. "Our wedding is not an inconvenience."

"Then why do you act as if it is?"

"Because..." He paused on his way to me then scraped a hand over his face. "Etta, we've got a lot going on, wouldn't you say? Two shootings in the space of a month? You know what my fathers and I have been trying to uncover."

I wouldn't ordinarily have been so insecure, but he'd been acting so strangely. So un-Tin that it frightened me, and our new normal wasn't solid yet, wasn't fixed in stone.

Then there was the fact that I was dealing with new guards and new faces when I hated change.

I missed Andrea; I *grieved* her passing.

And Mika hadn't been on my detail for two days either.

Call me a big baby, but my world was in flux. In the pressure cooker that was life at court, there was only so much I could take without feeling the strain. This was the last straw.

"You haven't told me anything, Tin," I cried. "Not since Devon came bursting into our bedroom.

"How am I supposed to know what's going on? You come in late and you go out early—" I gulped. "We haven't even..."

"Because I'm trying to save your family's collective ass. That's why."

I wasn't sure what pricked his temper the most, but it encouraged him to stride up to me, and as he placed a hand either side of mine on the armrests, he loomed over me.

A weird smell filtered into my senses, but I was more focused on the fire in his eyes.

"I was in a small town a hundred or so miles from Moscow."

"Moscow?" My mouth gaped. "What the hell were you doing in Moscow?"

"You don't want to know how Dad uncovered this, but a collective of Veronians moved to Russia and decided to sow dissent in the motherland."

"UnReals?"

"Yes and no. Anti-royalist, but capitalists. They were looking to make money off Veronia and the DeSauviers' misfortunes.

"They'd teamed up with an arms dealer who was ready to supply the UnReals with a bunch of weapons to arm them when a civil war broke out."

A gasp escaped me. "How could they trigger a civil war?"

His mouth tightened. "They'd uncovered the truth about you, Etta."

"What about me?"

"That you are the only true heir to the throne."

My brow furrowed. "Christel and Victoria are second and third in line—"

"No. They're not. You're Edward's daughter. His sole biological child."

"How would they know that?"

He sighed. "Mika was a mole, Etta. He snagged some of your DNA and your sisters' too—"

"I don't believe it!" I snapped. "Not Mika! He's loyal!"

But he hadn't reported for duty for two days.

I shoved at his shoulders, pushing him away so that I could leap to my feet.

Only, he didn't let me.

He held me captive in the armchair. "I wish I were lying, but I'm not. His father's recently been placed into a nursing home—the collective paid for that move."

Pain filtered through me because I'd known that about his father. Hadn't I? I just hadn't known Mika would betray me.

Betray Veronia.

Traitor.

Oh, God.

Andrea.

She'd died because of him. Because of his treason.

As I bit back a sob, Tin plowed on, "Once they determined you were the heiress, they wanted you out of the picture. The guy you killed was with the UnReals—"

"They told you that?" I demanded, my mind still reeling from Mika's betrayal.

He bowed his head. "It's a whole sordid mess of bastards who want to undermine your father's reign and destabilize the country at the same time. I didn't want you to know any of this, but—"

"But, what? I'm the future fucking queen of this country, Tin. If anyone should know, it's me."

"The goddamn king doesn't know," he snarled back.

My eyes flared wide. "You did this without Father's approval?"

"Of course we did. It was in Russia. We didn't need his approval."

"That's bullshit and you know it." I sucked in a breath as I thought about the political ramifications. "You used Veronian soldiers to—"

"We didn't. We used Bratva. They owed *Papa*. This was a covert operation. No one will ever know what happened outside of me, *Papa*, Dad, and now you."

"Andrei and Devon were there?"

He shrugged.

"You have to tell Father," I rasped. "How can he take steps to prevent this from happening again if he's in the dark?"

"There are no steps to prevent this from happening again aside from locking you in a gilded cage, but that's okay because I'll be your gilded fucking cage. No one and nothing will get to you without going through me first."

"Tin, don't say things like that," I breathed, and my hands moved to cup his wrists. My nails burrowed into the thin flesh there as I whispered, "Please."

"You seriously think I don't want to marry you when I'd lay down my fucking life for you, Etta?"

I swallowed. "You've been distant. I've made mistakes."

"And I've told you to forget them. We need to move on."

Lips quivering, I asked, "Where's Mika? He hasn't reported for duty in two days."

His gaze shuttered. "Don't worry about it."

"Jesus, Tin. You can't just—"

"I didn't have to do anything."

Stiffening, I demanded, "The Bratva?"

"*Papa* has many favors to call in."

I processed that, feeling my eyes turn to saucers as I stared at him.

He was the same Tin, but... different.

As much as I reeled from it, something inside me relaxed.

He *was* my partner.

But that didn't mean he didn't need corralling.

"What was their plan?" I demanded.

"Kill you, kill the DeSauvier line of succession."

"Daddy would be next in line if I died. And whichever of his daughters would follow in his path..."

He shook his head. "They're illegitimate, sweetheart." My mouth rounded as my mind whirred, but he filled in the gaps for me. "Xavier would be next, but he has no legitimate offspring either.

"And it would continue to bounce down the line until a DeSauvier who was not bred to sit on the throne would be crowned, and that was when they'd leap into the fray."

"That's a long-term plan."

"Is it?"

"They were going to kill all my fathers?" I whispered.

"They went for George after you. That's the second and third in line targeted."

"Why not—"

"Your father?"

I blinked as a thought occurred to me. "At the parade, I read in one of Father's reports that a man with a rifle was picked up and arrested."

"Shit. Really? I hadn't heard that."

"You should have coordinated with Father and Papa," I chided.

"Dad tried to. Edward wouldn't have it."

I sucked in a breath then stated, "If they dropped the truth about my paternity, about Christel and Victoria's, that would have shaken the country's faith in the family. You know how traditional Veronians are." His nod of agreement had me blanching. "Was that in the cards?"

"Yes."

"When?"

"They didn't have a manifesto, Etta. This was extracted through torture."

I swallowed. "You... you didn't bring them home to be arrested?"

"They're dead."

His flat tone had my nostrils flaring. "They should have been interrogated."

"I learned what I needed to know and I neutralized the threat. Dad set MI6 onto the arms dealer. Your family is safe."

"My family is never safe," I snapped. "We always deal with this kind of thing, and we will until our line ends."

"That could have happened a lot sooner than you think," he drawled.

I shoved into him this time, needing him to let me go so I could think without breathing the same goddamn air as him.

For whatever reason, he let me up, and I started striding back and forth in front of the fireplace, needing to think, needing to get my thoughts together.

But all I could think of was how many holes there were in the story that could have been filled if the appropriate authorities had been allowed to interrogate the terrorists.

Tin had acted without license. His family had too.

Father would be furious.

Yet the threat had been neutralized.

"I won't apologize for trying to protect you."

The flat words had me braking to a halt.

I stared at him, my mind twisted up, my heart racing as I tried to figure out how to make sense of all this, but his words made everything ridiculously simple.

"In the future, you do *not* act without my awareness," I intoned, a snap to the words that had him straightening up. "You do not leave the country to act on Veronia's behalf without mine or Father's approval.

"You do not interrogate criminals who have murdered Veronian nationals and then kill them without the country's authorities being there to determine every ounce of information has been wrung from them.

"You will be *my* consort, Tin. My husband. My *partner*."

"Partners don't need permission to act," he hissed.

My hands balled into fists at my sides. "You dare say that when, if our roles were reversed, you would be furious if I'd acted in the same reckless manner as you did today?"

He scowled at me. "That's different—"

"Why is it? Because I have ovaries?"

"No. Because you're my wife!" he growled as he rushed toward me.

One second, I was in front of the fire, the next, he'd pinned me to the wall beside it, charging against me with a force that nearly stole my breath.

Held in place, he grabbed my hands, held them to the wall at shoulder height, our fingers bridged so we were mutually locked in place, and he snapped, "You're mine, Etta. Mine."

"And you're not mine?" I snapped back. "I'm the one who claimed you first, Tin.

"You were too fucking slow to make your move. Too scared to wait for Father's approval. I know you wanted me four years ago, but you hesitated. You weren't confident enough to make your move, but

I was.

"You're mine as much as I'm yours—"

His mouth slammed onto mine, but before he could take things to the next stage, I bit down on his bottom lip, hard enough for him to jerk back with a hiss.

"Dammit, Etta—"

"You do not get to kiss me to shut me up, Tin. That is not how this is going to work."

"Yes, Your Majesty," he sneered.

His fingers began to untangle from mine, but I wouldn't let him. I tightened them.

"In this world, you are beneath me, but I don't want that. I want an equal. But you didn't treat me like that today. If anything, you acted as if I'm beneath you. Where in that is there a partnership?"

He froze at my words.

"Have I ever treated you as if you're beneath me?"

He was silent so long that I wasn't sure if he was going to answer.

But, slowly, he defrosted. "The wedding."

"Then and only then," I agreed. "And look at what happened. You faded from my life for four years, Tin."

"Are you going to 'fade' from mine because of today?"

Because I didn't sense any sarcasm, I told him, "No. But if you do it again, there'll be consequences."

He stared at me, deep into my eyes, and whispered, "I won't apologize for protecting you. For putting you first."

"Have I asked for an apology?"

Tin blinked. "No."

"Don't treat me like I'm a dumb female. I won't treat you like you're *just* my consort and not my partner." I sucked in a breath. "Do we have a deal?"

"We have a deal," he snarled, and that was when his mouth collided with mine again.

Only, this time, I let him in.

His tongue thrust against mine as his hands dragged up my skirt.

His fingers were chilly from so recently being outside, and I shuddered as he didn't stop until they were hooked into the sides of my panties, dragging them down until he shoved at them with his foot.

As he tore into my mouth, exploring and scavenging all at the same time, feasting on me with a hunger that I shared, he bent down and made to haul me into him, but he jerked back with a hiss.

"Fuck!"

I froze, unsure what was even happening, then I realized he'd hurt himself.

"Your wounds?" I demanded.

"No, they're okay," he ground out. "It's just a twinge."

I growled under my breath. "Are you trying to injure yourself even more? Maybe you're the one who needs protection." His eyes narrowed but I shoved my hands against his shoulders, not stopping until he was plunking down against the sofa, snapping, "It takes a fucking woman."

Pinning him in place by settling a knee either side of his, I reached between us and grabbed a hold of his dick.

Reassured by the presence of his boner because that meant he wasn't in enough pain to kill his arousal, I pulled it free from the fly I opened.

His hands slipped along my legs, starting at my ankle where he toyed with the anklet he'd given me years ago, before sliding higher.

With his caress sending sensation whirling through me, I moved until I found the perfect position. And, with my gaze locked on his all the while, I pressed his tip to my slit where my juices slid over his glans.

We both groaned, but I ducked down and pressed my teeth to his stubbled chin and nipped him there.

"We. Are. Equals," I grated out and punctuated the statement by sliding down his length.

His head angled back, but I followed, pushing my forehead into his as I started to rock into him, impaling myself on his shaft over and over as my hands went to his nape so I could dig my nails into him there.

"What are we, Tin?"

He remained silent, so I moved faster, faster until his breath gusted against my mouth and I felt how damn close he was—

I froze.

"What are we, Tin?"

"Witch," he sniped.

"You know it. We've already had this conversation," I breathed, bewilderingly close to an orgasm myself even though I was furious as hell.

"We're equals."

I rewarded him by starting up again, and this time, a scant second before I let our lips collide, I whispered, "I love you."

I didn't allow him to return the words.

I didn't need to hear them.

He needed to know that I would always seal every argument we had with that declaration.

That one truth.

Because fuckwit or not, I loved him.

And though this argument had been frustrating and disappointing, I'd learned he felt the same way about me.

As my pussy clamped down around his dick, my mouth continued dominating his, and as we both groaned through our mutual orgasms, his seed filling me up and drenching me with his heat, I knew that we'd just laid the first stepping stone for our future.

THIRTY-THREE

ETTA

THREE MONTHS LATER

"You look beautiful, baby," Mom rasped, and I had to hide a smile when I heard her tears, literally heard them in her voice.

If I looked beautiful, so did she in a champagne dress that showed off all her curves, draping down to the floor in a frothy cascade while discreetly revealing a slither of her décolletage.

I knew Sascha's dress was a little less formal, as would all the other women attending today, but Mom was Queen.

She'd be draping on the ceremonial surcoat the second she made it to Yorke Abbey and had to take her place on the throne at my father's side for the wedding service.

"She's right. You do."

Not having expected my father to make an appearance just before I was about to head to the cathedral, my eyes flared wide when I twisted around and saw him, complete in ceremonial garb, staring at me in the mirror.

My dress was everything I wanted it to be. Not fancy and finicky, not like anything a royal really should wear. It wasn't demure and tidy. I didn't look asexual or like a doll.

I looked like me.

The skirt was bouncy, but not too bouncy. It drifted around my legs, delineating my hips and butt, while surging upward into a bodice that was rounded with a sweetheart neckline that wasn't afraid to show off my tits to the only man I wanted looking at them— Tin.

Parts of my dress were covered in the lace Veronia was famed for, I even had some silk from a tiny fabricator in the East, but the design was nothing like my mom's dress. It wasn't formal and strict, didn't make me look virginal.

I looked like a woman.

A woman who was ready to be married.

And I knew I glowed, positively glowed, because I was so ready for this. So ready to be Tin's in the eyes of the world.

Mom reached up and rubbed her handkerchief to the corner of her eye so she wouldn't spoil her makeup, and Father lifted an arm and squeezed her, muttering, "Can I have a minute with her, love?"

As he pressed his lips to her temple, she gave him a tear-soaked smile before she disappeared, and with a wave of her hand, all the staff and the maids and the ladies-in-waiting dispersed too, leaving me alone with my father.

His smile was rueful as he murmured, "This is nothing like your first wedding."

"Complete opposite." I jerked my chin up. "I wouldn't change it."

"Even though it was a disaster?"

I winced. "No. Not even then. He's mine. Always has been."

Father sighed and raised his hands. "I didn't come here to fight."

"No?" I angled my chin to the side. "I hope you came to give me a kiss."

He laughed, strode forward, his fur and velvet surcoat draping behind him as he moved toward me. His arms opened and I settled into them with a sigh.

"I needed this," I muttered against his chest, careful not to scrape my makeup onto the suit jacket he wore.

He sported a Veronian iris as his boutonnière, and it scented fresh and reminded me of our summer vacations in Laurela where there was a field of irises nearby.

Memories of all the times we'd spent there, as a family, and with Tin's too, filled me with a kind of peace that made up for my nerves.

Like he knew, he asked, "You nervous?"

I squeezed his waist. "Not for myself."

A part of me was certain Tin would balk and would run away, but I had faith in him.

Faith in us now.

So I was just anxious on his behalf.

The man hated social situations, for God's sake. This was his idea of a living hell.

"He'll be fine," Father countered.

"I know he will, for the wedding." My nose crinkled. "It's the coronation bit I'm nervous about."

"It's easy. You know that."

"For us," I grumbled. "But he must be nervous. I wish I could see him."

"You've broken every other custom," he said dryly. "I'm surprised you didn't sneak out to see him—" He broke off, shaking his head. "Let me guess, you did?"

I grinned up at him. "Do you really want to know?"

"No!" he retorted forcefully, making me chuckle.

And I didn't blame him. Tin had stayed in the other side of the palace, far away from my quarters, last night, but that hadn't stopped him from coming to me and waking me up with a smile.

"He'll be fine," Father repeated, rolling over that little awkwardness with the ease of a consummate diplomat. "I don't want you to think about that; I just want you to think about today. About enjoying it. It's your day."

I pulled a face. "If it were down to me, I'd have Elvis marrying us again."

He touched my chin with his thumb. "You have never liked any of the pomp and ceremony, have you?"

"Nope, never."

"We're alike in that. I wish, for your sake, we weren't." Shaking his head, he pressed his mouth to my forehead. "Never think, my darling, that I don't love you for who you are—"

"Even if it means I'm awkward and difficult?"

"Even then," he said with a laugh. "I'd prefer you to be you, to knock heads with you than for you to be who you're not." A sigh escaped him. "I'm sorry if I made you conform—"

"You were doing what's best for me. I know that." I squeezed him. "You don't have to apologize, Father. I mean it."

"You're too kind." He blew out a breath that made the baby hairs around my hairline bob and dance. "But then, you always were the best of us, even if we were too stubborn to see it, trying to push you, a round peg, into a square hole."

My nose crinkled. "Thanks, Father. I really want to be likened to a round peg on today of all days."

He snorted. "You look beautiful. And you know it."

Eyes twinkling, I shrugged because he wasn't wrong. I looked epic, if I did say so myself.

"Why are you being all maudlin anyway? That's not like you."

"If a man can't take stock of his life on his daughter's wedding day, when can he?"

"Does that mean Christel and Victoria are going to get visits like this just before they're ready to drive to the cathedral?"

His smile was dry. "Maybe not. Maybe I'll be kind and just speak to them after the ceremony, but you?" He shook his head and squeezed my chin again. "You changed my life, baby girl, and I wanted to thank you for that."

Eyes wide, because I hadn't expected him to say that, I whispered, "You really mean it?"

"I do. I was older than you when I met your mother, and I never expected to love her the way I still do. It was a gift, and I think I forgot that where you were concerned. I'm glad Tin is that for you."

"He is," I whispered. "He's the love of my life."

"I'm glad, baby." A knock tapped at the door, and he grimaced. "That means I need to get moving." He sighed, kissed my temple again, then called out, "Two minutes."

Pulling away, he strode toward the door where I saw there was a large box perched on a dresser. Clad in a velvet that looked antique, my brows rose when he opened it and brought it to me.

Inside was a majestic crown. Hundreds of different gemstones were inset into a headdress that would offset the virginal white of my dress.

It was about four inches thick in circumference, and I knew, without even touching it, it would be heavy, and by the end of the day, my neck and shoulders would ache like a bitch.

"Great-grandma's crown?" I whispered, surprised because it was an ornate piece.

Father was still wearing the wooden circlet on his head—a message to our enemies that the fight was not over.

Having declared war on the UnReals back in February, and introducing several laws that the press called 'the purge,' a few dozen of the bastards were currently awaiting trial after the purge had borne fruit.

I considered it a wedding gift.

Especially as today's ceremony would be taking place without the UnReal threat hanging over our heads.

"I thought you might like to wear it today."

My mouth rounded. "I'd love to."

It was a more modern style and it suited me down to the ground, but I'd expected to wear one of the more commonly known crowns, one of the big ones that we tended to wear for matters of state like today.

"Hold it for me," he said, and I did, gently lifting it from the cushioned bed and resting it on my palms, accepting the gold pins he handed me next.

Lowering the case onto a nearby dresser, he reached for the diadem, and with an ease that few men would ever display where it came to hair pins, he raised it and rested it on my head. Then he secured it, and all the while, my eyes were closed because I hadn't expected him to do this for me.

It was more than an honor—I felt his love.

That was more of a gift than a crown.

We spent so much time at odds with each other, but it was like by giving me this crown, he was seeing me as the daughter I was. Not the queen he wanted me to be.

When it was secure atop my head, he murmured, "You look even more spectacular than you did before." Resting his hands on my shoulders, he said, "It's my wedding gift to you, darling."

Eyes flaring wide, I whispered, "Seriously?"

He dipped his chin. "Seriously. And, as for Daddy and Papa, we've all decided to let you have the Laurela Palace."

This time, I gaped at him. "The summer palace?"

"It's your favorite, and you're newlyweds. I think you need some freedom before we draw you into the fold."

I gulped, never having expected that. Newlyweds were traditionally given a palace, but they kept a weather eye on me. This freedom, the symbolism behind it, was unprecedented. "I-I... are you sure?"

"I'm deadly sure." His lips twitched and he chucked my chin. "Today's the first day of the rest of your life. I just wanted you to know that," he murmured, pressing another kiss to my temple, "I couldn't be prouder of you."

In a flash, he'd swirled around and was heading to the door before I could even process everything he'd said.

Still, I couldn't stop myself from calling out, "Dad?"

As he peered at me over his shoulder, his brows high at the unusually informal address, I told him, "I love you." Swallowing, I reached up and let my fingers gently brush the crown. "Thank you."

His eyes twinkled. "I love you too."

And with that, he left me, and for a few seconds, I had no choice but to look at myself in the mirror and see that, for the first time in my life, in my father's eyes, I was a woman. No longer his recalcitrant daughter, the naughty girl… a woman.

And he'd given me a gift to match.

Not just the crown and the palace, but acceptance.

Somehow, that meant more to me than anything else. I didn't doubt that, in the future, we'd butt heads, but maybe we were always supposed to do that. Maybe that was just how we were supposed to show each other we loved one another.

A knock sounded at the door, and I called out, "Come in!"

Mom's head peered through the crack, and she beamed at me when she saw my crown. "It looks amazing—it suits you. I always looked ridiculous when I tried to wear it, but I knew you'd look like the princess you are."

A laugh escaped me, maybe as she'd intended. "Thanks, Mom."

She winked. "Are you ready?"

Ready to marry Tin? For everyone to know he was mine? That I was his?

I grinned. "Hell, yeah."

THIRTY-FOUR

TIN

I stared at the stained-glass windows at the head of a cathedral that had seen God only knew how many DeSauviers getting hitched and smiled at the sun gleaming through the elaborate panes.

It was still only early spring, but God, as the reverend had told me earlier, was smiling down on Etta and me.

I figured we deserved more than a smile—more like a laugh—but I'd take it.

Today was the day.

Etta was about to become my wife—officially recognized by the king himself—and I was about to be crowned as her consort.

Was I nervous?

Yes.

Unequivocally, yes.

A hand grabbed my arm, and I knew it was Jack because he was my best man.

"What is it?" I whispered.

"She's here."

I twisted around, aware that Yorke Abbey's doors had opened, and took a quick glance at the first few pews on either side of the aisle.

As I did, I asked, "You got the ring?"

He huffed. "Yeah. I have one job, Tin. Not like I can screw that up."

"Make sure you don't."

"Jesus, between you, Mom, the dads, *and* Beau, if I lost this ring it would be a miracle."

"A miracle or a nightmare for you," I warned.

The cathedral was massive, to the point where I couldn't see Etta anyway, not without squinting, so I checked in with those I could see.

"Beau here?" I asked quietly.

"Yeah, she brought her girlfriend with her," he grumbled.

Shooting him a look, I asked, "You *like* her?"

"No," he sniped, glowering at me like I'd told him his Chevy car was slower than a Ferrari.

Cocking a brow at him, I merely said, "All right. Calm down."

When he huffed again, my lips twitched, but though I saw Beau and her girlfriend, sitting beside Rosie and Bethan, mostly, I zoomed in on Mom.

Naturally, she was crying, her hat askew from where Dad kept shoving his face to kiss her cheek to make her feel better.

While I knew my parents were undoubtedly causing a stir, I didn't give a damn. The sight of them all clustered together made my heart happy.

Theirs was relationship goals.

Daw held her hand, and she was surrounded by Father on one side, and *Papa* and *Vati* on the other, and they were all muttering among themselves.

They were doing me proud in that ass Jean Luc's suits, but I had to admit to being a little bit prouder of Daw.

He might not have wed Mom in a kilt, but today, for *my*

wedding? He was rocking the tartan all the way to the bank, and he looked damn good in it too.

No knobbly knees in sight—mostly because Mom's hand kept fondling them.

Didn't need to see that.

Did.

Not.

Need.

To.

See.

That.

But the sight was impossible to delete now it was in my memory banks, and a base contentment filled me regardless.

I wanted that.

When Etta and I were older, when other couples were getting divorced, I wanted to be so into her that she was the moon to my stars.

A smile danced on my lips at the fanciful thought, when being *fanciful* was not a trait I was known for, and I carried on looking around the pews.

This truly was a nightmare.

Thousands of people, nobles, celebrities, foreign dignitaries, all seated here, looking at me.

Watching every move I made.

It was enough to make me feel nauseated, but there was light at the end of the tunnel, and that was the only reason I was doing this.

In the eyes of the entire fucking world, hell, the universe, Etta was about to officially become *mine*.

"She doesn't have many friends, does she?"

Jack's words had me blinking. "Huh?"

"Well, I've never met any of these guys, and I had to be introduced to all her bridesmaids. I guess I didn't realize how few friends she has."

His insight had me frowning, but then, I stopped.

"We're each other's friends."

I had family, acquaintances, ex-colleagues, but on the friends' scale, my list was woeful too.

Not that I was complaining.

That was plenty of people in the grand scheme of things.

"You know how unhealthy that is, right?" Jack questioned.

My lips twitched. "You're the one who's jealous of your best friend's girlfriend."

He hissed under his breath.

"Remember," I taunted, "we're in church."

He glowered at me, but I switched focus.

Spying Etta's family, I saw they were seated to the left.

Well, most of them.

Her other fathers were there, along with her sisters, but Edward and Perry were at the side of the altar, seated on their thrones.

I was dreading the moment I'd have to approach them, where Perry would place a small crown on my head and Edward would decree me Etta's consort, but I'd do it.

I had to.

Etta was worth putting up with that crap.

Then she was there.

And she sucked out most of the oxygen from the cathedral.

Erasing my concerns and easing my social anxiety with every step she took toward me.

Resplendent in a white gown that was loose about her legs, not full-on like a princess dress, no meringue in sight, but swaying with her, making her sparkle and glitter, she was glorious.

The bodice pulled taut at her waist, and her tits were pushed up with just enough force that I resented gravity for torturing me—I wanted to get her out of that dress.

Or, maybe, I wanted to fuck her in it.

Then, I winced because I was in church.

But hell, God gave her to me, so why should he complain if I wanted to make her mine?

Again and again and again.

And again.

I sucked in a breath as I took in the glimpses I could spot of her face through the heavy lace veil all while a choir sang, the soprano voices echoing around the chapel, hitting the ceiling which was hundreds of feet overhead.

Amid the dingy light from the ancient abbey, she was surrounded by swathes of flowers.

Bright white thistle and elda, famous Veronian flowers that I knew were detailed on the lace of her dress.

She had a bouquet of roses and peonies in her hand which added to the floral chaos of her journey toward me.

It was only when she took those final steps to the altar, the prime minister at her side because the jackass had the right to walk her down the aisle—Etta was right, this was *democrazy*—did my heart start to slow to the point where I realized it had actually been racing.

As I looked at her, I could breathe deeper.

This was nuts, everything was insane, but she wasn't. She was my world, and this was just a formality.

Dotting an I.

Crossing a T.

I sucked in a breath when her hand slipped into mine, and as her matron of honor, a cousin, stepped forward to help her lift the veil, DeWitt, the prime minister, disappeared, and I was left looking into her eyes.

She was beautiful.

Everything about her was perfect. A jewel that outmatched the crown she wore on her head.

And she was mine.

It didn't matter that, together, we'd head over to her parents' thrones where I'd ask him for the right to claim her as my own.

It didn't matter that I'd be crowned and would be a duke by the end of this ceremony.

All that mattered was her.

Me.

Us.

I smiled at her, grinning because, at last, I was fucking happy, and when she grinned back, I had no choice but to lean forward and to press a kiss to her lips.

I heard laughter, tutting, and a few claps, but I ignored them.

Even ignored the reverend who told me that kissing was for after the service, and instead, I whispered in her ear, "I can't wait to fuck you with this dress on."

Her breath caught, and her eyes glinted with excitement.

And that's how we got married.

Not with nerves, not with worry about being a shitty consort or saying something wrong, or worse, *doing* something wrong and fucking up live on film that was being shown around the world.

Just with thoughts of later.

Thoughts of when we were behind closed doors and the world was suddenly filled with only two people.

Her and me.

Forever.

EPILOGUE

TIN

FOUR YEARS LATER

"What's wrong?"

Alice turned to me with a scowl. "What do you mean, 'what's wrong?' For God's sake, Tin, must you be so placid?"

For some reason, her words made me think of Andrei—my *papa*.

He could be considered placid, but he dealt with all kinds of crises with a soft smile on his mouth and with a calmness that I'd wanted to emulate all my life.

I didn't think I'd ever be that good at handling disasters, but *Papa* was one of the best counselors a man could ask for.

With a wife like Etta, I needed all the counseling I could get.

Because Edward had stepped back and had allowed Etta and I to have more responsibility, crises came in many forms now.

From dealing with the smattering of UnReals who'd survived the 'purge,' to arguing with Prime Minister DeWitt whose geography hadn't improved and who kept on insisting we needed nuclear arms.

With my pregnant wife living on Veronian soil, no way in hell was I about to allow *that* to happen.

"This isn't me being placid," I informed her, "it's just me not understanding why you're stressing over something you have no control over."

She squinted at me. "Are you purposely trying to piss me off?"

I grinned at her. "No, I wasn't, but it seems to be working either way."

A hiss escaped her as she folded her arms across her belly. "I won't allow it."

"You don't have a say in it," I pointed out, even though, technically, she did.

"That's what pisses me off the most." She jerked her chin up. "I know it's stupid."

Whether it was or not, Etta was mine—and whatever she wanted, she'd get. I really was just messing with her.

"It's what you want," I told her softly, not wanting to piss her off anymore.

I reached out to bring her into my arms, to fold her into my embrace. She was getting bigger, her belly rounder so I couldn't hold her as close, but I dipped my chin and rested it on her head.

She huddled into me as she muttered, "We have the right to call our daughter whatever we want.

"If I don't want her to have a gazillion names, then she won't have a gazillion. I'll make DeWitt pay if he doesn't come through," she snapped. "He owes me. I saved his ass that time he was drunk when the Saudi Arabian ambassador came to visit."

My lips twitched at the memory of our prime minister almost falling asleep at the table.

"What's your plan? To leak that to the press?" I teased.

She heaved a sigh. "I told you I should have taken a picture of him dozing."

"Secrets are a commodity," I disagreed. "Pictures make it blackmail."

"You'd know," she countered.

I would.

"I just want her to be normal."

"I know you do, sweetheart, but she'll never be normal. She can't be. She's our firstborn, and she's going to be your heir." My nose crinkled at the bridge. "Plus, she's related to me."

"Just a little," she joked.

I hitched a shoulder. "You know my family is a bunch of overachievers."

A breath gusted from her lips. "You're right. She's destined to be weird."

"Weird but successful," I tacked on.

"Do you think she'll be like her Uncle Jack?"

"God, I hope not," I said with a shudder that had her laughing.

"He's calmed down since he won the F1 Championship."

"That boy will never calm down."

"Beau has a calming effect on him," she countered.

"I wish she weren't gay. Then she really would be able to tame him. I'm sure he pulls half the stunts he does because he's trying to impress her."

"Impress her into turning straight?" She arched a brow at me. "Not sure that's possible. She could be all serious and somber like Bethan—"

"I hope she is," I inserted before she could continue:

"—of course, she's into what your mom and dads are—"

"What?!" I could feel my eyes bugging. "The—"

Chuckling, she raised a hand to her lips. "Don't say anything. I only know by chance."

"How?" I demanded. "And which... several guys? Or the BDSM?" I groaned. "Why are you making me have this conversation?"

Etta grinned. "Because I like to watch you squirm."

Growling under my breath, I demanded, "Which?"

"The BDSM. When Bethan was here last, I found her in the stables getting spanked by a footman," she joked, laughing when my mouth gaped. "Tin, are you a prude?"

"Where my baby sister is concerned, bet your beautiful ass I am."

She patted my chest—the exact spot where she'd given me heartburn. "Maybe she'll be like Rosie."

My brow furrowed. "Always getting into trouble?"

"Hardly. She's a vet now. Very respectable."

"You know the local police call her a menace, don't you?"

She snorted. "I don't think she's a menace. It's not her fault she comes across a lot of people who treat their animals poorly, is it?"

I grunted. "Maybe not."

"What's your cure-all there? That Bash will tame her?"

My eyes widened. "Good God, no. Bash is wilder than she is."

"Maybe she should tame him?"

"Impossible."

She smirked up at me. "Wanna bet?"

"How much?"

"Naming rights."

I shrugged. "I was going to let you choose anyway."

She sagged into me, her head tipping back and providing me with her mouth at the perfect angle for me to press a soft kiss to her lips.

While I thought I'd kissed her out of her funk, I hadn't.

"I won't put her through what Father put me through," she argued the second I let our mouths part ways. "If she's terrible at school, then I won't make her feel bad about it."

I had to grin. "She won't be terrible at school." I winked. "She's my kid too."

"Big head," she grumbled, shoving me, but I didn't go far, not when we were hugging the way we were.

"Big other things too," I countered which had her snickering.

Grabbing a gentle hold of her chin, I tipped her head back again so I could press another kiss to her lips.

"I didn't think you could look more beautiful until you got pregnant, and then, when you're fighting for our girl's right to be normal, you're even more gorgeous." I squinted at her. "What's your secret?"

"Lays' chips. They give a girl a glow."

"Is that so?" I hummed under my breath as, hiding a smile, I pressed a kiss to her forehead. "All will be well, Etta. You don't have to worry."

She stilled. "What have you done?"

I shrugged. "Pulled in some favors."

She was quiet for a second which meant she was thinking. Which was always dangerous.

Then her hand slipped between us and she cupped my dick. "Did I ever tell you how hot it is when you go all James Bond on me?"

"No, you didn't," I rasped, "but you can always remind me..."

And JACK'S story, with his Beau, is now live and free in KU!
To read about Tin's sibling, you can read HIS TO HOLD here:
www.books2read.com/QuintHisToHold

AUTHOR NOTE

Hello darlings!

As I promised, I hope you agree that you didn't need to have read my Reverse Harem romances to enjoy Valentin and Alice's story.

However, maybe you'd like to dip your toes into those books?

To enjoy Sascha, Andrei, Sawyer, Devon, Kurt, and Sean's story, you can find start here: www.books2read.com/HersToKeep

They're live on audio too, and the final book in the series will be dropping in audio with the marvelous Shane East and Hollie Jackson narrating on the 14th December! www.books2read.com/HersTo Hold

As for Perry, George, Edward, and Xavier, you can find their story here: www.books2read.com/TheirsVeronia

Don't forget that once HIS TO KEEP hits 200 reviews on the Zon, there'll be a bonus scene in my Diva reader group. You can join here: www.facebook.com/groups/SerenaAkeroydsDivas

I wish you all the happiest of holidays, and sending all my love from my family to yours,

Serena

xoxo

FREE BOOK!

Don't forget to grab your free e-Book!
Secrets & Lies is now free!

Meg's love life was missing a spark until she discovered her need to
be dominated. When her fiancé shared the same kink, she thought all
her birthdays had come at once, and then she came to learn their
relationship was one big fat lie.

Gabe has loved Meg for years, watching her from afar, and always
wishing he'd been the one to date her first and not his brother. When
he has the chance to have Meg in his bed—even better, tied to it—it's
an opportunity he can't refuse.

With disastrous consequences.

Can Gabe make Meg realize she's the one woman he's always
wanted? But once secrets and lies have wormed their way into a
relationship, is it impossible to establish the firm base of trust needed
between lovers, and more importantly, between sub and Sir...?

This story features orgasm control in a BDSM setting.
Secrets & Lies is now free!

CONNECT WITH SERENA

For the latest updates, be sure to check out my website!
But if you'd like to hang out with me and get to know me better, then
I'd love to see you in my Diva reader's group where you can find out
all the gossip on new releases as and when they happen. You can join
here: www.facebook.com/groups/SerenaAkeroydsDivas. Or you can
always PM or email me. I love to hear from you guys:
serenaakeroyd@gmail.com.

ABOUT THE AUTHOR

I'm a romance novelaholic and I won't touch a book unless I know there's a happy ending. This addiction is what made me craft stories that suit my voracious need for raunchy romance. I love twists and unexpected turns, and my novels all contain sexy guys, dark humor, and hot AF love scenes.

I write MF, menage, and reverse harem (also known as why choose romance,) in both contemporary and paranormal. Some of my stories are darker than others, but I can promise you one thing, you will always get the happy ending your heart needs!